Loving Her

Volume 1

by

Lauren Shiro

Vanilla Heart Publishing

Loving Her
Volume 1

by Lauren Shiro

Copyright 2013 Lauren Shiro

Published by: Vanilla Heart Publishing

www.VanillaHeartBookAndAuthors.com

10121 Evergreen Way, 25-156

Everett, WA 98204 USA

This book is a work of fiction. Names, characters, places, and incidents are either the product of the author's imagination or are used fictitiously, and any resemblance to places, events, or persons living or dead is purely coincidental.

ISBN-13: 978-0615926278 ISBN-10: 0615926274

10 9 8 7 6 5 4 3 2 1 First Edition

First Printing, December 2013
Printed in the United States of America

Series Dedication

I dedicate this entire group of stories to the loving memory of my grandfather. My hero, my rock, my greatest fan. He always encouraged and supported my writing. It is because of him that you are reading these and I wrote them. Thank you will never be enough. Rest in peace, RPK. You are greatly loved and missed.

The Ballerina

by

Lauren Shiro

Dedication

I dedicate this first book to my beautiful, wonderful wife, Vicki Shiro. My best friend, always a source of love and joy. Thank you for being my partner on this journey. I love you!

The Ballerina

Liz gracefully pranced onto the stage for her curtain call. The ending to another exhilarating performance. As she curtsied, the crowd's applause grew louder, and some audience members rose to their feet. The greatest perk to dancing the lead role. A wide, bright smile was painted across Liz's face as she and the company took their final bow before the heavy velvet curtain fell.

Back stage, Liz gathered all of her belongings; she was ready to go back to her hotel and call it a night.

"Good show, Liz." Karen, the stage manager walked by.

"Thank you, Karen!" Liz's strong southern drawl echoed out.

"Rehearsal is at one tomorrow," Karen said as she walked deeper into the group of dancers.

"Okay. I'll be there." Liz called back. Picking up her duffel bag, Liz walked out of the stage door.

"Ummmm...excuse me." A quiet voice barely interrupted Liz's thoughts.

Liz stopped to see a young, unassuming woman with bland brown hair watching her.

"Hi." The woman said sheepishly.

"Hi there. How can I help you?" Liz's voice was loud and boisterous compared to this meek woman.

"Oh! You gave an excellent performance tonight." The woman almost looked as though she was blushing, but she turned away so Liz couldn't really tell.

"Why, thank you!" Liz said with her undeniable twang.

"I...was wondering...how much longer the...company would be in town."

"One week. Then we're going up to Atlanta."

"Oh," the woman said with disappointment in her voice. She hesitated for a moment. "I...was wondering if you'd like to go out to dinner; have a local show you around." The woman shared a nervous, weak smile with Liz.

"Oh, well, to tell you the truth, I never did think about it."

The woman's face dropped.

"But...it sure does sound like fun!" Liz said, hoping to appease the woman.

She looked up at Liz with excitement in her eyes. "Here's my card," she said quietly.

"Thanks..." Liz looked at the business card. "Jen."

"Yeah," Jen smiled. "Call me any time." Her smile was brighter than the street lamps.

"I will." Liz smiled back. With a nod, Liz continued on her way.

"She gave you her card?" Stacie asked Liz as they stretched before rehearsal.

"Yeah. She wants to have dinner with me." Liz said with both confusion and cynicism in her voice.

"Are you going to call her?"

"I told her I would."

"What do you think she wants?" Stacie wondered.

"I don't know," Liz shrugged. "Maybe she's a real fan."

"Or maybe she's a rich woman looking for some poor dancer to spend her millions on!" Stacie joked.

"I wish!" Liz laughed. "Naw. She works at a shelter for cats. I don't think she's got money."

"She's a philanthropist!" Stacie roared in laughter.

Liz chuckled. "What do you think? Should I call her?"

Stacie thought for a moment. "I don't know it's kinda weird, but, you never know. Maybe she's harmless."

"She certainly looked harmless," Liz replied.

"Well then, yeah. Why not? What's it going to hurt? You could meet her after the matinee tomorrow."

Liz pondered Stacie's words. "Okay." She said. "I will! I'll call her tomorrow."

"Thanks for meeting me here." Jen said quietly as she looked up at Liz.

Liz towered over this quiet, mousy woman. Plainly dressed in an oatmeal colored button-down blouse paired with chocolate brown pants and similarly colored flat shoes, Jen did not compare to the 5'10" red head who stood regally before her.

"Thanks for inviting me," Liz brightly answered.

Jen pulled out the chair for Liz to sit.

"Why, thank you!" Liz said.

Jen smiled as she sat down. "So…how long have you been dancing?" Jen asked.

"My whole life. It's all I ever wanted to do. I'm really blessed that my parents could always find a way to make it happen."

"Oh wow. That's sweet. I'll bet they're great people."

"Oh they are!"

"That's great that you are so close with them," Jen squeaked. "Do you miss them? Do you get to talk to them often?"

"I call when I can. They know life on the road isn't always the greatest for staying in touch. But we manage." Liz paused for a moment. "Enough about me, tell me about you! Now, what is it that you do?"

Jen shifted in her chair, obviously uncomfortable about having the attention switched to her. "Oh! Well, I'm the director of Feline Haven, an all feline rescue organization and shelter."

"Well, isn't that nice! How did you get involved with that?" Liz cocked her head in interest.

"Oh, I've always loved animals." Jen said. "But I knew I couldn't be a vet or anything – not with euthanasia. So, I started volunteering at no-kill shelters as a teenager, and it just kind of went from there."

"Wow. That is really great. It sounds like you do great work," Liz sweetly answered.

"Thanks." Jen blushed and turned away. After a moment, she said, "so…are you seeing anyone?"

"Naw." Liz replied. "It's so hard when you're always on the road. Plus, I have classes and rehearsals on top of all the performances – sometimes we do two or even three a day! It's a pretty demanding schedule."

"Oh I see," Jen quietly retorted. She looked at her plate somewhat dejected.

"Are you seeing anyone?" Liz asked. She wondered why Jen would ask such an unusual question, but she chalked it up to nothing more than small talk. So she figured it was ok to ask in reciprocation.

"Me? Oh no." Jen waved her hand in dismissal of such a thought.

"Why not?" Liz asked. "You're nice enough and you're pretty."

13

Jen's face expressed a myriad of emotions. "*You* think *I'm* pretty?!"

Liz was beginning to wonder about this girl. She must have terrible self-esteem. Jen was a little plain, but she wasn't hideous. There was no reason for her not to date. "Well Sure!" Liz replied.

"Thank you." Jen blushed again. After a few awkwardly silent moments, the waitress approached their table. "Are you ladies ready to order?"

"Thank you for a nice dinner." Liz said as they approached her truck.

"You are very welcome," Jen answered with a smile.

"Well, this is it." Liz said, about to open the door to her behemoth.

"*This* is your truck?!" Jen asked. Her face lit up as she smiled in utter shock.

"Yeah," Liz said with great pride. "My daddy gave it to me. It is a 1977 Chevrolet K-10 pickup. I've got a bored out 454 with a cowl induction hood, quad exhaust, and..."

"Wow!" Jen said.

Liz could see the wonder in her eyes. "Would you like to go for a ride in it?" Liz's smile was as grand as it had been during her curtain call.

"Yeah!" Jen said with an equally impressive smile. Never before had she seen a beast like this.

The truck looked down at her with large circular headlights. The chrome grille glistened in the moonlight. Although the truck was black, the paint was shiny as if it was a brand new truck. Red metal flakes sparkled throughout the jet black paint. This was more than a truck. It was a work of art.

Liz walked Jen around to the passenger door and opened it. She held out her hand for Jen to climb in.

"Thank you." Jen said.

Liz walked around the gargantuan truck and let herself in. After settling into the seat, she turned the key and pressed the gas pedal to the floor. She started and revved the incredible, deafeningly loud motor. The truck roared with power.

"Boy that's loud!" Jen shouted over the grumbles of the big block engine.

"Yep!" Liz agreed with a devious smile.

14

Save for the noise of the big block motor, Liz and Jen drove a short, but rather silent jaunt to a nearby scenic view of the infinite Floridian beach.

Like a pilot, Liz seamlessly pulled the monstrosity into a spot with a view that rivaled the best postcard. Finally, Liz turned off the truck.

Jen rubbed her ears. "I think my ears are ringing." She joked.

"But it sure was a rush, wasn't it?" Liz asked with great enthusiasm.

Jen hesitantly agreed. "Yeah." She said after a brief pause.

They both looked out on the endless ocean.

"Wow. That is some view." Liz whispered.

Silently, they watched the waves dance under the moonlight. Words would only detract from this incredible moment.

Jen quietly slid over the long vinyl bench seat until she was next to Liz, taking in this breath-taking scene.

"This is great." Jen whispered.

"Huh?" Liz asked, turning to look at her.

Jen placed her soft hand on Liz's face, slowly leaned in and gently kissed her. Jen's lips were warm and soft.

Liz briefly lost herself in this moment, before her rationale came back to her and she pulled away. "Whoa!" She said, putting her arms up.

"What? What's wrong?" Jen asked with concern in her eyes.

"Uhhhh...I...it's just I...never. I never kissed anyone before." Liz sheepishly admitted.

"What?! How is that possible? You're so beautiful, and..."

"Well, thanks, but it's true. I've never dated anyone before."

Jen looked at Liz inquisitively.

"Between my farm chores and dancing; classes, rehearsals, touring and all, I just never dated anyone. Ever."

Jen paused. "Oh my God! I am so sorry. I didn't mean to..."

"It's okay." Liz replied. She didn't want to hurt Jen's feelings.

"I didn't know. I didn't mean to assume anything. I just thought with you saying I was pretty and..." Jen said softly. Her shoulders rolled forward and she sank in her seat, her head hung low.

"Well, I do think you're pretty. I just didn't mean it like that. I'm not..."

Jen turned her head to look up at Liz. "Oh my God! You're not gay?!" She paused. "Oh Jesus, Jen!" She chastised herself. "I am so sorry, Liz! I never meant to offend you!"

15

"No, no. You didn't offend me." Liz tried to cover her words. "I'm just...I...I..."

Jen's face was buried in her hands. "You're not a lesbian. I get it. I'm sorry." Slowly, Jen uncurled. "I can leave now, if you like."

"No. That's not necessary." Liz looked pitifully at Jen.

"I feel awful! I am just so sorry. I stupidly assumed by some of the things you said and the way you opened the truck door for me, and drove me here."

"Oh, I'm sorry. I didn't even think about that. I thought I was just being nice. I didn't mean to send you the wrong message."

"Oh, it's okay. You were nice. Extremely nice, Liz. And for that, I thank you. I just thought you were gay."

Liz breathed deeply. "I don't know, to be perfectly honest. I've never really thought about whether I was or not. I just never thought about things like that."

"Oh." Jen said with a quiet confusion in her voice. "Well, now I don't know..." Her voice trailed off momentarily. "Ummmm," Jen sought to compose her thoughts and turn them into cohesive words. "If you don't mind my mistake, we can be just friends. I don't want you to feel forced in any way. Or..."

"I...I don't know right now. Do you mind if I just take you back and then go to my hotel room? I need to think." Liz said.

"Sure. Whatever you want. I really am sorry, Liz." Jen softly replied.

Liz started the loud truck motor again. She quickly began driving back to the restaurant where Jen's car waited. The two women sat in an awkward, heavy silence; even the truck seemed more quiet.

After just a few minutes, they arrived at Jen's car. Liz pulled right up next to it so she could get out of the truck.

"Good night," Jen said softly. "And again, I'm sorry."

"It's alright," Liz weakly smiled. She watched Jen climb out and get into her car. Then Liz drove back to her hotel.

Liz lay awake all night. Thoughts sped through her mind like race cars. And like cars, they raced in circles.

Jen was pretty and very nice. But she *kissed* her! That was pretty brazen of her.

Jen's a lesbian. She knows who she is. She's dated people.

Liz had never identified herself as gay or straight. She just never thought of it. Sure she found people attractive, but dance was her first love. She couldn't allow herself to be distracted by people. She had found men attractive. But she would look at some of the girls in her classes and company and thought they were beautiful, too. Maybe she *was* gay.

Even if she was, this wasn't how she wanted her first kiss to be. Couldn't she just go back in time and erase this whole experience?

Liz marked her way through rehearsal. She was too exhausted to dance full out just for a rehearsal. As they were finishing up, she noticed a stage hand brought in a vase of flowers and left it in front of the stage.

As soon as they were finished, Liz jumped down and ran over to the bouquet.

Dear Liz,

Please forgive me. I hope you can accept this as a token of my sincerest apologies and of what I hope will be a new friendship. Take your time. I'll wait for you.

Jen

Liz's performance was mediocre at best. Between her exhaustion and confusion, she could feel that she was not dancing well.

"I'll wait for you." She said to herself repeatedly. The more she thought about it, the clearer a fuzzy memory had become.

"The right person will be patient and will wait for you." Liz's father had once told her. Liz still wasn't sure if she was a lesbian, but if Jen would wait for her, she would certainly give her a second chance.

Liz's heart was pounding in her chest. "Ummmm...hi...Jen." She struggled to find the words. "This is...Liz O'Kane calling. I'm...sorry for freaking out on you the other night. I've been doing a lot of thinking and...I've decided...I...I'd like to see you again." A wave of fear enveloped Liz. "If...you're interested, come by the theatre tonight at nine. We're doing an early show at seven, so the performance will be over at nine. I'll be waiting for you after the show. Thanks. I guess I'll see you later." Liz hung up the phone hoping that she hadn't sounded like a complete idiot in her message, and that Jen would actually show.

Liz looked out on the sea of faces. Her statuesque height helped her well. No one was recognizable. It seemed Jen hadn't come.

Liz couldn't blame her. Things had gone so badly the other night, why would Jen want to see her again? The one person who might actually be good for her and Liz screwed it up.

Liz sighed out of frustration; she couldn't help but be mad at herself.

"Liz!" A voice called out.

Liz looked around. Jen was making her way towards her.

Liz began working her way through the crowd. When she finally reached Jen, she embraced her greatly. "I am so glad you came," she whispered.

"Let me be honest with you," Liz started. "I don't know if I'm – I'm not sure I'm like you."

"You're not sure if you're gay?" Jen asked.

"No," Liz firmly answered. "But, I do like you. And I do think you're pretty. I'd like to get to know you. But I have to travel a lot. And I have never dated before...and I just don't know how to do this."

"Well, let's start." Jen answered radiantly. "There's no need to rush anything. You still have to tour, but we can talk on the phone and just see how things go. We'll do things based on your schedule, okay?" Jen was so calm and level-headed. Her serenity helped to ease Liz's red-headed anxiety.

"We can do that?!" Liz asked in shock.

"Of course! This way, there's no pressure and you can take your time figuring things out."

Liz smiled and sighed a great sigh of relief. "Thank you," she said quietly.

Jen smiled back. "You're welcome. Thank *you* for giving me another chance."

Liz continued to smile. She was really happy. Things were working out so much better than she had imagined. After a few moments of silent bliss, Liz worked up the courage to ask Jen an important question. "Can we...uhhhh...try that kiss again?" Liz's light skin flushed with color.

"Of course," Jen gently replied. She slowly leaned in and pressed her lips against Liz's. Her lips were warm, moist, and sweet. The kiss was gentle and considerate. It was wonderful, incredible, and emotional. Liz was quickly losing her heart to Jen. This moment – this kiss – was absolutely perfect.

"North Carolina. You?" Liz said into her hotel room phone. She was in Georgia now, and she and Jen were embarking on their new and unusual long-distance relationship.

"Philadelphia, actually." Jen quietly answered.

"Well that explains your accent!" Liz teased.

"Yeah." Jen laughed. "So, how did a country girl like you become a ballerina?"

It was Liz's turn to chuckle. "I was always dancing as a kid. I would even dance in church!

"So when my parent took me in..."

"Wait, what?" Jen cut her off.

"Huh?" Liz paused a moment to think. "Oh! Sorry. Let me explain. See, my parents are not my biological parents. My real parents had five kids, but couldn't afford to take care of any of us. It wasn't a clean home...or even a good home.

"My parents saw us in church and saw me dancing all the time. They talked to my real parents and agreed to take me in as their own.

"My real parents didn't mind much at all. I was one less mouth to feed; one less headache."

"How did that make you feel?" Jen softly asked. "Was it hard on you?"

"Oh no, not at all. I was so little at the time, that it really didn't bother me at all.

"At first, I'd visit my real folks every now and again, but the visits were never really nice. I hated staying there. My folks were always drunk. Bad stuff always seemed to happen to me there.

"I guess I was about seven when we all decided I should stop seeing them. So I did. That was really the best thing."

"Wow. That's quite a story," Jen whispered. "You don't seem bitter or hurt at all."

"No. Why should I be? My parents gave me such a good life. I know I wouldn't be here if I had stayed with my biological family. I have gotten the opportunities I have always dreamed of thanks to my parents. Things are good, why should I be bitter?" Liz happily answered.

"Wow," Jen said in quiet astonishment.

"So anyway," Liz continued without missing a beat. "When they took me in, the deal was I could go to dance class if I helped around the farm.

"I'm sure I complained a bit. All kids do, but any help helped the farm to make money, and then my parents could afford dance classes for me.

"It was hard at times, especially if we didn't have much to sell. But we all did our best and my parents sacrificed a lot, too. All so I could dance.

"I try never to forget that. I don't make much as a dancer, but I try to help them if I can. My parents are good people, even though I really am the redheaded step-child!" Liz laughed at herself.

Jen laughed with Liz. "I'll bet they are. They sound wonderful!" Liz could hear Jen's smile through the phone.

"Higher! Higher!" Myrna, the choreographer shouted. Liz's company was trying to condense their show to a much smaller stage.

"Miss O'Kane! Why are you *en atitude*?!" Myrna screamed.

"Because look how close Devyn is to me! If I *developpe* out, I'll kick her in the head!" Liz sternly answered.

Myrna walked around the dancers. "Damn," she whispered. "Okay. You're doing the best you can. This stage is too damn small." Myrna paused. "Let's just call it a day. I want to see everyone at six a. m. tomorrow!"

The group groaned.

Liz quietly walked over to the corner of the room. She took off her pointe shoes and gathered her towel, water and belongings. With her hands full, she walked out of rehearsal alone.

She got in her truck and drove the three miles back to her hotel. She wearily weaved her way through the semi-familiar roads until she finally pulled into the parking lot.

Tired and frustrated, Liz wearily walked through the hotel. With what little energy she had left, she opened the door to her hotel room.

Slowly, the door revealed rose petals scattered over the floor. Jen peeked her head from around the corner. "Surprise!" She said softly.

"What are you doing here?!" Liz asked in shock.

"I flew out to see you." Jen smiled.

"To Toledo?!"

Jen's face fell. "You don't want me here?"

"No, no." Liz walked over and hugged Jen. "I'm thrilled you're here. I just had a rough day and I wasn't prepared to see you is all."

"Should I not have come? Are you not happy?" Jen asked with great concern.

"No. You make me very happy." Liz whispered in Jen's ear.

"Heavy metal." Liz said into the dark.

"Heavy metal?! Are you serious?" Jen laughed as she cuddled in closer to Liz.

"Yeah. Why?"

20

"Okay, so you're an old pick-up truck driving, heavy metal-listening ballerina?" Jen laughed again.

Liz began to chuckle as well. "Well, when you put it that way, I guess I do sound weird, huh?"

"Not weird. Just not what one would expect from a ballerina." Jen tried to reassure her.

"I suppose. But I am more than just a ballerina."

"Oh, I know you are!" Jen sweetly replied.

"Maybe I just get sick of hearing classical music all day. I don't know."

"I think it's great. What bands do you listen to?"

"Metallica is one of my all-time favorites. I like Rob Zombie..."

"Rob Zombie?! Holy crap!" Jen exclaimed.

Liz lay silently for a moment.

"Oh, I'm sorry." Jen said quietly. "I didn't mean to..."

"Naw, it's ok. I just didn't expect it from you."

"Sorry." Jen said.

"It's okay."

"Are you sure?"

"Of course! I wouldn't say it if I didn't mean it."

"Thanks." Jen's relief was audible. "Ok, so who else do you listen to?"

"Well, another one of my favorites is a German band called Rammstein."

"Huh?"

"They're a German heavy metal/industrial band. Their music is really good. I've heard so much music over the years dancing, and I gained an ear for groups or people with really good musicianship, and they are one of them. They may sound coarse, but their musicianship is some of the best I have ever heard."

"Wow. Okay, if you say so." Jen replied, unsure of what to say.

Liz glanced at the clock on the nightstand. "It's almost eleven, and I have to be at rehearsal at six in the morning. I'm sorry, but would you mind...?"

"Say no more." Jen slowly got off the bed. "I hope you get some good rest."

"You too. Thanks for coming." Liz said as she rose to her feet.

Liz walked Jen to the door of her hotel room.

"Good night." Jen said with a sweet smile.

21

"Jen, I'm sorry. I don't know how to do this." Liz pleaded.

"Liz, it's fine. I have my own hotel room. I wouldn't expect anything from you. Like I said before, take your time. I'll wait for you." Jen's smile grew bigger.

"Thank you so much for understanding." Liz said.

"You're more than welcome." Jen reached up and gently kissed Liz. They both closed their eyes and savored this sweet moment.

"Good night." Jen whispered.

"Good night," Liz weakly replied. She quietly closed the door behind Jen.

"That male dancer really had his hands all over you." Jen said with a smirk on her face as she and Liz once again relaxed on Liz's hotel bed.

"Yeah. They always do." Liz replied.

"Do you think he liked it? You think that's why he became a male dancer?" Jen chuckled at herself.

"Dan? I don't know. I don't think so. I don't think he's into women. He seems pretty light in the loafers." Liz replied naively.

"You mean he's gay." Jen sat up, resting on her elbows.

"Oh…yeah. I guess so." Liz chuckled.

"Did you like it?" Jen asked flirtatiously.

"Me? Nah. I'm just used to it by now. When you dance your whole life, you get used to having hands in all kinds of places – even where you don't want them. It's just one of those things you have to get used to." Liz replied, unaware.

Jen sat quietly, unsure of how to save her failed teases.

After a few awkward moments, Liz turned to her. "What?" Liz asked, her drawl peaking at an unusually high pitch.

"It's nothing." Jen smiled. "I was just teasing you. That's all."

"You were? Well now don't I feel like a silly little country girl! I guess it's a good thing I'm a dancer and not a rocket scientist." Liz laughed at herself.

"I think it's cute, actually. It's very endearing. You're a genuine person, Liz. There aren't many people out there like you." Jen softly replied.

"Cute? How cute can a 5'10" amazon be?" Liz laughed.

Jen reached over and began tickling Liz. "Very cute, actually!"

The two rolled around the bed, laughing and ticking each other.

After a few minutes of childish fun, Liz somehow found herself on top of Jen, staring down deeply into her rich brown eyes. "Wow.

You really are beautiful." She whispered. She gently leaned down and kissed Jen passionately.

"How's the tour going?" Liz's mother, Kathy, asked into the phone. "You know we miss you."

"I miss you too, mom. It's going really well. Almost every performance has been sold out. And Jen just booked another flight to come see us when we're out in Las Vegas!" Liz said excitedly.

"Jen? Who is that?" Liz's father asked. His voice almost sounded hollow from them using two phones to talk to her.

"Oh!" Liz quickly struggled to figure out a way to describe Jen. "She's...a gal I met down in Florida. She came to a performance and is quite a fan, I guess. She and I talked after one of the shows, and we...keep in touch. She made a trip to see us in Toledo. And now she'll be coming out to one of our Vegas shows next month."

"Wow! She really is a fan." Robert, Liz's father, replied.

"It's nice that you're getting such a following already." Kathy said. "Just don't let it get to your head."

"I won't. It's just nice to have a friend – someone that you know you're gonna see when you're out on the road like this. It gets kind of lonely." Liz answered.

"I know it." Her mom said. "It's nice that you're getting fans and friends. I sure do wish we could come out and see you as much as this girl is."

"I know, mom. But y'all are still coming to the Charlotte performance, right?"

"You bet!" Robert replied enthusiastically.

"Good! I can't wait to see you then!"

"Us too," Kathy said. "Well, sweetheart, it's getting late. Your father and I need to get to bed."

"Oh yeah. I forgot about the time difference. Sorry!"

"It's okay, sweetie. We love talking to you." Liz's father said.

"Okay. Good night, mom. Good night, dad. I'll call you again soon. I love you." Liz said.

"We love you too. Good night." Her parents said in unison.

Liz gently hung up the phone. As she placed the receiver back in the cradle, she greatly wondered how she'd ever be able to explain Jen. Her parents had always been so accepting and supportive of everything she ever wanted to do. But would they accept their adopted daughter as a lesbian? Liz took a deep breath before turning off the light and attempting to sleep despite her new fears.

"Wow," Jen whispered as she admired the pointe shoes Liz had just worn in the performance. The pink satin held a secret. They appeared soft and delicate, but the toe of the shoe was hard and square. The elastic seemed to constrict, rather than expand. These shoes were unlike anything Jen had ever seen before.

She knocked on the toe of the shoe. "It's hard." She said in sheer amazement.

"Yeah," Liz replied. "Those are made by a Russian company. I prefer the Russian shoes because they're harder than then the French of Italian shoes. They use more paste and material to make a harder box and shank. They're sturdier for me, they feel more secure. And, I don't know... I just like how they feel."

"You like how they feel?!"

"Comparatively speaking!" Liz chuckled.

"These seem...painful."

"They are. It's really hard when you first start. Your feet bleed and stuff. You eventually build up to it, sort of. I mean, it still hurts a bit, but you just deal with it. It's never like walking on a cloud, though. It's not what it looks like."

"It did look so effortless watching you up there."

"Yeah, it's not. It's pain and discomfort. But you just smile and keep on going."

"Wow! You know, you hear about how high heels are bad for your feet. These must be murder!"

"They're not the best."

"What do your feet look like?" Jen asked curiously.

Liz, sitting with her feet tucked underneath her legs, started to look uncomfortable. "Oh, well...they're not pretty."

"No? What do the shoes do to you?"

"They just wreak havoc on your feet. That's all."

"Can I see?"

"They're not pretty," Liz repeated.

"I'd like to see."

Liz took in a deep breath. Slowly, she uncurled. With trepidation, she gradually slid her feet forward.

Liz's long, lean, infinite legs stretched before her. Jen studied her feet. Boney and bruised, they were anything but attractive. The bottoms of her feet were layered sheets of callouses. Her toes appeared misshapen, flat and squished together. Even her toenails were discolored and appeared unhealthy. On her feet, Liz's normally fair skin was red, cracked and peeling. Blood blisters and wounds of all sorts were sprinkled all over the tops of her feet. Indeed, there was nothing pretty or dainty about them. "See, they're ugly." She said, and she quickly hid them again.

"Wow. I am so sorry." Jen said softly.

"You have nothing to be sorry about." Liz looked down at the bed, keeping her gaze away from Jen.

"But...I just don't get why."

"Why I would knowingly do this to myself?" Liz's twang echoed through the dark room.

"Well, yeah."

"Because it's what I love. I just feel like I was born to dance. It's a small sacrifice to pay for pursuing your dream. I just wish I wasn't so ugly."

"You?! Are you kidding?! You're beautiful!"

"But my feet..."

"They are beautiful in their own way. The fact that they are the way they are because of you pursuing your dream and your passion makes them beautiful," Jen said. "Come here," she rose off the bed.

She took Liz by the hand and led her to the full length mirror hanging on the wall of the hotel room. "Look at you." Jen gently led Liz in front of her. "You have the most amazing, beautiful red hair. Your eyes are the most unusual but simply gorgeous shade of green I have ever seen. You are tall and lean. Your body is pure muscle." Jen wrapped her arms around Liz's waist. "Your legs are long and slender. And your feet are just perfect." She softly kissed the nape of Liz's neck. "Just perfect," she whispered again.

"So, which one of you is the man?" Stacie asked as she and Liz warmed up for yet another rehearsal.

"Why, I am of course!" Liz tried to deepen her voice, but her laughter broke through causing her voice to return to normal. "I don't know. I don't think either of us is, really. She's no tomboy or anything. And I'm just me. Is that normal?"

Stacie paused for a moment. "I don't know. I guess I just never thought of it. I mean, you hear about the boyish ones – I don't know. I guess I just assumed that one was always more manly than the other."

"Hmmmm," Liz said as she pondered the concept. "I don't know. Maybe I should ask her. Is it okay if we're not? I just don't know how these things work."

"Okay folks. Let's go!" Myrna's voice soared over all the others.

Stacie shot Liz a look and a grin as the two got up and took their places for the rehearsal.

THE BALLERINA

Seinfeld played on the TV, but Liz wasn't paying attention. It was a swirl of noise and colors in the background. The hotel bed was small, hard and incredibly uncomfortable. Life on the road seemed endless. She didn't even know where she was any more. Cities blended into each other. Miles became exponentially longer. Home was just a distant memory. Familiarity resided in the unknown. Everyone was tired, uncomfortable, miserable. This was a hard life. Liz was fortunate enough to have been picked up by a company right out of school, but she wondered how much longer she could live out of her suitcase. This was a lonely life and she was greatly missing Jen tonight. Excruciatingly slowly, the night ticked away.

"Attention, everyone!" Karen's voice was an audible lasso, roping everyone to her direction. "Stacie has sprained her ankle. A doctor confirmed it after class this morning. Veronique is her under study and will be dancing the role until further notice.

"Liz and Veronique, I want you two to stay after so that we can rehearse your duet."

Liz and Veronique both nodded.

Liz quickly glanced over at Veronique. She was significantly shorter than Liz. Her skin was a deep, rich, dark mocha. Her jet black hair was perfectly slicked back into an incredibly tight bun. Her long, lean muscles glistened under the shimmer of her mahogany skin. Her almond shaped eyes were focused intensely on Karen. Her profile was immaculate and unique. She was one of the most beautiful dancers to watch. Her movement was so fluid, so flawless. She was simply gorgeous.

Liz made sure she didn't stare too long, she liked Veronique. She didn't want to make her feel uncomfortable. And yet, she would have loved to take in her beauty even more.

Liz slowly peeled her glance away from Veronique. She closed her eyes and tried to focus on Karen's words.

"You dance incredibly well." A very sweaty and out-of-breath Veronique said.

"Thank you," Liz's reply was muffled as she wiped off her own sweat with a towel.

"I really mean it. You have talent...natural talent. You're gonna go far.

"Have you ever heard of the World Ballet Competition?"

"Have I?! It's only been my dream!" Liz answered brightly.

Veronique leaned in closely to Liz and softly said, "you should audition."

"Awe, thanks. But I'm not that good."

"Yes, you are! Trust me. You should really consider doing it. It can really boost your career."

"Well, thank you, but I just don't know. I'm just starting out with the company. I don't wanna..."

"Listen, you're good. You're damn good. You're young, I get it. You don't want to burn any bridges. I don't blame you. But you would do well. You would be seen by the best people and companies around the world. I know you're just starting out, but do you really want to tour for the rest of your career?"

"Not really." Liz whispered.

Veronique nodded her head. "You have real talent. Go. You never know who will be watching."

Liz cocked her head to the right. "How can you be so sure?"

"I did it last year." Veronique answered.

"And?"

"And when we finish touring, I am going to the Alvin Ailey American Dance Theatre!" Veronique smirked a devilish smirk. "I know what I'm talking about."

"Oh wow! Congratulations!" Liz said, completely oblivious to Veronique's last remark.

"Thank you. Look, I know talent; I can admit when someone is better than me. And you are absolutely one of the best dancers I have ever seen. I want to see you go far, and I know this is the way to do it.

"I can even help you get your video audition and application together if you want."

"Oh wow. Thank you. I would love some help. I'd be afraid I'm doing something wrong."

Veronique placed her hand gently on Liz's arm. "Let me help you. You are so much better than this company. I want to see you succeed." Veronique's smile was contagious.

"Wow. Thank you. That means so much to me! I cannot thank you enough."

"Arch your back more. More!" Veronique shouted at Liz.

Liz performed an arabesque, her long, lanky arms and legs reaching outward infinitely. When she came back down, she panted out of breath.

"Listen, if you want to do well, you need to execute these moves like no one ever has."

Liz took a sip of water from her bottle while Veronique continued.

"You're going up against the best of the best. If you want to stand out, you have to make yourself stand out. Make them watch you. Make them remember you. Make them *want* you." There was something erotic and seductive to Veronique's smooth, rich voice. Liz lost herself for a moment, taking in the lovely sight of Veronique and the innuendo heard in her voice.

After a brief pause, in between deep breaths, Liz said, "I'll try."

"Okay, from the top. And hurry. We don't have much time before rehearsal starts."

Liz rolled her eyes. "I don't know if I can keep going like this."

"If you want it that badly, you will."

"Okay," Liz huffed. She walked back to the center of the room and started over.

Liz yawned into the phone. "Honey, can I call you tomorrow? I'm so tired."

"Yeah, okay." Jen replied disappointedly. "Liz," she started. "Is everything alright? Our conversations have been getting shorter and shorter. What's going on?"

"Nothing," Liz's speech was long and weary. "We've just been rehearsing so much and I have no down time right now." She yawned again.

"Okay, if you say so. I just – if you don't want to do this, I would prefer you just say so."

"Oh no. It's nothing like that. I'm just worn out. I promise."

"Okay. Well, I don't want to keep you up any longer. Good night. Sleep well."

"Good night." Liz's words were garbled from her exhaustion. She had only just hung up and she instantly fell asleep.

Veronique mirrored every precise movement Liz made. The music finally began to fade. Liz held her final pose until the room was filled with silence.

"Much better," Veronique said. "You just really need to watch your turn out on the pas du chat."

"Okay, I will." Liz's voice was breathy after having rehearsed with Veronique all day.

"You really emote when you move. The music isn't in the background. It comes out of you as you move. You are amazing to watch. I really think you're going to do well.

"You'll be fine as far as style. Just make sure your technique is infallible." Veronique took a towel and buried her face in it. "Okay, let's do it one more time. We're filming tomorrow. I really want to make sure you've got it down."

"Okay," Liz huffed. She took a large swig from her water bottle.

Veronique moved in close to Liz, "Don't worry; I'll be gentle with you." She winked and brushed her hand against Liz's arm as she walked back into the center of their rehearsal room.

Liz could hardly contain her excitement as she waited for Jen to pick up the phone. Jen had just answered when Liz suddenly shouted into the receiver. "Honey, guess what!"

"Whoa! What?!" Jen replied.

"I got picked! They picked my video for the WBC!"

"Uhhhh....okay? What's the WBC?"

"The World Ballet Competition, silly! I got picked! They want me to compete!"

"Wow! That's exciting! That's great! Congratulations!"

"Thanks! I'm so excited! I gotta tell Mom and Dad!" Liz exclaimed.

"Yeah! They'll be so proud of you!"

"I sure hope so!"

"Liz, of course they will! Why wouldn't they? This sounds like it's a really big deal! When is the competition? Are you going to finish your tour?" Jen asked.

"Yeah, but it's close. The competition is in Orlando and I'll only have two weeks between finishing up here, going to Florida and practicing for the competition."

"Well, come here! Once your tour finishes, you can just come and stay here. Bring everything with you. I have plenty of room. And I'll stay out of your hair so you can do whatever you need to do to prepare."

"Are you sure?" Liz asked nervously. She didn't know what to make of the offer. It sounded too good to be true. Was it? What would it be like staying with Jen? Would Jen have expectations of Liz? Would she really let Liz do what she needed to do? Was it a good idea – was it safe to stay with Jen?

"Sure, I'm sure. Orlando is only 20 minutes from here. Why not? I'll even buy your plane ticket so you don't have to worry about a thing, okay?"

"Wow!" Liz responded. It was too good of an offer to pass up. She decided to forego her fears and insecurities and allow herself this opportunity. "You are the best! Thank you so much!"

"You're welcome. I'm happy to do it because I love you." Jen said brightly.

"I...love...you, too." Liz nervously replied

Liz looked at the picture of Jen.

How odd was it that they met after her performance in Florida. Was it fate? Were they meant to be together?

Everything up until this point had been so good...too good. Was Jen too good to be true? She always seemed like such a good, honest person. Was she really?

Was it just her nerves about ending the tour, the upcoming WBC and the thought of moving in with Jen, even if it was temporary?

There were so many changes, so much left in the air, still. Where was she going? What was going to happen next?

Liz studied Jen's image. She was plain, but pretty. She had such a good, generous heart. She supported Liz in all of her endeavors. She had been so patient with Liz as she tried to figure herself out. She was a soft, gentle soul. As she admired Jen's eyes in the photograph, she realized that Jen really was a good and true person...and that she loved her.

"How did tonight's performance go?"

"Well. Fairly packed house. Everything went smoothly until James lost his grip on me during the *pas de deux*. Luckily, I was able to maintain the position until he could get a grip again." Liz chuckled. "Honey, I am beat. Do you mind if I just go to bed?" Liz said wearily.

"No. You do what you need to do. You're under a lot of stress and pressure right now. I understand."

"Thank you so much, baby. You are so good to me." Liz yawned into the phone.

"Good night, sweetheart. Sleep well. I love you." Jen said softly.

"I love you too."

The final few weeks of Liz's tour whizzed by in a blur of rehearsals, performances and preparations for the WBC. In the blink of an eye, Liz found herself in Florida riding in the passenger seat of Jen's Subaru station wagon.

"I can't believe you're sitting here!" Jen said with a giant grin as she shifted gears.

"I can't believe you know how to drive a stick!" Liz teased.

"Ha ha," Jen retorted. "How does it feel to be here?"

"I don't know." Liz answered. "Everything has just been so hectic lately, that it almost doesn't even feel real. Maybe once I've settled in...or once I'm actually at the WBC. We'll just have to see, I guess."

"Okay. Whatever you need, just say the word."

"Somehow I need to find a practice space." Liz muttered quietly.

"In my purse, in the side pocket, I have a list of all the local studios with their phone numbers and rental fees." Jen said, watching the road ahead.

Liz bent down and pulled the paper out of Jen's purse. The list was long and ripe with information. "Oh wow. Thank you! This is so thoughtful of you. I can't believe you did this for me. Thank you so much! I don't know what to say."

"You don't have to say anything. It's the least I can do. I want you to be happy and I want you to do well."

"I love you!" Liz exclaimed.

"I love you more," Jen winked at Liz.

Liz's two weeks in Florida flew by in a blurry tornado of rehearsals and work outs. She spent her evenings as quiet time with Jen. Liz found herself more and more at ease with Jen, and found they had a routine and a life style she could easily become accustomed to.

In the blink of an eye, Liz found herself waiting in the wings, about to compete. Her nerves were exceptionally high knowing that not only was she competing in the largest ballet competition in the world, but also knowing that her parents were sitting next to Jen, having no inclination as to the true nature of their relationship. Thoughts raced through her mind until she heard her name announced. Liz took in a deep breath, exhaled and walked on to the stage.

The music began to swell, the lights brightened on and around her, and Liz simply danced with all her heart.

Liz's parents and Jen surrounded Liz after each round, watching her go further and further in the competition. They all shared in her joy as she continued to do well. The final round had come. Along with Liz, her parents and Jen all shared in the same excitement and nervousness.

Jen, Kathy, and Robert all sat with their hearts racing as Liz took the stage one last time.

Liz moved so fluidly on the stage. Her long limbs were graceful and beautiful, not lanky or awkward in anyway. Liz hit each movement with such precision and perfection. Her energy – her soul – emanated from her, creating an elegant moving sculpture on the stage. Her movements were adroit and effortless. She was the personification of beauty as she danced, twirled and leaped. Every movement from the slightest tilt of her head to the grandest arabesque was exquisite. This was a seamless execution of her dance. An intense quiet fell over the audience as they all found themselves engrossed in this amazing performance. In lissome form and in perfect synch with the music, Liz's dance was truly the expression of her soul. The music faded, the lights dimmed, and this flawless, artistic performance ended stunningly.

Albeit still nerve-wracking, it came as no surprise to Jen or Liz's parents when Liz's name was called as the winner of the competition.

Liz suddenly found herself in a whirlwind of press and pictures. Countless names and nameless faces came up to congratulate her. Jen and her parents stood by, watching with immense pride as Liz was the belle of the ball for the evening.

The celebration continued well into the wee hours of the morning. Liz's parents promised her an elegant congratulatory dinner the following night.

Exhausted and yet enlivened, Liz and Jen finally left to go back to Jen's apartment.

As they drove the dark Floridian roads, Metallica's Nothing Else Matters played through the radio in Jen's car.

"Turn it up, honey." Liz said.

Jen carefully turned the knob so the song could be better heard.

"This is our song," Liz said quietly.

They rode in silence, carefully listening to the words. "Never opened myself this way, life is ours, we live it our way...Couldn't be much more from the heart. Forever trust in who we are and nothing else matters...Trust I seek and I find in you. Every day for us something new. Open mind for a different view, and nothing else matters."

After the song ended, Liz turned to Jen. "That's how I feel about you, honey. I am so glad you were by my side tonight. I couldn't think of a better person I would want with me than you. I love you."

"I am so proud of you, Liz." Jen replied. "And I am honored to have been by your side tonight. I love you."

The two women glanced at each other and smiled brightly.

"Stay with me," Liz quietly pleaded.

"Huh?"

"Stay with me. Please. Stay with me forever."

"I would love to." Jen beamed.

Liz slowly awoke and stretched her infinite limbs. She rolled over to see Jen was gone, but there was a small note on her pillow.

"Hi sweetheart. I am at work but will be home between 4:30 and 5. See you then. I love you. Jen."

Work. Liz hadn't even thought of that. Life for everyone else had returned to normal. But she had just won the WBC yesterday! It was over. It was time for...Liz didn't even know. "Well, now what?" Liz said out loud to herself.

"Honey!" Liz exclaimed as Jen walked through the door.

"Well, hi." Jen sheepishly replied.

"I am so excited! I have the best news!"

Jen chuckled. "What is it?"

"Well, I was so afraid when I woke up this morning. You were gone and working and I just didn't know what to do with myself. I was all scared and worried 'cause I didn't know what was gonna happen now."

"Okay. So, what did happen?"

"I got a phone call, sweetheart! The Pacific North West Ballet! They offered me a position in their company, no audition needed! All because of the WBC!"

"The Pacific Northwest Ballet. As in Pacific ocean...west coast?!"

"Well, yeah!" Liz's enthusiasm was overwhelming.

"That's great baby, but what about here? What about us?" There was fear in Jen's eyes.

"Well, you're coming with me, right?" Liz nervously asked.

"I'd like to honey, but I can't just up and leave. I have a job, a lease on this apartment, the cats..."

Liz's excitement crashed to the ground.

"Sweetheart, I'm sorry. I want to go, but I need time to figure things out. I need to figure out what will happen with the shelter, where I can find new work. I have to get things in order first."

Liz looked at the ground, afraid of what Jen's answer might be. "Do you want to be with me?"

"Of course! It's not that I'm not excited for you. I am. I just need some time. I want to go, and I want to be with you, Liz. I promise." Jen paused. "When do you need to be out there?"

"August first."

"Okay. Let me think and see what I can do. Worst case scenario, I move out there a little later after you, okay?"

Liz's eyes were watery, but they still lit up. "Okay." She smiled.

Liz packed the last of her belongings into the bed of her truck. "That's everything," she said anxiously.

"Okay," Jen replied with equal apprehension. "Please call me from the road, honey."

"Oh, I will."

"This is a huge drive. I'm really worried about you."

"It'll be fine. Don't worry about it, I won't do anything stupid."

"It's not you being stupid I worry about. It's everybody else!" Jen replied.

"I know, I know. You'd think I'd be tired of driving after coming off a tour." Liz joked.

"I know, right?" Jen feigned a weak smile.

"Well, I'd better get going."

"Okay," Jen fought back the tears. "Be careful, baby."

"I will," Liz said as she embraced Jen. You're coming out in two weeks, right?"

"Yeah," Jen said sorrowfully. "The moving truck will get there next Wednesday, though. Okay?"

"Okay, honey. I can't wait till you get there."

"Me either!" Jen cried.

"I'll see you soon then. I love you."

"I love you too." Jen sniveled.

Liz hadn't been dancing long with Pacific Northwest when she was promoted from ensemble to second soloist. Her name was becoming quite well-known within the dance community after the WBC and her first few performances in Washington.

By the time spring was attempting to bloom under the grey Washington sky, Liz was about to dance the lead in Giselle.

Opening night was a tremendous success. The house was packed, and some of the greatest names in dance had come to watch Liz along with her parents and Jen.

Just two days after opening day, Jen sat Liz down after dinner.

"Honey, we need to talk." Jen said.

"Uh oh," Liz mumbled under her breath.

"I came home from work today and there was a message on the machine."

"Okay...?"

"It was from a woman named Christine Minetti. She is the artistic director of the Los Angeles Ballet. She wants you to call her so you can schedule an audition. I guess they saw you on opening night and they really liked you."

"Wow. I didn't expect that," Liz said.

"I know. You just got started here. What are you going to do?"

"Well, it's just an audition, right?"

Jen looked at Liz.

"It doesn't mean that we are going to pack right up again and move."

Jen stared at Liz, unmoving.

Liz continued. "I have a contract here, so I have to stay for the season. If they really want to have me, they will work with me."

"So, you're gonna go?!" Jen's voice cracked with fear.

"I'll just make a short trip down there and we'll see what happens."

Jen looked down.

"Honey, nothing's gonna happen for a while."

"But even still. That means we're going have to move again," Jen argued.

"We might. We might not. We don't know. You're just assuming that they'll hire me on the spot. It doesn't work that way."

"It does for you."

"I've just gotten lucky, that's all."

"Liz, you're talented. Whether you admit it or not, you stand out. Everybody else sees that. You're a hot commodity in the dance world. They *will* offer you the position, I'm sure of it."

"And," Liz breathed deeply. "If they do, we will cross that bridge when we get there."

"I just don't want to up and move every few months." Jen protested.

"I understand that, honey. Unless they have some amazing offer, we won't. And if they do, we will settle down in Los Angeles. Alright?"

"I suppose," Jen replied begrudgingly.

Liz hurried through the airport as quickly as she could. Although she had only been gone for two days, she could not wait to get back home to Jen.

Once in her truck, Liz drove the behemoth quickly down the slick Washington roads until she finally pulled in to the apartment complex's parking lot.

Grabbing her bags, she ran through the rain and hurriedly entered the apartment.

"Hi honey," Jen turned to greet Liz as she walked through the door.

"Hi baby," Liz responded out of breath.

"How'd it go?"

Liz put down her bags. "You really wanna know?"

"Yeah," Jen answered.

"They offered me a principle position."

"I knew it!" Jen said.

"That's not just it, though. They offered me money. *A lot* of money. Significantly more than what I'm getting paid now."

"Seriously?!"

"Yeah! They understand I am under contract for the season. So I am signed with them for next year."

"Wow," Jen said both excitedly and with disappointedly.

"Trust me, honey. This is going to be worth it. It's a bigger venue in a bigger city. There's much more down there than there is up here. You'll love LA. It's so sunny and bright. And crowded. You're used to that, coming from Philly. I bet you'll be happy being in a big city again."

"I hope so," Jen quietly replied.

Jen pulled out another sheet of newspaper. She placed the next plate on it and began to fold the paper up over it when Liz called from the other room.

"Look at this, honey! I think this would be perfect for you!"

Jen maneuvered her way through the small path between the boxes. She walked in and leaned over Liz's chair to see the computer screen.

"LA Cats, huh?" Jen chuckled. "Ha! That's kind of funny."

"What is?" Liz turned so she could uncomfortably see Jen.

"LA cats. It's almost like alley cats...with an accent. Well, it would sound that way if you said it! I think that's cute. I wonder if that's why they did that."

"You are weird!" Liz laughed.

Jen was engrossed by the site on the computer screen. "Oooh, look at that!" Jen's tone had immediately changed.

"What?"

"Here. Look at this." Jen pointed on the monitor.

"Oooh, that doesn't sound good." Liz said.

"I know. That's really bad. I hate to see an organization get all messed up like that. I'm sure they didn't start out that way. But if you get just one bad person in there for long enough, it all falls apart. And you know who loses? The cats!"

"Well, maybe that's a reason for you to go there, honey. You could turn it around and help the cats."

"I don't know," Jen argued.

"I do! Look at what you did in Florida. And even in our short time in here in Washington. You've done some amazing things at both places. Think of what you could do there. You know what to do and how to fix it."

Jen just looked at Liz.

"You do. Whether you realize it or not. You could be the one to help those cats."

"You really think so?"

"Yes! Go for it, honey. Just do it. You'd be helping the cats."

"I guess I could try." Jen supposed weakly.

"Well, I have faith in you." Liz retorted.

"Okay, okay. I will contact them." Jen said.

"Good!" Liz replied, quite proud of herself.

Liz ran to answer her cell phone.

"Hi honey!" Jen said.

"Hi sweetheart! What's going on?"

"It looks like I'm going to have to stay late again. I'm sorry."

"Really?"

"I'm sorry honey. I really am. If I don't get this stuff straightened quickly, I may not have a job to come back to."

Liz exhaled deeply in disappointment. "Well, I guess if you must."

"Honey, I am so sorry. Please don't be mad. I will get home as soon as I can, okay?"

"Yeah," Liz said dejectedly.

"I'll call you when I'm leaving, alright? I love you!"

"I love you more." Liz hung up before the tears began to blur her vision.

"Well, this is a lot like Philly. Just way hotter!" Jen said to Liz as they walked through the crowded L.A. streets. The hot summer sun beat down on them both.

"Do you like it here?"

"Oh yeah I do! I don't like the traffic or the roads around here. Philly was never this bad." Jen laughed. "Overall, I love it here. I have a great job, I love our apartment. I feel like we have a good life here. Don't you?"

"Well, yeah. It is crazy here, but the company is awesome. I love our apartment, too." Liz smiled down at Jen. "And mostly, I love you!"

Jen smiled back up at her; she snuck a quick kiss before continuing on their walk.

Liz watched the television on the opposite side of the couch from Jen. She looked over at her out of the corner of her eye. Jen was engrossed in her work. Leaning in, focused solely on the screen of her laptop, she typed away fervently. She paid no attention to her lonely partner on the other side of the couch.

"Honey, why don't you put that down? Relax for a bit. Come watch the movie with me." Liz implored.

"Soon, honey. I have got to get this done." Jen said without turning her eyes away from her monitor.

Liz quietly huffed, longing for some time and attention from her lover that would never come.

Liz jumped off the couch and leapt to the phone so quickly. Jen lowered the volume on the television for Liz to hear.

"Hello?" Liz's drawl dragged out one little word. The voice was familiar, but his speech seemed strained. "Oh, hi Gary."

"Liz, is Jenny there? I need to talk to her."

"Sure, Jen is here. Let me just get her right quick. Hold on." Liz gently placed her hand on the bottom of the phone and she walked over to Jen.

"It's for you. It's your dad." Liz whispered.

Jen got up and took the phone from Liz. "Hello?"

Jen paused while her father spoke. "Oh hi, dad. What's going on?"

Liz could hear the tone of Gary's voice leaking from the receiver.

"Of course, dad. What is it?"

Liz held her breath while Jen listened.   After a few painfully silent moments, Jen finally spoke. "Mom? What's wrong with mom?" Jen's voice cracked with fear.

Liz strained to hear Gary.

"Sick? Mom is sick? Is that what you mean? What do you mean mom is ill?"

"She has...stomach cancer." Gary's voice could hardly be heard despite the quiet that surrounded them.

"Mom has..." Jen's voice trailed off.

Jen was silent for several moments.

"Oh really?" Tears broke through Jen's voice.

Even away from the phone, Liz could hear Gary struggle to speak. "Yes. Mike is coming down tomorrow morning. Adam is already here."

"Okay," Jen swallowed some tears.

There was silence for several moments.

"I don't know, but I'll go now. I don't know how or when, but let me go pack some things and I'll leave right away." Jen said anxiously.

The other end of the phone was silent.

"Dad?"

Jen stared blankly at the phone.

Liz ran over to Jen. "What's wrong, honey?"

Jen's eyes darted away from Liz to the floor. "Mom has cancer." Jen paused. "I have to go," she said hurriedly as she turned from Liz to go pack.

Liz gently grabbed her arm. "Jen?"

Reluctantly, Jen turned towards Liz, tears streaming down her face. She buried herself in Liz's arms and wept.

The family walked into the home somberly. Liz slowly traipsed behind Jen. There were no words, so they entered wordlessly. Each person's breath could be heard, each on their own pattern of deep inhalation and exhalation.

The funeral and luncheon had gone as well as they could have. The memorial service was quite fitting for Elaine. Even the weather was cooperative. For all the positive things Liz could count, it pained her to see Jen cry. Jen's bright smile had been gone for a while. Her brown eyes seemed dark and dull. Even having known Elaine for a few years, it was still a very painful experience, even for Liz.

Jen flopped down onto the couch. Liz walked and stood next to her. She gently rubbed Jen's back. The pair looked around the room. Everyone sat quietly with their eyes staring blankly at the floor. Liz took in one last deep breath, hoping to somehow relieve Jen of her pain.

Jen shook her right hand repeatedly.

"Are you alright?" Liz asked, watching Jen with a fearful curiosity.

"Yeah. I'm fine. My hand just feels...weird. That's all."

Liz glared at her with concern.

"I'm sure it's fine," Jen dismissed it. "With all the stress from Mom and everything else, maybe I over did it or strained my hand or something."

Liz's face expressed clear disbelief and concern.

Adam walked into the room with impeccable timing. "What's going on?"

"It's nothing." Jen smiled weakly.

"Your sister has been shaking and rubbing her hand all morning. She says it feels 'weird.'" Liz spoke austerely to Adam.

"Weird? Weird how, Jenny?"

"It's nothing. It's just pins and needles. No big deal. Liz is making a mountain out of a mole hill, I promise."

Adam turned back to Liz. "Is that true, Liz?"

"I don't know. You tell me. She's had things like this before. She drops stuff a lot. She's exhausted and has been for a while. I don't know. Maybe it isn't anything. It just seems odd to me that this has been going on all morning and it doesn't let up. Could that just be from stress?"

"I suppose, but that's not typical. You probably should get that checked out, Jenny. Just to be sure."

"Just to be sure of what? It's no big deal." Jen defended herself.

"Just humor me. Make your older brother happy and go over to HUP. I'll make a couple of calls to make sure you get the best of the best over there."

"HUP? Seriously? I don't need to go to the hospital. Especially the one where you work. You'll conspire with your coworkers against me or something."

Adam sighed. "Come on, Jenny. Just go."

Jen looked at both Adam and Liz. "I'm outnumbered. Fine, I'll go."

"I'll take you." Liz said firmly. "Adam, where am I going?"

"To the Hospital of the University of Pennsylvania. It's on Spruce Street. Do you know how to get there?"

"I think so."

"Here, I'll drive, but you come with us. Jenny will need you with her, whether she says it or not."

Adam grabbed his keys and the three left.

Liz stood nervously by Jen's bedside. She hovered over her in anxious silence.

"Have you had episodes like this before? Have difficulty speaking? Ever get really fatigued?" Dr. Lynch asked Jen. Liz bit her lip, having nearly answered for her. Liz thought if maybe she had the answers, she had some control and this wasn't of any real concern.

"Well, yeah." Jen answered casually after a moment. "But I never thought anything of it. I work a lot, and my mother just passed away last week, so we've been under a lot of stress lately. I'm sure it's just stress."

"Well stress can certainly aggravate things. But, it's not stress that's causing this."

Liz's head quickly turned and her eyes grew wide as she intensely watched him.

"What do you mean?" Jen and Liz asked in unison.

"Your MRI showed several plaque lesions on your brain. Four, to be exact."

"Plaque lesions? What does that mean?" Jen asked.

"You have multiple sclerosis," Dr. Lynch responded somewhat coldly.

"What?" Jen asked sitting up in the hospital bed.

"I'm sorry, but you have MS. The tingling sensations, brain fog, fatigue, loss of motor skills – those are all signs of MS."

"That can't be right." Jen's words reflected Liz's thoughts.

"And living out in LA, a hotter climate makes it worse. Heat exacerbates multiple sclerosis."

"So, being out in California has brought this on? LA made her sick?" Liz asked, feeling both incredibly nervous and incredibly guilty for having made Jen move to California.

"No." He answered. "But the heat out there aggravated things – it can make the symptoms worse. She might not have noticed the symptoms so quickly or so severely." Dr. Lynch explained.

"So, what I do? What happens now?" Jen asked tearfully.

"Well, I have the name of an excellent neurologist. I've already put in a call to him. He will see you on Tuesday. He'll explain MS and what type you have, come up with a treatment plan and so on. I really want you to stay here, Jen. I think the climate of Los Angeles is a hazard to your health."

"Okay," Jen sniffled.

Liz still stood nervously, continuing to hover over her in anxious silence. Feelings of guilt consumed her.

"Hi Mom and Dad," Liz spoke nervously into the phone.

"Hi Liz!" They said in perfect harmony.

"How are you doing, honey?" Kathy asked.

"Good."

"You still liking the fast life out there?" Robert asked.

"Well, that's the reason I called." Liz's voice began to shake.

"What's going on, honey bee?" Robert probed.

"Ummmm...well, you see, Dad...I'm gonna be moving soon."

"Where to, now?"

"Philadelphia." She answered in utter fright.

"Why there?" Kathy spoke.

Liz sighed into the phone. "You remember Jen, right?"

"Of course!" Her parents both answered brightly.

"She's been a good friend to you," Robert added.

"Well, she has MS. She was just diagnosed with it. And she wants to go back home. To be closer to her father and brothers and some old friends."

"Oh that's too bad. She's such a nice girl. So, where is home for her, sweetie?" Kathy inquired.

"Philadelphia."

"Wait, what?" Kathy asked, confused. "What does her going home have to do with you? I don't understand."

"Mom, Dad. Jen has been more than just a friend to me. She's my..." Liz took in a deep breath. "She's my girlfriend...or partner...whatever you call it."

There was silence on the other end of the phone.

"I'm...I love her. She's a wonderful person. And she moved out to Washington and then California for me. She's always supported me. She takes good care of me. And now I need to take care of her. She needs to be in Philadelphia, and I want to go with her."

There were several more moments of silence before Liz could hear her mother take in a deep breath. "You know we've always liked Jen," Kathy started. "We've enjoyed it when you brought her with you for holidays. She is a lovely girl."

"Truth be told, we have always wondered about her."

Liz didn't know how to respond to her mother.

"I guess what your mother is trying to say," Robert chimed in. "Is that we're not terribly surprised."

"Okay, well..." Liz swallowed hard. "Is that alright? I mean, do you mind? Does it bother you?"

"It's not what we're used to," Kathy answered. "But we do like her. I think she has been a good, supportive person for you."

"So, it's okay?" Liz repeated herself.

Liz heard both of her parents inhale deeply.

"Uhhh...yeah. I guess so." Kathy responded.

"Yeah," Robert said. "Yeah, I guess it is. If she wasn't such a good person, I don't know if I could accept that. But I've seen you two together. I've watched her come to the WBC and all of your appearances. Like you said, she has moved a lot for you. I think that says a lot about her character. I think you made a good choice when you picked her, honey bee.

"As your parents, we just want you to be happy. And we want you to be safe wherever you go."

Liz became choked up with tears. "Thank you, daddy!"

"We love you, sweetheart." Kathy said.

"I love you too," Liz answered as a smile crept its way onto her face.

Liz braced herself before walking into Christine's office. Slowly, cautiously, she entered.

Christine was on the phone. She looked up and saw Liz. She smiled and motioned that she would be with Liz in just a moment.

"Yes. Okay. That would be perfect. Okay, great. Thank you." Christine finally hung up. "Well hello, Miss O'Kane. What can I do for you today?"

"Well...you see, Jen was just diagnosed with MS."

"Jen..." Christine muttered as she tried to remember who Jen was.

"My partner."

"Oh yes! Okay. I'm so sorry to hear that. What can we do for you two?"

Liz swallowed hard. "She needs to move back home, to Philadelphia. She has her family there and some great doctors are treating her."

"Oh, I see." Christine said casually.

"So, I need to go with her. I need to talk to everyone about terminating my contract."

"Miss O'Kane, you have been with us for the last three years. Everyone in the company and on the staff absolutely loves you. You are one of the best dancers we've had in our existence. It will be a terrible shame to lose you, but I understand it completely. I will speak to everyone and we will pay out your contract."

"Are you sure?"

"Oh absolutely! I hate to lose you, I really do. But I understand. If you are ever able to come back to LA, just call me. You will always have a place here with us."

Tears of both gratitude and sadness filled up Liz's eyes and quickly began running down her face. "Thank you!"

Christine smiled and nodded her head.

Liz nervously packed the last of her belongings. She inhaled deeply. This was nerve-wracking. She had asked Jen to move twice, both times were for her career. This move was different, though.

There was no career advancement to be had here. This move held no new opportunities. This move held a very uncertain future for both Liz and Jen.

How would they live? What was life with multiple sclerosis going to be like? Liz had her savings, but how long would that last? After that, what would they do? Could Jen ever work again? Would life become mundane again, or were they doomed to a life of infinite doctor and hospital visits? What was going to happen a week from now? A month from now? A year from now? A decade from now?

This was a move that was founded in fear: the more Liz thought of it, the more fear consumed her.

She took one last deep breath, prayed a quick prayer and walked out of the room to bring her last bag out to the moving truck.

Liz and Jen sat down one night to create a new and humble budget.

"Okay, this is what I have saved up." Liz started.

Jen shuffled through some papers. "Here, this is it. This is my savings and 401(k)." Jen handed the papers to Liz.

"Okay Well...wow." Liz sighed. "That's not much for us to live on."

"Even all of it combined?" Jen's voice reflected apprehension.

"If this was temporary, we'd be alright. But it won't. We don't know when I can dance again...if at all. You won't be working. We'll need rent money, money for food, money for the cats, money for the cars and then regular bills like electric and heat and..."

"Okay, I get it. I need to apply for SSI disability." Jen said, defeated.

"That'll help a little bit. But it is still going to be tight." Liz buried her face in her hands.

"I talked to Dad yesterday." Jen admitted. "He did offer to help, as did Adam."

"They're so good. I appreciate that. It's very nice of them. Hopefully, we won't have to."

"I know. I hope not, but..."

"We'll cross that bridge when we get there." Liz said. "For now, let's just go to bed. It's late. We're both tired. We can work on this some more tomorrow."

Jen looked sick with worry. "Are we going to be okay, Liz?"

Liz looked lovingly back at her. "Yes, honey. I don't know how, but we'll make it work. Right now we've got to get you better. Alright?"

Jen reached her arm across the table and took Liz's hand in her own. "Alright. I love you."

"I love you too." Liz smiled.

"Classic Car Care." A raspy voice answered the phone.

"Hi, my name is Elizabeth O'Kane. I have a 1977 Chevrolet pick-up truck. It looks like I might need some new leaf springs. Is that something y'all can do?" Liz asked.

"Sure! I love working on a classic. Beats working on the street cars all the kids have nowadays. Come on down, I'll take a look and see what I can do."

"Well, you see, that's where the problem is. I am new to this area and I don't know where you are."

The voice on the other end chuckled. "I'm in Bala Cynwyd, right off of the Schuylkill."

"Excuse me?" Liz asked.

"The Schuylkill. The expressway. Seventy six."

"Oh, okay." Liz said, though she wasn't really sure if she knew what seventy six really was.

"Yeah. I'm on Belmont, just a quarter mile off the exit."

"Alright, well thank you. I'll be there shortly."

"Okay."

Liz hung up the phone. "Honey!" Liz called out. "How do I get to the expressway?"

A tall, thin woman with dark shaggy hair stood outside the garage, smoking a cigarette when Liz pulled in with her truck.

Liz jumped out of her truck and walked over to the woman. "Excuse me," she started. "I just called a little while ago. Is the mechanic inside?"

"Nope." A smirk came across her face.

"Well, do you know where I'd find him?" Liz asked.

"You're looking at *her.*" The woman said with a smile.

"Oh dear lord! I am so sorry! I didn't mean..."

"It's cool. I'm Linda." She put out her hand.

Liz shook her hand, "Liz."

"Nice to meet you Liz. Nice truck."

"Thank you. It was my daddy's, but he gave it to me when I graduated from college."

"That's one hell of a present."

"It sure is. It was always his dream to have a nice truck, but he's a farmer. So I've done my best to trick it out and maintain it."

"From here, it looks like you've done a great job." Linda said. "Pull 'er right in and I'll take a look."

Liz and Linda began to forge a good friendship thanks to Liz's truck. The more Linda worked on the truck, the more Liz trusted her.

As she would work on the truck, Linda would talk with Liz and they became quite familiar. The mechanic and the ballerina had little in common, save for a love of cars.

Liz had really felt out of sorts in such a large city. Linda became Liz's first real friend.

It didn't take Liz long to feel comfortable enough to come out to her new friend.

"I'm actually kind of surprised." Linda said.

"How come?"

"Well, you just don't strike me as the type."

"How would you know?" Liz innocently asked.

Linda chuckled. "I am too."

"You are?! Oh. So...?"

"You just don't set off my 'gaydar,' if you know what I mean." Linda laughed.

"Okay?" Liz didn't quite know what to make of Linda's statement.

"You know – when you can just tell a person is just by looking at them.

"People have always picked up on it with me. Hell, my parents knew when I was little. My mom didn't want to accept that her one and only little girl was a dyke, but she knew.

"It's just something I've always known about myself, too. So, I've just always known. I know I'm gay, I act gay, I consider myself gay. I don't know. It's just a way I identify myself."

"Oh, okay!" Liz responded brightly.

"So, do you think of yourself as gay?" Linda quietly asked Liz.

"Hell yeah! I'm a rootin' tootin', lady-lovin', pick-up truck driving lesbian! Yee haw!" Liz said loudly before falling into laughter. After a few moments, she composed herself and her tone quieted. "To tell you the truth, I never really thought about it, Lin. I just know that I love her and she loves me. If that makes me gay, then so be it."

"It's great that you have that. You're really lucky."

"Yeah. She's great."

"No, I mean what you have. You have a house with someone you love and they love you back. You have a life, a family. It's nice. I hope to have that someday."

"You don't have a girlfriend?" Liz asked gently.

"Nah." Linda dismissed.

"Well, why not?"

"I don't know. Lots of reasons, I guess." Linda paused and quickly changed the subject. "There. Your timing is all set. You should be good to go for a while."

"You got any plans for Memorial day?" Linda asked from under the truck.

"Why yes we do! We are going to have a barbecue at our house. Jen's brother, Adam, will be there. Her friend Maria is coming. Just a small get together. You?"

"Nah, nothing really. I'll probably just stay home, drink a couple of beers."

"Why don't you come over?" Liz asked brightly.

"Thanks. I just...I don't...I don't normally mix business with pleasure. It's gotten me into trouble in the past."

"Well, I...you're the only friend I have out here right now." Liz stated sadly. "I would love to have you there."

Linda slid out from under the back axel. She swiped sweat off her forehead and smeared oil in its place. "Oh, don't kill me with that pitiful stuff."

"Well, it's true. And I really would like to have you there."

"Oh, alright. I'll go. You're not going to try to hook me up with anyone, are you? Are there going to be any single lesbians that you're going to play match-maker with me and them?"

"Maria is single, but I didn't plan on getting you two together."

"You didn't? Okay, good." Linda smiled. "Write down your address for me and I'll be there. What time?"

"One o'clock."

"Okay, I'll be there." Linda smiled.

Alicia's brown hair was pulled into a perfect ballet bun. She plain and was far shorter than Liz, but she was a graceful and elegant dancer. "I'll tell you what," she started. "I will gladly work with you privately and you can work it off by teaching classes yourself. Sound like a plan?"

"I think so. I'm just worried. I don't want to commit to too much because I need to be available to help my partner."

"I understand that. We can just play things day by day or week by week and work accordingly."

"Oh, that would be wonderful! I cannot thank you enough!"

"It's my pleasure. Your resume is incredible and I understand your situation. I'm always happy to help a fellow dancer."

"Thank you," Liz grasped Alicia's hand and held it for a moment before walking out the studio door.

Linda came back in to the room with beers in both hands. She handed them out to Liz, Jen and Maria and lastly Stephania. "Here," she said to each of them as she handed them out.

"So, how do y'all know each other?" Liz asked as she pointed at Linda and Stephania.

"Steph's a model." Linda said. "She shoots with some of the classic cars I work on for HRC."

"HRC?" A perplexed look washed across Liz's face.

"Human Rights Campaign. The sale of the calendars is donated to them for LGBT rights." Stephania answered in a nearly condescending tone.

"Oh." Liz replied curtly.

"Tell me more about you," Stephania leaned in closely to Maria.

Linda rolled her eyes and then turned to Liz and Jen. "You know, you should bring your truck down next time she has a shoot."

"That would be great!" Jen smiled. "Just think, honey! People could admire your truck and it would go to a good cause!"

"What would it cost me? I haven't worked in a while and Jen..." Liz started.

"Nothing but your time. You'd bring the truck, hang out with us for a while and once the shoot is done, you'd be good to go." Linda explained.

"Oh. Well then maybe alright. We'll see."

"Yeah. I'll call you once we start scheduling everything."

"Sounds like a plan, Lin!" Liz smirked at Linda.

Linda quickly glanced at the large television just past her right shoulder. "Oh hey! The game's started, you guys."

The group of women all turned their attention to the Super Bowl game that was now underway.

"Good job, girls!" Liz called out as the class of preteen girls exited the studio.

Alicia wormed her way through the small group to enter the studio. "Hey Liz. How's it going?"

Liz plopped down on a chair. "It's alright, I guess. I am tired, I'll tell you that."

"I know. You've been working your butt off and I appreciate it." Alicia paused. "How's Jen?"

Liz sighed heavily. "She's alright, I guess. She's walking with a cane now because she's been falling a lot."

"Wow. I am so sorry."

"Thanks. It's hard to see, you know. She's young. She shouldn't have to walk with a cane." Tears began to escape from Liz's eyes. "And I know it's even harder on her. She doesn't want to have to live this way."

Alicia reached over and gently rubbed Liz's back.

"It's not fair. She didn't do anything wrong to deserve this." Liz stared ahead, fearful of making eye contact with Alicia.

"I know. You're right. It's not fair. It's not fair to her and it's not fair to you. Life just sucks sometimes, you know?"

"Yeah," Liz sniffled. She slowly stood up. "I'm gonna get goin' if that's okay."

"Of course!" Alicia replied. "Have a good weekend. Try to take it easy, alright?"

Liz nodded. "I will," she replied through her tears.

The parking lot of Linda's shop was filled with classic and muscle cars, and what seemed to be an infinitely large number of people.

Liz stood behind everyone next to Linda. "This is so cool!" She whispered.

Linda chuckled. "Yeah."

"So you do this every year?" Liz asked in awe.

"Yup."

A woman with rich, chocolate brown hair walked over to Linda. "Hey," she said quietly.

"Hey Heather! How are you?"

"Good. You guys haven't started yet?"

"Nah. They're still getting Steph all put together." Linda teased.

"Good, so it's okay that I'm late!" Heather laughed.

"Yeah," Linda laughed with her.

Liz watched them.

"Oh, I'm sorry. Liz, this is Heather. She owns that MG over there," Linda said as she pointed to care that was merely a blip in amongst the giant crowd.

"Heather, this is Liz. She owns that Chevy truck."

"Oh, I love that one! So unique. What a great ride." She said in an almost sickeningly sweet tone.

Liz shook her hand, saying nothing in response.

"Well, I have someone I want you to meet." Heather said turning to Linda.

She reached out and pulled over a blonde woman who wasn't paying attention.

The blonde pushed her curls out of her face.

"Linda, this is my girlfriend, Donna. She's a cop." Heather bragged.

"Hey," Linda said extending her hand. Donna's grip was firm.

"Hi." Donna answered. The two looked at each other for a moment.

"Honey, Linda is the one who owns this shop." Heather leaned over and whispered in Donna's ear.

"Oh hey." Donna said again, still gripping Linda's hand.

"This is Liz." Linda said, finally breaking Donna's hold.

"Hi," Liz said with her bright, strong drawl.

"Hi." Donna said as she shook Liz's hand.

"Okay, everyone. Quiet on the set! We're shooting with the Camaro first. Everyone to their positions!" A man yelled over the group.

Linda, Liz, Donna and Heather all turned their attention to Stephania as she began to pose with the cars.

Liz, Jen, Linda, Maria, Stephania and Donna sat around the table.

"This is nice. I like this." Liz said, smiling.

"It is always good to be in the company of family," Maria agreed.

Stephania moved her chair in even closer to Maria and she rested her head on Maria's shoulder.

"Thanks for inviting me." Donna said to Linda.

"Yeah, any time."

"Hi ladies. What can I get you for drinks?" A young waiter asked the group.

"An apple-tini!" Steph shouted out.

"A Corona, please." Maria looked up at the young man.

"I'll just have a Bud," Linda said.

"Make that two, please." Donna requested.

"I'll just have water." Liz said.

"Can I also have a water, but could you put lemon in mine?" Jen asked.

"Certainly!" The young man flashed a smile and quickly disappeared into the restaurant.

"This is going to be a good night." Maria said, nodding and smiling at them all.

"Excellent work, Liz." Alicia said as they finished up another hour of class for Liz.

"Thank you," Liz said before she took a large drink of water.

"How is Jane doing?"

"Better." Liz replied. "Her technique really isn't that bad. The problem is, her turn out isn't very strong. I think her hips are inverted or something. That poor girl tries so hard, and I think at best she can only get like a thirty degree turn out!"

"That's tough. I'm glad she's doing better, though. She has struggled a lot in the past and I've had a couple of teachers try with her, but no one could ever seem to get it right with her. Know what I mean?"

"I do. It just takes a little extra time and patience is all. She's a good kid and she really does try with all her might."

Alicia smiled at Liz. "I'm really glad we've got you on board here. I think you're one of the best things to happen to this studio."

"Awe, thanks!" Liz smiled, her cheeks turned a slight rose color.

Alicia smiled back. After a moment, she checked her watch. "Okay. It is almost eight o'clock. I think we both call it a day."

"Sounds good to me!" Liz took another sip of water.

"Okay then. See you tomorrow morning?"

"Yeah. What time?" Liz asked.

"Ten should be fine." Alicia said.

"Alright. Sounds like a plan. I'll see you then." Liz stood up and walked out of the studio into the darkening night.

"How have you been?" Liz asked.

"Not bad. Pretty busy. How is Jen?" Linda asked as she removed the old brake drum of Liz's truck.

"She seems to be doing well. She is in remission right now. She has that relapsing/remitting kind of MS or whatever it's called."

"Uh huh."

"So anyway, she's been pretty stable."

"That's good. What are your plans from here on out?" Linda strained to speak as she lifted the heavy new brake drum and placed it on the truck.

"I don't know. We don't really have one. We've just been taking it day by day."

"Okay."

"Why, Lin? What's up?"

"Hang on." Linda got up and walked over to her small, crowded desk. She grabbed a tiny newspaper clipping. "Here," she said.

"What's this?" Liz asked.

"I just saw this in the Philadelphia Inquirer. I thought it might interest you. Are you and Jen in a place where you can go back to dancing full time?"

"I think so. I want to ask her first, but to audition and to be a part of a company again would be amazing. I don't have to be a principle dancer. I just wanna dance!"

Linda chuckled. "I hope you can." She smiled.

"Are you *sure*?" Liz asked for the fifth time, while still grasping tightly onto the clipping.

"Yes!" Jen laughed. "Go! We're doing ok. I want you to dance. I never wanted to hinder your career."

"You didn't honey. I just want to make sure you're okay."

"I am. I will be. I have Dad, Adam, and even Donna if ever needed anything. Ok? It will be fine. Just go out there and kick some butt!" Jen's smile lit up with pride as she looked up at Liz.

"Honey, you are simply the best. Thank you. I love you!"

"I love you more." Jen winked before kissing Liz.

Liz stood in front of the full-length mirror. Her black pin stripe suit sat beautifully on her tall, lean figure. Her flaming red hair was pulled into a perfect bun. Not one hair was out of place. She continuously rolled the suit with a hair roller to ensure that there wasn't any cat hair on her suit. Today was too important to lose on account of cat hair.

Jen walked out of the bedroom, leaning heavily on her cane. She came up behind Liz, and wrapped her arms around Liz's tiny waist. She kissed her on the back of the neck. "You are going to knock them dead today, sweetie." Jen said gently.

"I sure hope so," Liz replied.

"You taking the truck?"

"Nah. I ain't driving into the city at this time in the morning. The Schuylkill will be a nightmare. I'll just take the train in. It'll be easier."

"Ok, sweetie. Give me a call when you're on your way back. We're supposed to go out with the gang tonight. We're gonna meet Katie, Linda's new girlfriend."

"Ooh, that's right! I forgot all about that! Thanks for reminding me, honey. I should be back in plenty of time for that. We'll take the truck out tonight for that. She needs to get run." Liz paused for a moment. "You gonna be okay while I'm gone?" She asked gently.

"Yeah. I'm not gonna do much of anything until you get back home. I'll be fine. You just go and knock 'em dead!" Jen said with a smirk.

Liz leaned down and kissed Jen on her forehead. "Thanks honey. I'll do my best. I'll call you later on. I love you." With that she grabbed her large duffle bag, and started heading towards the door.

"I love you more!" Jen called back. With her brown hair a mess, and her light blue terrycloth robe wrapped tightly around her, Jen hobbled to the kitchen to get some breakfast.

"Well, Miss O'Kane," one of the stuffy judges started. "Your resume is extremely impressive. You've danced with some of the finest companies in the country. But, why such a break between your last company and now?"

"My partner was diagnosed with MS a couple of years ago, and so I took some time off to be with her. I just felt that I needed to be there with her through various tests and treatments and all. Things are more stable now, so I'm ready to dance again." Liz's Southern accent echoed in the nearly empty theatre.

"There is also some concern about your age, and the length of that gap" he stated coldly.

"I understand," Liz replied. "Thirty three can be kind of a tricky age for us dancers, especially when we haven't danced in a while. Some people view their thirties as the time when they lose their youth and vitality. But, I have been practicing and attending class daily even during this 'break.' So by no means has it been a real break.

"You know, I look at people like George Balanchine. One of the most incredible dancers and choreographers ever. Someone whose work this company follows. That man danced for so many years. He danced well beyond his 33rd birthday. He even kept dancing while having heart issues and his other medical problems.

"Martha Graham danced for over 70 years.

"I know it's been a while, but if they can do that, I know that I can dance at thirty three...and beyond." Liz stood proudly on stage.

"Why the Pennsylvania Ballet?" A woman asked.

"Why not?" Liz retorted. "I'm here; Philadelphia is my home and has been for quite some time now. This ballet troupe is a wonderful company. There is such a rich heritage here, and I would be honored to be a part of that heritage. I know that I would gain from this experience as much as I would be able to contribute."

"Well, let's just see if that's true." The first man remarked.

"We've already reviewed your video," a third man chimed in. "On film, you appear to dance well. Now, we can really see how good you are in person."

Liz took a few steps backwards. She closed her eyes and inhaled deeply. "God be with me," she prayed. With one more deep breath, she opened her eyes and took her starting position.

As Liz rode home on the train, listening to Metallica's "And Nothing Else Matters," she felt her cell phone vibrate. "Damn," she thought. "I forgot to call Jen. She's gonna have my hide!" Liz picked up the phone, and saw that the caller ID was not Jen's number. She answered hesitantly. "Hello?"

"Hi, Miss O'Kane?"

"Yes, this is she."

"This is Gary Bruden from the Pennsylvania Ballet." Liz's heart stopped. The gentleman on the other end paused before continuing. "This is very atypical for us to do, but I must tell you that the board members, the artistic director and I were all thoroughly impressed by your audition today. We'd like to offer you the position of Prima Ballerina."

Liz had to use every ounce of strength not to scream right there on the Septa train. She took a few deep breaths to try to calm herself.

"Miss O'Kane?"

"Yes, I'm here. I'm sorry. I just wasn't expecting to hear so soon. I am flattered, truly. I would be honored to be the Prima Ballerina. When do we have our first class and rehearsal with the rest of the company?"

"Well, as you may know, we're actually on a break right now; classes and rehearsals start in four weeks."

"Well, okay then." Liz said excitedly. "I know I'll be speaking to you before then, and then I'll see you in four weeks."

"Sounds good. Thank you very much." With that, he hung up.

Liz so desperately wanted to scream, shout and jump for joy on the train, but she figured that the other people on the train may not appreciate it. She took a few more deep breaths to calm herself down. Time to call Jen. "Hey honey."

"Hi sweetie! How did it go?"

"Good! It went real good, actually."

"I'm pretty sure the 'Ohne Dich' piece surprised them."

"Oh really?"

"Yeah. Most ballet people aren't expecting you to dance to a song by a heavy metal band." Liz laughed.

"Yeah, I guess not." Jen also chuckled. "But you do feel it went well?"

"Yeah! I definitely have some good news."

"What do you mean you have some good news? Did you hear right away? When did they say they would let you know?"

"If I wasn't on the train, I'd tell you. But, I'll tell you when I get home, okay?

"Now, how are *you* doing?"

"I'm alright. I'm just doing some laundry at the moment, nothing crazy."

"Don't push yourself," Liz warned.

"I won't." Jen replied meekly. "I wish you'd tell me what's going on. It's not like you to keep things to yourself."

"I know, I know. I just don't want to be one of those loud, obnoxious people on the train. Just wait till I get home, okay? I should be home in 20 minutes or so."

"Okay, sweetie. I love you."

"I love you more," Liz said.

As the group of seven women sat around enjoying their dinner, the conversation flowed freely. Katie definitely fit in with the rest of the crowd.

"I think it's great that you're a vet student." Liz said.

"Thanks," Katie said.

"Hey! Now you know someone who can care for your herd!" Stephania joked. The table broke out into laughter.

"Herd?" Katie asked.

"We have seven cats." Liz explained.

"Seven?!" Katie's pitch rose up in utter shock.

"You see," Jen quietly explained. "I used to be the director of an all feline shelter in Florida. Cats have always been my passion, and so I've taken in countless kitties over the years."

"Wow. That is amazing!" Katie said with great enthusiasm. "I'll be more than happy to help out with the troops. And maybe if you know any good rescue organizations here in the city, we can work something out there too!"

Liz and Jen smiled at each other.

"I like her," Liz whispered to Jen.

"Me too! She's unlike anyone Linda has dated before. She's a keeper!"

Liz raised her glass and said, "To Katie!"

Jen interrupted. "Wait! That's not all! We have an announcement to make. My amazing woman just became the new Prima Ballerina for the Pennsylvania Ballet!"

"Why didn't you tell us?!" Linda asked.

Liz simply blushed.

"Here's to Katie *and* to Liz!" Linda toasted.

Everyone raised their glasses.

"Watch your end of the table," Donna barked at Linda as they tried to enter the tiny Philadelphia apartment doorway.

"It's a good thing you don't have too much, Katie." Stephania huffed as she carried a box behind Linda and Donna.

"Thank you all so much for helping me move!" Katie's reply echoed down the hallway.

Jen carried a small, light box full of Katie's toiletries. After she placed the box in the bathroom, she started to walk past Liz who was carrying a very large and awkward box.

"Sit," Liz ordered.

"But, I could…" Jen protested.

"No, honey. Please, just sit. There are only 3 boxes left and we're done. Just relax." Liz said gently.

Jen grudgingly complied and sat on the couch, watching the others heave all of Katie's belongings.

The group had just placed the last box and began to rest when someone knocked on the door.

Katie jumped up and answered it. "Hi Keith! Good to see you again."

"You too," the awkward young man replied.

He handed her two large pizza boxes. Two bags full of soda sat at his feet.

Katie eagerly took the pizzas and turned back into the apartment. Linda jumped up and grabbed the bags.

"Thanks!" Katie said enthusiastically as she handed him money. Keith turned and began to walk away as they shut the door.

"This is my way of saying thanks, ladies!" Katie said with great joy. "Dig in!"

The group took Katie's order quite seriously; they quickly indulged themselves in the food.

Only a few minutes into their meal, the phone rang. Linda jumped right up to answer.

"Hello?" She paused for a moment as the person on the other end spoke. Linda put the phone down and walked over to Katie. "It's for you, babe," she whispered and she brushed a kiss on Katie's cheek.

Katie rose, and picked up the phone. "Hello? Oh, hi Mom." She paused. "Yes, that was Linda, my new roommate."

"Roommate?" Stephania asked Linda, her face conveying an expression of disapproval.

"Yeah. Katie's parents are tough. Her dad is a pastor, so she has to watch what she says. It sucks." Linda whispered in reply.

"No mom, she doesn't smoke." Katie said in the background. "No, she doesn't have throat cancer. That is her normal voice." Katie paused for a minute. "Yes, mom, I know she has a deep voice. But that's..."

"They're more than tough," Jen whispered to Liz.

Liz nodded in quiet agreement.

The group waited silently until Katie's strenuous conversation was finally over. Katie finally hung up and proceeded back to the table.

"Everything okay, honey?" Linda asked.

Katie sighed. "Yeah."

"Your father is a pastor?" Jen asked cautiously.

"Yeah," Katie sighed again.

"How do you plan on explaining this to your parents?" Steph asked.

"Well, my parents are in Iowa. If I can find work here in Philly after I graduate, then I won't have to answer to them anymore."

"There is a ton of work to be had around here." Maria said. "With Liz and Jen alone, I'm sure you'll be fine!"

The table broke out into a light chuckle.

"Of course she will." Linda said, pulling Katie close to her. "She's bright and talented. If she can do everything she's doing now, she'll be fine. She's awesome."

"There's no doubt that she is. We all love you. You know that, Katie." Jen tenderly chimed in again. "I'm just uneasy about this whole thing, though."

"Jen fell a couple of weeks ago." Liz said as Linda turned her ratchet.

Linda looked up, and nearly hit her head on Liz's truck's hood. "What?!"

"Yeah. She called Donna. I wouldn't have known about it had Donna not called me while the Paramedics were there.

"I mean, I would have weaseled it out of her when I saw all the bruises and stuff, but she'd rather not tell me this stuff, Lin."

"You realize she's trying to protect you, Liz." Linda said. "She doesn't want you to see how sick she really is."

"That's the worst part!" Liz exclaimed. "I *do* know! I see it.

"I know it's killing her that she can't work anymore. I know she'd like to have some pride and dignity. I understand how hard she has it staying at home and struggling to do simple daily chores. She just wants things to be the way they used to be."

"Can you blame her?" Linda asked, her face practically buried in the truck's big block.

Liz paused and sighed. "No. I would love nothing more than for her to be healthy again. But dang it, Linda! Why the hell does she have to push herself so hard and end up hurting herself?! There's no reason for it."

"It's like you said, she wants to have pride and dignity. Look at you and me. Imagine how you'd feel if you couldn't dance any more. Imagine how I'd be if I couldn't be a mechanic any more.

"Hell, look at all of us. We all define ourselves by our jobs. Donna is undoubtedly a cop. Even off duty, she is still a cop.

"Maria eats, sleeps, drinks, and lives writing.

"Stephania models all over the world.

"Our jobs are more than just jobs to us. We are a circle of career-oriented lesbians. Jen just wants to be her old self...and like the rest of us." Linda explained.

"But..." Liz began to argue. She sighed heavily. "I know you're right. I wish it didn't have to be this way. I wish she could see that she's more than a shelter director."

"She does, Liz. She just misses life. She misses getting out of the house. She misses doing the things that you and I consider mundane." After a few more tweaks of the ratchet, Linda slowly stood up, put the ratchet away, and dove back in to the engine to pull the air filter.

"I'm just gonna hose this real quick," she explained as she walked over the hose. Within a few seconds, all the dirt was being washed down the bay, and the truck's air filter looked brand new again. Both women were silent as Linda made her way back towards Liz.

Linda quietly placed the air filter back end and carefully closed the hood of Liz's truck. She then wiped her hands on a small hand towel, but they still were black as night.

As she looked up, she noticed tears welling up in Liz's eyes. Cautious of her mechanic's hands, Linda gently hugged Liz. "It's gonna be ok, sweetie."

Liz was utterly exhausted. It had been a long, long day. The head mistress had pushed her hard; today's rehearsal seemed unending.

She wearily drove Jen's Subaru home, fighting to keep her eyelids open.

Finally, she saw the most beautiful oasis she had ever seen: her home awaiting her.

Liz's tired, weary body dragged through the house until she finally made it to the bedroom.

Cautiously and silently, Liz dropped her dance bag and gently made her way onto the bed.

She lay behind Jen. She began gently running her fingers through Jen's hair. She began to whisper a prayer. "Lord, please take care of Jen. Please heal her. God, if there was ever a person who had your heart, it's her. She's bright, beautiful, smart, and strong. She's everything we should all aspire to be. God, I love this woman. I hate to see her in so much pain and getting worse. Please heal her. She deserves the best, and to not suffer like this. This is the one thing I want more than anything, so if you could find it in your heart, I'd appreciate it. Thank you. Amen." She softly kissed the back of Jen's arm. Liz wrapped herself around her, and drifted off to sleep.

Liz wore a huge smile surrounded by bright red lipstick as her family and fans all surrounded themselves around her. She signed autograph after autograph and gave hug after hug. She reveled in the excitement of this incredible moment.

"I think that's the best I've ever seen you dance." Kathy said, joyfully and proud.

"It was fantastic," Linda agreed.

Donna made her way through the crowd, and was leading a beautiful brunette by the hand. "Liz," Donna started. "This is Brynn. Brynn, this is my friend Liz."

"You were amazing," Brynn said in admiration.

"Why, thank you!" Liz exclaimed, her southern accent surprising Brynn at first.

Liz continued to sign autographs and stand for pictures for quite a while.

"You up for a celebration?" Donna asked once the crowd began to dissipate.

"I am if you are!" Liz said with great enthusiasm.

"Well alright then! What are we waiting for? Let's go!" Donna shouted.

Linda raised up her glass. Over the noise of everyone in the restaurant she called out, "to Liz!"

"Here, here!" everyone concurred, they all took a drink.

"Well done, honey bee!" Robert said squeezing his daughter into his side.

"That was a beautiful performance, honey." Kathy quietly said to her. "I really think it was one of your best." She beamed with pride.

"Thanks, Mom." Liz smiled in return. She clanked her fork against her glass to quiet down the group. "Actually, I have a toast of my own."

Everyone in the group settled and all eyes were on her.

"First, I'd like to thank all y'all for coming out tonight. You are all my friends and family. I am so blessed to have all of you in my life.

"But there is one person who has been there through it all." She rose from her chair and walked over to Jen. She seamlessly turned Jen's chair to face her, and then she knelt down. "Jen, we've been together for seven years now. Through cross country moves, auditions, competitions and just life, you have been there. We've been through some great times, and some terrible times. But no matter what, you were always right by my side.

"You waited for me to figure myself out. You allowed me to grow and change as a person and you never passed judgment on me. You taught me what true love and devotion are all about.

"Jen, I love you. I always have, I always will. If we can weather what we've been through so far, we can get through anything. I want to be with you for all time. I want to always take care of you. I want to savor every moment of life with you by my side. Will you marry me?"

With that, a small, black box appeared. Liz opened it, and inside was a beautiful, delicate solitaire diamond ring. Liz could hear the group gasp quietly, but her focus was solely on Jen.

"Yes!" Jen replied tearfully.

Liz's smile was bigger and brighter than it had ever been previously. She rose and gently placed the ring on Jen's finger.

Jen looked down at the ring. "It's...it's...amazing." She said quietly.

Liz smiled down at her. "I love you."

"I love you...more." Jen winked at her.

The Cop

by

Lauren Shiro

Dedication

To my brother, Bryan. Someone I could always look up to. Someone whose actions I wanted to emulate. You are a gift to those who know you. I don't say it enough, but I love you!

The Cop

Donna lay in bed. It had been a long, restless night. Knowing what today was consumed her every thought.

One year had passed. One full year. Her parents had been dead for a year. Donna was only twenty three, and she was already an orphan. Though time had passed, her pain had not eased in the least.

The phone rang, Donna rolled over. Her alarm clock said it was just a little after nine in the morning. She decided it was a decent time for someone to call, so she answered. "Hullo?"

"Heya kid. How you holding up?" It was John. John and his wife Beth were good friends of Donna's, and her parents'. John and Beth had watched Donna grow up, and soon they would see her graduate from the police academy. They would, but her parents wouldn't.

"Got a pulse, John." Donna answered dryly.

"I'm sorry, Don." John sighed into the phone. "Why don't you come over today? Beth will make something good for dinner."

Donna was silent.

"Okay, so Beth is a phenomenal cook. Anything she makes would be good. All the more reason to come over." John insisted.

"I don't know, John. I just don't feel like gettin' outta bed."

"I know, Don. But we don't want you to be alone, either."

"I appreciate that, John. I do. I just – I don't know. How the fuck am I supposed to deal with this?!"

"I don't know. But it's a hell of a lot easier to not deal with alone. Okay?"

"Fine, John. I'll come over in a little while. Just don't expect me to be Little Mary Sunshine."

"No expectations here, Don. Just lots of love."

"Yeah," Donna choked back the tears and quickly hung up.

Donna reluctantly rolled out of bed and got into the shower.

THE COP

After a brief but scalding hot shower, she stared at herself through the steamed mirror. At first, her face was blurred by the condensation. As time progressed, her face became increasingly clearer. She was definitely a good cross section of her parents.

She had her mother's curly blonde hair and bright blue eyes. Her jaw line and tall, lean, muscular build were definitely from her father. She could see them both reflected back at her, almost as if they were standing right behind her.

"Damn it!" Donna screamed at the mirror's reflection. Tears raced down Donna's cheeks. She couldn't escape it. The people she cherished and missed the most were staring right back at her.

Donna knelt down in front of the grave, placing the bouquet of flowers gently down in front of the headstone. "Happy Father's Day, Dad." She said quietly. "This sucks, ya know. Father's Day without you. What's the point?" Her voice began to tremble. "I mean, what's a girl supposed to do on Father's Day without her father?" A tear began rolling down her cheek. "And ya know, it's not like this is getting any easier. Even after a year, it's the same. It sucks, Dad. It just plain sucks." Emotion engulfed her. "Why the fuck did you have to go and die anyway?!" Donna reached her hand out and touched the top of the grave stone while she wept in silence. A light, misty rain lightly danced on her skin as she continued to cry in solitude and silence.

After several taciturn moments, her cell phone gently vibrated in her pocket. Donna slid it out and answered. "Hullo?"

"Hey Don," it was John. Again.

"Hey John." Donna sniffled and wiped away the tears. "What's up?"

"Well, we were wondering what you are up to." John asked. "Are you coming over or what?"

"Ummm..." She sniffled again. "I'm just visiting Mom and Dad's graves." Her voice began to break again.

"That's what I thought." John paused for a moment. "Why don't you come over, Don? You don't need to be alone today."

"K. I'll be there in a bit." Donna quickly hung up the phone. "Sorry Dad." She wiped away one last tear. "I'll catch ya later. Love ya." She sat for just a moment longer with her eyes closed. She slowly pried her hand off the grave stone. She rose, glancing at her parents' graves one last time. She then turned and walked away. Her brand new black Mustang sat running just a few feet away, welcoming her with warmth and shelter from the rain.

Donna sat on the couch at John and Beth's home. Beth was busy cooking away in the kitchen, and John had just come over and sat next to her.

She studied his face. Although she knew him better than the back of her hand, he almost looked...different today. John was a short, stout man with very broad shoulders. His light brown hair was dissipating by the day. To compensate, a thick brown moustache resided above his upper lip. His dark brown eyes displayed sympathy and intensity.

"Donna," his low, gruff voice interrupted her thoughts. "I know this hard. You have no idea how much Beth and I want to take away your pain."

Donna looked at the floor. Tears began to stream down her face. "I know, John. You guys are good people." Donna took in a deep breath. "How – why is it that whenever there's a drunk driving accident, the asshole walks away from the scene and everyone else dies? It's not fucking fair!" She cried into the palms of her hands.

"I know, Don. All we can do is hope that she gets hers in the end."

"God damn teenage punk. Thought it was so fucking cool to drink. Who the hell gets piss ass drunk on Father's day and then feels that she's just perfectly fucking fine to drive herself home?!"

"Donna, I know you're angry. You have every right to be..."

"They wouldn't have been driving home that night had I not taken them out to dinner!"

"You can't blame yourself. You did nothing wrong."

"I should have gone with them instead of going back to the apartment. At least I could have saved them."

"Don," John said softly but firmly. "Stop. You don't know that. You probably couldn't have done anything if you were there anyway. You did nothing wrong. You didn't set them up."

"There were so many things I could have – I should have – done different." Donna protested.

"Honey, I love you. But you have got to stop living in the past. I know this hurts – and you do need to heal. But you also need to focus on your future. You're about to graduate from the academy."

She cocked her head towards him. "So?!" She shouted. "Who cares? Seriously, who gives a flying fuck?! My parents won't be there. What the hell does it matter?" Donna placed her hands over her face again and sobbed.

"Donna," John said putting his arm around her. "Do this for them. You know they would be so proud of you."

69

"I don't know, John."

"What do you mean? You're carrying on the family tradition! Of course they'd be proud of you!

"Remember when you were in high school and you told your parents you wanted to go into the force? You should have seen your father's face when he told me that story.

"And then when you went to college to study criminal justice before going into the academy. He was beaming with pride!"

Donna's expression showed her doubt without a word.

"It's true. You know I wouldn't lie to you."

"I know." Donna mumbled, rubbing her hands over her face. She paused. "John, my parents never knew – I never came out to them.

"I was afraid. Mom wanted grandkids so bad. And I don't know what Dad would think, he was so traditional."

"I can tell you for a fact that he was proud of you no matter what, Don. He didn't care. He adored you, I promise."

Donna looked up at him through her tears.

"And, you never needed to. They knew, and neither one of them cared. It didn't matter."

Donna's tearful, crystal blue eyes were still fixed on John.

He nodded his head slightly. "It's true. They knew. They didn't care. They loved you. They were proud of you. And they accepted you for who you are. All they ever wanted was for you to be happy and to have a good life.

"Beth and I love you like you're our own daughter, too. We're proud of you. And we love you no matter what.

"All four of us simply want the best for you, okay?" John paused, reached over and pulled Donna in close to his side. "Do us all a favor. When you go to work every day, do it for them. Think of them and work hard for them. Do your best and honor their memory by doing so. Do everything for them...and for us." John turned and held her as she cried uncontrollably into his broad but soft shoulder.

The clock read 11:08. This horrid day was almost over. Donna appreciated John and Beth's hospitality. They were wonderful people, but Donna still felt hollow. She sat motionless on her couch, unaware of the world around her. All she knew, all she could think, all she could feel was pain.

"Fuck it!" Donna shouted. Only her lonely little cactus heard her. As if on auto-pilot, she stood up. She grabbed her coat and went out to her favorite lesbian bar, No Name's.

She briskly walked the fairly quiet Philadelphia streets. The light rain continued to sprinkle the city.

It didn't take long for her to get there, and Donna wasted no time in getting right up to the bartender. She ordered a beer and began to scope out the women who came out to the bar tonight.

Standing quite a ways away, in the far corner with her back to Donna, was a tall woman with striking auburn hair. She turned around slowly; Donna could she could easily see this woman's face was beautiful. Her skin was flawless. Her deep brown eyes were mesmerizing.

Donna took a large gulp of her beer, held on tightly to the bottle and bravely walked over to the gorgeous woman. "Hey, I'm Donna." She said extending her hand.

The beauty took her hand and shook it. "I'm Nicole."

"Nicole? That's a beautiful name."

"Thanks. So, what do you do, Donna?"

"I'm a cop. Well, I'm graduating from the academy next week."

"A cop? Wow! That's impressive!" Nicole took a step closer and gave Donna a flirtatious wink.

"How about you?"

"Nothing exciting. I'm in marketing."

Donna had no idea how to respond. "Marketing? That's...uhhh...neat." She hoped she didn't sound like an idiot. "So, what brought you down here tonight?"

"I just wanted a break from work. I figured I'd just hang out. You?"

"I ...needed a break from life. Just dealing with some bad stuff right now and I just don't want to think about it."

"I can understand that," Nicole replied. She turned and placed her hands on Donna's hips. The two stared deeply into each other's eyes. Nicole leaned forward and kissed her. It was hot, intense and sensuous. Almost immediately, Donna got lost in the moment. She melted into the kiss, and she wanted more. She wanted to kiss Nicole more. She wanted to feel this warmth more. She wanted more of Nicole. She could feel that she was losing control of herself.

Gently, Donna pulled back. "Do you want to come back to my place, and we can forget the world together?"

"That sounds wonderful," Nicole smiled.

Donna wrapped her coat around Nicole and took her by the hand. Quickly but carefully, she guided her through the bar and down to her apartment. Donna opened the door for Nicole, but walked in right behind her so as not to lose any time or contact with her.

Once inside, they immediately resumed their kiss. There was tremendous desire between the two women. It was fast and it was strong. Both women lost themselves to the intensity of the moment.

They quickly began undressing each other. Sensuously, they kissed, touched, teased and caressed the other's soft body.

Donna was flying. Her thoughts could not be any further from her life. She was completely immersed in Nicole.

The two women spent most of the night fondling, savoring, pleasing and enjoying each other.

Donna stood on the stage with all of her fellow graduates. The big day had arrived. She kept her mind focused on the thought that on the day after tomorrow, she would hit the road with her FTO. Thinking of the pressure, the scrutiny and the potential events that awaited her made this event slightly less painful.

All the usual speeches were made by all the usual suspects. Donna couldn't care less what the politicians or the Chief or anyone else had to say. They were making sounds, not words. She went through the motions because it was what she had to do.

After the ceremony was over, she feigned her way through small talk with whoever approached her. Being one of only two females that graduated in the class, she attracted far more attention than she wanted.

She even mustered her way through a superficial conversation with John and Beth. Hoping they couldn't see through her, she faked her way through the dialogue and left as quickly as she could.

She hopped into her Mustang and drove swiftly back to her empty apartment.

She hustled her way through the hallway and rushed in through her own door. She slammed it closed and locked it. Donna took a deep breath.

Solitude. Not a soul around. Just a cactus. A cactus that didn't speak; didn't pass judgment on her. Silence. A safe silence. She was alone and loved every second of it.

She pulled off her shoes and took off her uniform, making sure to hang that perfectly. Settling herself in a pair of silk boxes and a ribbed white tank top, she grabbed three beers out of her refrigerator and plopped herself on the couch.

She quickly opened the first and guzzled it down. As she drank, she flipped through the channels until she found something mind numbing enough to distract her.

First beer down, she quickly went on to the second. She drank and stared at the television for hours on end.

Donna squeezed next to Beth so the gang of three teenage girls could pass her. They talked and giggled like silly teenage girls do. She kept her eye on them and shot a dirty look in their direction after they passed.

"Look, I know this is hard on you." Beth continued without missing a beat. "It's hard on all of us. John and I lost people that we consider family, too."

"But not your parents." Donna snipped.

"No. But I have lost mine. I know what that feels like."

"Beth, no offense, but..."

"I know what you're going to say, honey. And I get it. I do. You're right. I did not lose my parents to a drunk driver. I did not lose them at the same time and I was much older than you when I lost mine.

"Our concern for you is that you're not letting go of the past."

Once again, Donna found herself squeezing her way through mobs of teenagers. She hated teenagers, hated crowds and hated malls. Why did she even agree to this in the first place anyway? What was she thinking? If there was a hell, she was living in it at this very moment. Beth's lecture wasn't helping the situation. Donna clenched her jaw and gritted her teeth as they continued to aimlessly wander.

"I know that this is going to take a long time to heal. I respect that. What John and I worry about is that you're still living in the past. That you haven't accepted their passing."

"You're right. I haven't accepted their passing...and I'm not going to. Why the hell should I accept that they were killed by a fucking drunk driver?!" Donna's voice echoed down the mall corridor.

"There is a big difference between accepting and approving. Accepting just means that you acknowledge that it happened. By no means are we telling you to justify or permit or even excuse her. We would never do that. You just need to come to terms with it so that you can move on with your life."

Donna sighed heavily. She was not going to win this one. This was probably the last time she would ever agree to join Beth on one of her mall visits.

Donna anxiously stood in the hallway. She fidgeted with her hands, not knowing what to do. Her body was tense with excitement and anticipation. She had no idea what to expect. She constantly shifted her weight while waiting.

The door opened yet again. She had lost count after ten. She looked up, wondering if this was the one. A big burly man came out. He had thick dark brown hair and narrow hazel eyes. He was well over six feet tall and his shoulders were broad.

"White?" His deep voice echoed down the hall.

Donna nervous nodded her head and extended out her hand. His mammoth hand wrapped around hers and gripped it tightly. "Frank Kirkpatrick. I'll be your FTO."

"Okay." Her voice quivered with anxiety.

"Let's go." He commanded. Donna sheepishly followed.

"Come on, White!" Kirkpatrick barked.

Donna ran her hands down her face, trying to focus and give him the right answer. She thought and thought. "Fifty two seventy six." She answered.

"Yes." He slowly leaned in over the table. "You know why I push you so hard?"

Donna's weary eyes looked up at him pathetically. She shook her head ever so slightly.

"You're good. You're probably the best rookie I've had in years. I push all of my rookies to be the best that they can be. But you can make one hell of a cop. And sure as shit, I will not allow you to do a subpar job. Got it?"

She nodded.

"Okay. Go home. Get some rest. I'll see you in the morning."

Again, Donna simply nodded.

"Okay. Today you are all on your own. I'm standing back. If you need an extra set of hands, I'm here. Otherwise you're leading everything. This will go into the eval I'm giving to the lieutenant." Kirkpatrick said.

"Okay," Donna said as they sat in the patrol car. She took in a deep breath, trying to calm her nerves. She wanted to do well. Everything she had worked for rested on the outcome of today. Dad, please help me! She prayed.

The car slowly wormed its way through the crowded Philly streets. Donna's eyes darted from side to side watching every car, every pedestrian. She was intensely focused on the world around her. She occasionally turned, wondering what might happen on the next street. Though much time hadn't passed, it was an excruciatingly quiet fifteen minutes for Donna.

Finally, the car in front of them tore through a red light.

She pressed the gas pedal down and quickly caught up to the other car. She turned on her lights. The car didn't pull over. Instead, they tried to elude her and drive even faster. Donna then added the siren as she, too, drove faster. The other driver still continued to drive. She watched her speedometer climb. Seventy. Eighty. Eighty five.

More and more cars began to fill up the streets again. The traffic thickened and finally there was no way out for the other car. After a quarter mile chase, the car finally pulled over.

Donna carefully exited her patrol car. Guardedly, she approached the car. A young man in his early twenties sat in the car, staring straight ahead.

"Do you know why I pulled you over?"

Beads of sweat raced down his forehead. His face drained of all color. "I...uhhh...the red light?" He fidgeted in his seat.

"Yeah. That's just the beginning, but yeah." She responded in a nasty, nearly cynical tone. "License, registration, proof of insurance, please."

Donna looked up out of the corner of her eye. She could see Kirkpatrick standing close by.

The driver nervously fumbled with his wallet. His grip slipped off his license, dropping it on the floor. As he leaned over, Donna saw an unusual wooden box tucked underneath his left leg. After several moments, he finally sat back up. His hands shook as he handed her the necessary papers.

"You're nervous. Why are you so nervous?"

He twitched and fidgeted. He began to open his mouth, but he could not make a sound.

"You ever been pulled over before?"

"No!" He exclaimed harshly. He paused for a moment and regained his composure. "No ma'am."

"Hmmm. Okay. I'm gonna run these. I'll be right back." Donna's look lingered before she went back to the patrol car to check his paperwork. Kirkpatrick eventually got back in the car.

"So, what's up?' Kirkpatrick asked.

"He's super nervous and fidgety. I also saw something I wanna check out."

"And what was that?"

"You know those boxes...the ones that they put those one hit pot cigarettes in. It looked like one of those."

"Interesting."

Both Donna and Kirkpatrick waited in silence. The voice on the radio called back. The insurance had lapsed on the car; the driver's license was suspended.

"Well this is very interesting." Donna said as she exited the car.

She approached the driver with caution. "Hey, so what's up with your insurance?"

"Huh?" He avoided eye contact and his face was so washed out that he had turned nearly grey.

"Yeah. I got that your insurance lapsed and that your license is suspended. Wanna explain that to me?"

"What? That can't be right." He became increasingly nervous and twitchy.

"Hey, can I see something?"

"Uhhh...yeah. Sure."

"What's that thing you're sitting on?"

"Huh?" His eyes skipped around, avoiding contact with Donna's eyes.

"What's that thing you're sitting on? I wanna see it. The wood thing."

"Oh! Uhhh..." He could hardly speak.

"Come on. Lemme see it." Donna commanded.

The young man reached underneath himself and slowly pulled out the box. Apprehensively, he handed it to her.

Donna inspected the box front to back, top to bottom. She carefully slid the top over. She pulled out the ceramic cigarette. Before she even looked at the cigarette, she could see a little bag with what appeared to be marijuana sitting on the bottom of the compartment. She tilted the box so the bag slid right into her hand.

She sniffed the contents. That was definitely weed. She looked at the cigarette. There was burnt up pot jammed into the open end.

"Okay. Out of the car."

The young man sat motionless.

"I said get out of the car."

Still no response.

Donna pulled out her gun. "On the count of three. One…two…"

The young man slowly unclipped his seatbelt. He anxiously opened the car door. Moving at the speed of a snail, he rose out of his car.

"Put your hands on the car."

Again, he stood silently.

"I said put your hands on the car!" Donna shouted.

Still moving incredibly slowly, he turned and rested his hands on the top of the car.

"Kirkpatrick, can you come here and keep an eye on this guy while I check out the car?"

Without saying a word, Kirkpatrick walked right over to the young man and stood uncomfortably close to him.

Donna inspected the car. She looked under the seats, in the glove box, in the doors. She found no evidence in the cab of the car. She hit the trunk release button. She strolled over to the trunk, expecting nothing. The trunk opened revealing large square bricks of marijuana wrapped up in cellophane. Donna immediately walked back to the young man. "Do you have any weapons on you? Anything on your person that we should know about?"

"No," he mumbled.

"Pat him down and then cuff him." She said to Kirkpatrick.

Donna watched as Kirkpatrick did as he was asked. His large hands seemed even more enormous as they moved around the thin frame of the young man. He clamped handcuffs tightly around the driver's wrists. He roughly guided him to the car, and nearly pushed him into the back of the patrol car. Once the young man was seated and locked in, Kirkpatrick approached Donna.

"Whaddya got?"

"This," she answered as she led him to the trunk of the car.

"Very nice!" Kirkpatrick said. "Okay, so you have him in custody. Now what?"

"Well, I wanna catalogue and document everything before we bring him down for processing. So, I need to start that."

"Okay. And how will you go about doing that?"

"First, I'd start with pictures. Then I would catalogue the cigarette box with the pot in it, the one hitter and then the four kilo bricks of pot. And then, I will write my report."

"You got it. Nicely done, White."

Donna smiled. "Thanks!"

Beth's apricot Cornish game hen was to die for. Smothered in apricot juice and pieces of apricot, the meat was juicy and tender. Sided by a Caesar salad, baby carrots and corn, the meal was extravagant...for Donna.

"Okay, enough small talk." Beth said.

Donna looked up and watched her sitting across the table. Beth was a sweet, middle aged woman. She wore a large, fluffy blue shirt which made her appear larger than she really was. Her hair was a combination of wheat and grey all curled and entangled. It was short in length, just barely reaching her ears. Thought clearly aged, her eyes were a soft shade of brown. Small wrinkles made their ways around her eyes, forehead and mouth. Her lips were too thin for lipstick, but her smile was grand.

"It's time to get down to business."

Donna snapped back into the conversation. She quickly looked down at her plate. There was one tiny piece of apricot left. Maybe if she tried to eat it...slowly, she would distract herself long enough to ignore this conversation.

John jumped in. "Look Donna, we don't want to force you into anything. You know we love you like our daughter. This is your choice; we just want you to know we're thinking about you."

Her face twisted and contorted in fear and apprehension as to what they might say.

"Donna, do you remember I told you my friend Julia's daughter is gay?" Beth asked.

"Yeah...?" she replied hesitantly.

"Brynn is single." John blurted out.

"Oh, Jesus, John!" Donna said as she buried her head in her hands.

"No, hear me out." John briefly paused. "Brynn is a local cop up in Doylestown."

Donna's eyes peered up from just above her hands. "Brynn's a cop?"

"Yes," Beth said. "Ralph and John went to the academy together. Just like you, Brynn followed in her father's footsteps."

"So if Ralph and John went to the academy together; and then, John, you got partnered with Dad, did my parents ever meet her parents?"

"They met a few times. But Ralph stayed on patrol, so they didn't run into each other all that often." Beth answered.

"Did they ever meet Brynn? Did they like her parents? Did they like her?" Donna spoke quickly and anxiously.

"Does it matter, Don? We're not saying you and Brynn have a date tomorrow. We just wanted you to know." John answered.

"It does kind of matter to me, John. If Mom and Dad thought they were good people..."

"I see what you're getting at," Beth said gently. "Yes, honey. They did. Your dad and Ralph would laugh it up any time they were together."

"Ok, good." Donna fought back the tears. With one good swallow, she was a little more composed.

"If you ever want, just tell us and we'll call Julia. We can arrange everything." John sighed. "We worry about you. We just don't want to see you continue in this pattern."

"Thank you. I don't want to continue like this either. I hate the single life. It's just that...not many women want to sign on for what's involved. I'm in my mid-twenties. I want to truly fall in love and settle down with someone!"

"I know." Beth said in a quiet, nurturing tone. "That's why we brought this up. Brynn would understand. Brynn has a good head on her shoulders."

"She lives like you do," John added.

Donna glared at John.

"She lives alone, leads a fairly quiet life. Just works on the force. I think she even has a matching 'lonely cactus!'"

"So...she's not your typical dramatic lesbian?" Donna asked.

John laughed heartily. "No, no. She's mellow, like Julia. Like I said, that girl has a good head on her shoulders."

"Alright. I'll think about it." Donna took in a deep breath. She wanted a girlfriend, but she hated the idea of being set up. This was not what she wanted. Not now, anyway.

Donna flipped on the lights and siren. She slammed the gas pedal down with all of her weight.

"Armed robbery in progress, right?" She shouted to Kirkpatrick.

"Yeah," his voice bellowed over the noise of the sirens.

Donna raced through the Philadelphia streets, making sure that she was safe as well as speedy. Both she and Kirkpatrick held on while the car swerved through the crowds and corners.

Two other patrol cars were there when their car screeched in. Donna looked over at Kirkpatrick only to find him looking back at her.

"Be careful out there." He grunted.

Both reached for their guns before opening the car doors.

Three thieves stood with their own weapons drawn on the other officers.

"Put the guns down!" Donna shouted.

No one moved.

"I said, put the guns down!" She shouted again.

"No chance in hell, bitch!" One of the thieves shouted back at her.

Out of the corner of her eye, she saw another officer approaching one of the thieves from an alleyway behind them. She stood as still as she could, waiting for her moment.

For as hard as she was breathing, her body felt as though it could not get enough oxygen. She focused on her breathing pattern while still watching the other officer.

Inch by tiny inch, he moved his way closer. Slowly and silently he moved until he knew he was in the right place. He suddenly leaped forward, pushing the thief to the ground face down. He grabbed one of the thief's arms and pulled it behind his back. As he did so, Donna raced forward with her gun aimed at one of the other thieves.

Suddenly, Donna felt an incredible pain in her back. She felt as though a great force pushing her forward. All the air escaped her lungs. Her eyes rolled up towards the sky as she lost all control of her body. She felt her body slam against the concrete in a tremendous impact before blackness enveloped her.

"Donna?!" John's familiar voice spoke.

Donna weakly opened up her eyes. Her vision was blurry at best. She tried to speak. All she could do was exhale deeply. She could feel tubes and...things across her face and down her throat. Somehow, she forced a squeak out.

80

"Oh thank God!" Beth's voice gently filled her ears.

Donna tried to inhale deeply. She felt a tremendous weight or pressure on her chest. Breathing was painful.

"Donna, can you hear me?" John's voice reached out to her.

Donna managed to slowly roll her eyes over to see a blurry version of John. As best she could, she managed a smile.

"Hey! There's my girl!" John's voice cracked as he jumped up and ran over to her. His warm hands encased hers. "You're gonna be alright. It's gonna be alright." He broke down into an audible cry. "Don, you have got to stay strong for me, okay? I need you to be strong. I know you can do this. You will get better. Just do what the doctors say so we can get you out of here."

Donna could feel John's tears landing on her arm. She squeezed his hands as tightly as she could.

"How do you feel?" Doctor Smythe asked.

"Like shit," Donna grunted. "This pain is horrible."

"I'm sure. This is by no means an easy recovery."

She shifted in her bed, trying desperately to get comfortable. "How much longer do I have to say here?"

"That depends on you. I want to continue IV fluids for at least a week; and then we need at least three more consecutive blood tests with good, steady renal – kidney values."

Donna sighed heavily. "This is bullshit. I was two days away from finishing my field training and I fucking end up here and lose a kidney."

Doctor Smythe stood over her bed, unable to respond.

She looked up at him. "This just fucking sucks."

Donna looked up at Kirkpatrick.

"They say you're lucky. You were within inches of being shot fatally. Supposedly, losing a kidney isn't that bad." He said.

"I don't know. I'm thinking death would be a hell of a lot easier and less painful than this shit." Her voice was weary and scratchy.

An awkward silence sat heavily in the room.

"I came to apologize."

"For what?"

He looked down at her. His hazel eyes were more green than brown today. "For why you're here. I should have seen that guy."

"And me too. But we didn't. Neither one of us spotted him. No one would have expected a fourth, and especially not behind us. It was an accident."

"That was no accident."

"Okay. Mistake. Whatever. Shit happens."

Kirkpatrick turned his gaze away from her. "Well, no worries. Your eval is done. You've passed your field training with flying colors. I've spoken to the Lieutenant about you as well. Gave you a commendation."

"Wow! Thank you. I...don't know what to say."

Kirkpatrick looked back down at her. "You don't have to say a thing. You just need to get better. We need you on the force. Got it?"

"Yes, sir." Donna smiled as best she could.

"White!" Lieutenant Harris called out.

Donna turned around and began to walk back towards him. "What's up?"

"Nice job on that traffic stop." He paused briefly. "And oh yeah, on that twenty six twenty, too." He winked.

A smile painted its way across her face. "Thanks."

"It's good to have you back." He paused for a moment. "I hear you want to go into Narcs like your father."

"Well, yeah. Eventually."

"Listen. You passed your field training with flying colors. You know the standard. You patrol for three years before you can get into any departments."

"Well yeah. That's why I said eventually." She replied.

"Right. You know typically we try to find safer jobs – desk jobs – for people in your position."

"In my position?" One of Donna's eyebrows raised.

"Wounded."

"Ah, I see." She said, watching him cynically.

"Based on your family's history, the traffic stop, the twenty six twenty, and a glowing recommendation from your FTO, I am bending the rules for you. Just between you and I. You can go into Narcs, but..."

Donna's face lit up with exhilaration. She was so excited that it took a moment for her to register what he had just said. "But...?"

"Eh, you know what? Never mind." He paused briefly. "Just report in on Monday."

"Yes sir!" She said with great enthusiasm. "Thank you!"

Donna's pace quickened. Her heart began to beat faster and faster and faster. She opened the door feeling alive, brisk, and full of energy.

She looked around at all the cubicles and people walking around. There was electricity in the air. She breathed it all in, enjoying this sight. This was indeed where she belonged.

She continued to look around and study the faces when she felt someone touching her shoulder. She spun around to see John standing next to her.

"Hey!" She said with great enthusiasm.

"Hi. Welcome to the floor." He replied.

"Thanks. I can't believe I'm here. I'm really excited to do this. Where do I go? I gotta find out who my partner is."

"You're looking at him."

"Shut up! You are not!" She exclaimed, gently pushing him.

"Yes I am. Here, look." John handed her a paper.

New Assignment Start date: October 12.

Crenshaw, Jonathan H, senior narcotics detective.

White, Donna M., new transfer to Narcotics. Partner with experienced detective

Partnership to commence on date listed above. It read.

"What the...?"

John began to crack a smile.

"Did you do this?!"

"I may or may not have had some input on this." He teased.

"But, isn't there a conflict?"

"Nah. It's all good." John briefly paused. "So, are you ready for your first day as a Narc?"

"Yeah, I guess so." A smile slowly crept its way onto Donna's face.

"Alright, then. Let's go." John allowed her to walk in front of him as they walked into a conference room where other detectives were already seated and waiting.

"Only a handful of women have ever won this award. Never before have we had a rookie winner.

"But you see, Officer White is different. That's why she's here. She works diligently day and night.

"Not even being shot while still on field training would keep her down. No. Instead, she lost a kidney and came back in pure fighting form.

"Since completing her field training, she has received glowing commendations from her FTO and her colleagues alike.

"Six months ago, she joined the narcotics team. In that time, we have made over five hundred arrests in narcotics and drug-related crimes. Over all, we have seen a thirteen per cent decrease in our crime rate; I am sure that Officer White has a big hand in all of this.

"So without further ado, let me introduce you to this year's George Fencl Award: Officer Donna White!"

Donna's heart pounded as she walked across the stage to receive her award. She could hardly see the commissioner as she walked over to him. All she could see was one giant, blinding spot light. Smaller flashes would jump around the big spot light, in the darkness of the audience like smaller stars flashing around the giant spot light moon.

"Thank you." She said as she was handed her award. "I gotta say, it really is an honor to be up here. I never expected to win an award like this. That's not why I go out and do what I do. I'm a cop because...I'm a cop. My father was a police officer, I had to become one!"

The Audience broke out into a light chuckle.

"I do what I do because of my father. He instilled good morals into me. He taught me about honesty, integrity, doing the right thing, fairness. All the things that a police officer is meant to encompass.

"And I work in the department that I do because of my father. Not only because I am following in his footsteps. But because of how he died. A drunk driver hit and killed both of my parents on Father's Day." Donna's eyes began to fill with tears. "It was a drug related crime as far as I'm concerned. And I don't want other people to suffer through what I went through. I want to make the streets cleaner and safer by getting rid of the chemicals that cause people to lose their sound judgment and their humanity.

"I do what I do because I love it and because it's important to me. Thank you." Donna allowed the last few tears to fall while also smiling for more pictures.

Donna White was one of only two female cadets in her class to graduate from the Philadelphia Police Academy ten months ago. Within that short time span, White has made a name for herself.

She is the only child of Tony and Amanda White. Her father, Tony, was a Philadelphia police officer. John Crenshaw, now Donna White's partner, was originally partnered with her father, Tony.

White says she had a good upbringing and that her family was tightly knit. Police work was simply the norm for her family, so it came as no surprise when Donna said she wanted to go to the Academy. Her parents embraced her career choice with open arms. She studied and received her degree in Criminal Justice from Chestnut Hill College. Sixteen months ago, White went into the Philadelphia Police Academy. Her parents watched her succeed as one of the top students in her class. Sadly, they would never see her graduate. Her relationship with her parents was ended early by a drunk driver.

Carrying on the family tradition and on a mission to avenge her parents' death, Donna White has worked tirelessly in the Narcotics division. Over five hundred arrests have been made since White joined Narcotics; the Philadelphia P. D. has seen an over-all decrease of thirteen per cent in the crime rate.

White was this year's recipient of the George Fencl Award and has just recently been promoted to detective.

"Hey, that's a pretty good article, Don!" John looked up at her, smiling. "It's impressive that you got your name into the Philly Enquirer. And not for something bad!" He chuckled.

Donna laughed.

John's lips curled into a devious smile.

She looked over at him. She knew there was something behind that smirk. "What?" She asked.

"I have to admit it: I love that they even mention my name!" He laughed.

Donna smiled back. "Yeah! I made sure of that. And I made sure your name isn't in there for anything bad, either!" She quipped.

They both laughed.

"Personally, I love how they're making me out to be some kind of a hero: 'avenging' my parents' death." Donna put her hands on her hips, stuck her chest out and posed as if she was a super hero.

"That's not a bad thing, Don. And you do deserve credit for all that you've been through and the kind of work that you're doing now. You should be proud of yourself. I know we are, and I know your parents would be too."

A weak smile appeared as her lips quivered. "Thanks."

Donna slammed her beer on the bar counter. A cute young girl with crimson hair and very little clothing tended the bar. She walked over to where Donna was seated. "Another?" Her cute, perky voice pitched even higher.

Donna simply nodded.

The young girl stepped away, and came back with another cold bottle. She winked before she walked away.

Donna glanced up at the TV. Some stupid show on sports highlights played on mute. She didn't care about sports, she just didn't want to think or feel.

"Hi there." A soft, smooth, sensuous voice breathed right into Donna's ear.

Carefully, Donna turned her chair around. A tall woman with dark, rich brown hair and green eyes smiled at her. She could not help but be taken aback by this woman's beauty.

"Hi." She replied.

"You seem pretty upset tonight."

"Oh, it's nothing." Donna avoided eye contact. There was such intensity in the woman's eyes that she feared she would lose all capacities.

"What is it?" The woman leaned in closer.

"Well, it's my birthday." She muttered.

The woman sat up. "It is?! Then why are you so down?"

"It's...because...I don't have anyone."

"You don't want to be single on your birthday?" This woman's voice was hypnotic.

"Yeah, that too. I just don't really have any friends or family."

"You don't?!"

"Nah, not really." Donna looked up and got sucked in by the emerald green shade of this woman's eyes. It was so easy to get lost in them.

"Well, there's nothing I can do about your friends or family tonight. But I can make sure you're not alone tonight on your birthday." She winked flirtatiously. "I'm Heather." She said as she gently wrapped her hand over Donna's.

"Donna." She replied, completely lost in this moment.

Heather smiled. "Donna. It's nice to meet you."

Donna felt silly, but she couldn't stop smiling at this amazingly stunning woman.

"Why don't you come with me back to my place? You can have all the beers you want while you tell me a little more about why such a beautiful woman as yourself is alone and single on her birthday."

Heather slowly rose out of her chair, and Donna followed suit. They walked out of the bar into the crisp, cold night. "See that little MG over there? That's my car. Come follow me."

Heather's touch lingered just long enough for Donna to crave more. She walked hurriedly to her car and then drove off to follow Heather home.

Donna curled in even closer to Heather. "A girl could get used to this." She gently kissed her on the back of neck.

"Mmmmm," Heather moaned as she woke up. Her eyes slowly opened. She wore a smile until she saw the clock. "Shit!" She exclaimed. She leaped out of bed and ran to pull clothes from her closet.

Donna sat up. "What?!"

"The shoot."

"The shoot? What shoot?"

"Yeah, the photo shoot I was telling you about. The one my mechanic does for HRC. She uses my car. We were supposed to be there ten minutes ago...and it's gonna take us at least another twenty to get there!"

Donna climbed out of bed and grabbed her clothes off the floor. They hurriedly dressed and readied themselves. They rushed out the door and Heather drove her little MG as quickly as she could.

The parking lot of the shop was filled with classic and muscle cars, and what seemed to be an infinitely large number of people.

Heather parked her car next to a behemoth of a truck. The vehicles contrasted greatly, and yet they were both here for the same reason.

Heather grabbed Donna by the arm and pushed them through the horde of people. As they pushed and shoved their way through, Heather seemed to pick up the pace. Heather led her to some specific voices that Donna could hear over all of the other voices. "They're right over there." She said, keeping her focus forward as they trudged through the masses.

"So you do this every year?" A woman with a loud southern drawl asked.

"Yup."

Heather finally made her way to a small group. "Hey," she said quietly to a thin, nearly androgynous brunette with short, shaggy hair.

"Hey Heather! How are you?" Her voice was deep and smooth.

"Good. You guys haven't started yet?"

"Nah. They're still getting Steph all put together. You know how that goes!" The brunette joked.

"Oh good! So it's okay that I'm late!" Heather laughed.

Donna began looking around at the mob of people. She listened to Heather's conversations, but allowed her attention to wander.

"Yeah," the brunette laughed with her. After a moment, she introduced the tall redhead standing next to her. "Oh, I'm sorry. Liz, this is Heather. She owns that MG over there." The woman's deep voice paused for a few moments. "Heather, this is Liz. She owns that Chevy truck."

"Oh, I love that one! So unique. What a great ride." Heather said in an almost sickeningly sweet tone.

"Well, I have someone I want you to meet." Heather proclaimed. She reached out and pulled over and pulled Donna in next to her.

Donna pushed her blonde curls out of her face.

"Linda, this is my girlfriend Donna. She's a cop." Heather bragged.

"Hey," the androgynous woman said, extending her hand. She grabbed it. Linda's grip was just as firm as her own.

"Hi." Donna answered. The two looked at each other for a moment. There wasn't an attraction, but there was some kind of a connection. There was a commonality, almost a camaraderie between them. Without saying a word, they somehow understood each other.

"Honey, Linda is the one who owns this shop." Heather leaned over and whispered in her ear.

"Oh, okay. Hey." Donna said again, still gripping Linda's hand.

"This is Liz." Linda said, finally breaking their hold.

"Hi," Liz said with her bright, strong drawl.

"Hi." Donna said as she shook Liz's hand. She looked up at her. She was a tall, beautiful woman with amazing red hair. Her handshake was gentle, but firm. Her smile was bright, warm and sincere. There was something very genuine about her – about both of them. She liked them. Normally leery of strangers, Donna felt very unusually comfortable and familiar with these new women.

A bullhorn went off. "Okay, everyone. Quiet on the set! We're shooting with the Camaro first. Everyone to their positions!"

"There's something I need to tell you." Heather said.

"What?" Donna asked. She wasn't even looking at her. Her eyes were closed; she held Heather's hand and gently rubbed it against her own cheek.

"Donna!" Heather snapped.

Donna shot up, opened her eyes and dropped Heather's hand. "What? What's up?"

"Donna, I got offered a promotion."

"Oh that's great, baby! Congratulations!"

"It's in Chicago."

"Oh! So...uhhh...what are you going to do?"

"Take the promotion." Heather said without missing a beat.

"Wait, what?! Why? What about your friends and family? What about your home here? What about us?!"

Heather leaned in. "Donna, you and I both know this wasn't going anywhere. It was fun while it lasted, but there's nothing between us. It's not like we even had great passionate sex or anything."

Donna's jaw dropped. She felt all the color drain from her face. She had never seen Heather be so callous. She was struck by her words. How could she do this? How could she say this? There was a connection: Donna felt it! This was a solid relationship, or so Donna thought. This was devastating. She felt as though the world around her had just crashed and crumbled. This was a pain Donna had not felt before.

"What are you talking about? What do you mean?" Tears began to flow from her eyes.

"Seriously?! Donna, you know damn well that this is not long term. Yeah it was fun. But it's over. It's been over. It was a great little fling."

"But, I..." Donna choked on her own words. She had just been thinking of telling Heather that she loved her not ten minutes before. But now this. What was this? Why was it happening? How could she say all these hurtful things?

"I'm leaving on the twenty fourth. I just wanted to tell you in person. Good luck!" Heather rose out of her chair and walked away. "By the way, if you could get going, that would be great. I have some people coming over in about an hour!" She shouted from the other room.

Donna struggled not to make any noise as she cried. Aside from her parents, this heart break had to be one of the worst she had ever endured. How could this have happened? How could Heather have done this? Donna was gob smacked.

After several minutes of silent tears, she slowly stood up. She looked down and watched the floor as she walked towards the door.

"Have a nice life!" Heather called out.

Donna quietly exited the apartment. She walked to her car. She got in as rapidly as she could and she simply broke down.

Donna nervously walked up to the shop. She peered into the front door. No one was there. Linda must have been working on a car. She decided that this was a bad idea anyway. She turned around and began to walk away when she heard a voice call out to her.

"Hey!" It was Linda.

Donna spun around. "Oh hey." She said nervously.

"Donna, right? Heather's girlfriend. The cop."

"Yup, that's me. Well, except for the part about being Heather's girlfriend."

"Oh man, I'm sorry. I didn't mean..."

"No, that's okay. Seriously. I didn't expect you to know. I..." Donna let her voice trail off. She had no words.

"So, what's up? What can I do for you?"

"Well...ummm...that's actually why I'm here."

Linda looked perplexed.

"I...was just wondering if we could grab beers together some time."

"Are you asking me out on a date?" Linda took half a step back.

"No!" Donna shouted. "No. I'm sorry. I didn't mean it like you're not attractive. You are. I'm just not...I don't even know what I mean." She took a deep breath, trying to get her thoughts straightened out. "No. I wasn't asking you out. I just...I like you. I don't know. I just felt like we connected that time. I don't have many friends, and I like you and so I thought maybe we could hang out. As friends. I don't have many friends and..."

"Okay, I think I got that part down." Linda said lightly. "Sure, we can hang out. Is that gonna be a problem with Heather, though?"

"No. She's going to Chicago. Shit, no now she's already in Chicago. She's gone. And I'm all alone and..." Donna's eyes filled with tears.

"Dude, what did she do to you?!" Linda stepped forward again.

"I loved her. I was about to tell her I loved her and then she told me she was moving. She said there was nothing between us and that I suck in bed and I knew that we weren't going anywhere and that this was nothing and..." Donna rambled. "My parents are dead and I work a lot and I have no friends..." Tears rolled down her face while she blubbered endlessly.

"Whoa! Jesus. I'm sorry, man. That is not right. I am sorry." Linda gently hugged her.

Donna cried even harder in Linda's arms.

Linda sat at a ninety degree angle to Donna. They both had their feet propped on the edges of Linda's living room table. Keeping her eyes on Donna, Linda drank from her beer again.

"Why aren't you dating?" Donna followed suit, taking a large mouthful from her beer.

"I don't know. Too much drama. Too much bullshit. Fake people. The freakin' uhaul's at your house after the second date. All the usual shit, I suppose."

Donna laughed. "And that's exactly why I don't date much."

Linda leaned in. "So how did Heather happen then?"

"Your guess is as good as mine. We met at a bar, just like how I usually pick girls up. But she was different. I don't know. A one night stand turned into a week which turned into a month and then two and..."

"And then you got burned. Big time. I've seen her be a little fake, but I didn't think she was an out and out bitch."

"I don't know. Maybe I was ignoring the signs. Maybe it was just because I met her when I was so down. Fuck if I know. But here I am, alone." She took another drink. "Fucking bitch." Donna grumbled.

"Hey, I know it's hard. It was good while it lasted."

She rolled her eyes. "Spare me the clichés."

"Dude, I'm just sayin'."

Donna sighed. "I know. It's just that none of that shit helps anyway."

"I know, right?" Linda paused. "But really, what do you say to a person who goes through that? You know? Heart break fucking sucks, and people want to try to help. They want you to feel better, so they say whatever they think will help. But none of it works. It's a long, shitty process."

"Yup." Donna replied. "Ya know, you see happy couples on TV or in the movies – hell, you even see all the cute gay ones on South Street. What the hell is their magic key that makes it work? Or is there even one? I bet it's all fake; nobody can have something like that. It's just not real. Maybe in a fairy tale, but definitely not in real life."

Linda sat quietly for a few moments. "You remember Liz? That tall redhead at the shoot. She has that tricked out old Chevy truck."

"Oh yeah!"

"Dude, she and her girlfriend have the best fucking relationship. They're like something out of those movies or shows or books or whatever. It's crazy. They have the best relationship I have ever seen or heard of. If it wasn't for them, I wouldn't think it's real either. But they have it and they are for real." She paused. "I hope one day I can have that."

"Yeah." Donna replied, unable to hold back the tears. "Thanks for reminding me of what I don't have."

"Yeah. You and me both. Maybe someday."

"Maybe." Donna said skeptically.

"Whoa!" Donna said when she walked into Linda's kitchen and nearly bumped into Maria.

"Oh, I'm sorry! Let me just get out of your way. So sorry." Maria scurried out of the kitchen.

Liz hurried right behind her with a drink in each hand.

"Holy shit," Donna said quietly to Linda. "Did you know there were gonna be this many people?"

"Uhhh...sorta. I invited Liz, and of course Jen. Maria is friends with Jen, so they asked me if she could come...and she just started dating Steph, who I had already invited and then she asked me if Maria could come too, so..."

Donna looked at Linda with a mystified expression.

"Oh, you know Steph. She was the model at the shoot!"

"Oh, okay." Donna said, putting all the pieces together.

"And that should be everyone."

"Geez! I would never want this many people in my house!" Donna chuckled.

"As much as I like being alone, I love my big screen TV and I love having people come over."

"No thank you!"

Linda laughed. "It's not that bad."

"Whatever. Not my deal, but go for it! That's all you! I will, however, gladly partake in the festivities, food, and especially the beverages."

Linda laughed and teasingly swatted Donna's arm. "Smart ass! C'mon. Grab your beer and let's go."

"This had better be good!"

"It is! If there's one thing I'm good at, it's finding the worst B movies to watch and laugh at!"

"We'll see about that!" Donna winked and turned to go find a seat in Linda's living room.

Donna stomped heavily towards her apartment door. Why was someone knocking? She hadn't invited anyone. She peered into the peep hole in the door. She could see Liz's face on the other side. Why on Earth would she be here? Slightly more slowly than usual, Donna opened the door.

In front of her stood Liz and Jen both with several full shopping bags and a cardboard box unlike any other Donna had seen before.

"Uhh...hey guys. What are you doing here?"

"Well," Jen started.

"With everything you've been through." Liz interrupted and walked right past Donna carrying in the overstuffed plastic bags. "We decided you needed a roommate."

Donna's face fell. A roommate? Them?! What the...? Who were they to decide something like that? Why didn't they talk to her about it first? How on earth could they have fit their belongings into a few plastic bags and a weird cardboard box? Donna buried her face in her hands and shook her head. This could not be happening. She walked over to where Liz was standing.

"It's not what you think." Jen said.

Donna turned and looked at her as she brought in the odd box.

"We thought you could use some company. And with the connections I have, we were able to find you the perfect companion." Jen carefully opened the top of the box. A small calico face appeared, looking up and around.

"A kitten?!" Donna was shocked. "I don't know how to take care of these things. My cactus is lucky I haven't killed it yet!" Donna protested.

Jen chuckled. "It's fine, Donna. She's a little older, so she'll be a little more docile than a younger kitten. She is already spayed and vaccinated. We've got food, dishes, toys, a litter box, litter...all the kitty essentials you'll need." Jen smiled.

Donna bent down to look at the little face. Her white, orange and black marbled head seemed so tiny compared to her large hands. Carefully, she began to gently pet the kitten. Almost instantly, the cat closed her eyes and began purring. Donna smiled brightly as she looked up at Liz and Jen.

Jen elbowed Liz. "I told you it would only take a minute." They both smiled back down at her.

"But I can't take all of this..." Donna started.

"It's fine. Please take it. I have access to so much stuff it's not even funny. You'll use it and when you need more, just let me know." Jen replied.

"But..."

"Please don't fight us, Donna." Jen said gently. "We know how hard things have been for you and we thought that maybe having a little companionship would be a good thing. We just wanted to do something nice for you. It's about time someone did." Jen's smile grew.

"Wow," Donna stood up. "I just...wow. Thank you. That is so incredibly nice of you and I don't think I could ever thank you enough. That is a really nice gesture and I appreciate it. I really do. Thank you." She awkwardly hugged both girls.

"The only thing you need to do is name her!" Liz said.

Donna walked around the kitten in the box. "Priscilla? "No, you don't look like a Priscilla."

"What about a favorite person or character from a book? A movie? Musician? Friend's name? Car or Motorcycle? Uhhh...a favorite food, maybe?" Jen asked, hoping to help.

"Hmmm. Well ya know, Laffy Taffy has always been my favorite candy. And her orange is kind of a taffy color. I think I'm gonna call her Taffy."

"Boy that was quick! You know, for someone who was unprepared to have a pet, she seemed pretty prepared with that name!" Jen winked at Liz.

Liz laughed. "Yeah, no kidding!"

"Wow. Thank you guys again. I really mean it."

"You're welcome." The pair said in harmony.

"Do you need anything else, or should we leave you two to get to know each other?" Jen asked.

"You said everything is in the bags, right?"

"Yes," Jen said quietly while nodding her head.

"Then I guess I'm okay."

Jen smiled again. "Sounds like our job here is done. Enjoy, Donna. If you need anything, just call either one of us, okay?"

Donna smiled in return. "Yeah. Thanks again."

Liz and Jen walked out of the apartment, still trying to observe the interactions between Donna and Taffy.

Donna sat across from Linda, watching a cigarette dangle loosely from her lips. "Sometimes I forget how nice this city can really be."

Linda chuckled. "Is it really that bad?"

"Ya gotta remember, I see the worst of the worst. I think only Homicide has it worse than us. But ya know what? We do so much shit with them: a lot of our cases are tied together."

Linda removed the cigarette so she could take another sip of her coffee. "Makes sense."

"It fucks you up, man. You don't appreciate days like today. You don't see people sitting outside drinking coffee. All you do is watch everyone's moves. Find people acting suspiciously. You analyze every face, every action."

"If it's that bad, why don't you switch...or quit all together?"

"I can't. This is just who I am. I have always wanted to be a cop. It's the only thing I know how to do."

"So leave Narc, then." Linda suggested.

"Nah. I don't want to. As much as it warps you, it's just something I have to do. This is how I know I'm making a difference.

I don't think I would get the same sense of satisfaction doing anything else."

"Hmmmm." Linda took another sip.

"I know, I shouldn't bitch. I think part of it is that I'm alone and that's hard. I have no one to come home to. Well, I do have Taffy now, but you know what I mean."

"I do. The loneliness factor is a bitch. It does make everything harder. I agree."

"Yeah, well." Donna shrugged her shoulders. "It is what it is, I guess."

"Just don't lose yourself in your work."

"I'll try not to." She replied.

Linda looked down at her watch. "Well, I should probably get back to the shop. I'll catch ya later?"

"Yeah," Donna answered as she pushed her seat back against the concrete patio. When she stood up, the sun was blazing right in her eyes. She ducked, closed her eyes and then covered them with her right hand. "Geez, that sun is bright! I'll see ya later."

"Bye." Linda stood up and started walking back towards her shop.

The television played in the background. Donna took another swig of her beer as she scrolled through the pictures of women. They came in all sizes, colors and shapes. Some quickly grabbed her attention, but the interest would fade as quickly as it had arrived.

Out of nowhere, Taffy jumped onto the couch. She strolled over to Donna's lap where she curled up and purred away. Donna looked down at her and smiled. She began to pet Taffy, forgetting about the women on her computer screen.

"I guess maybe this isn't so bad." She whispered to Taffy. "I mean, I'm not really alone, right? I have you. I have John and Beth." She huffed deeply. "I just don't have a girlfriend...or my parents." A solitary tear rolled down her face. "But that's okay, isn't it? I guess I'm just supposed to live like this. Without the people I care about the most. But I have a cat. I have you, Taffy, and that just makes everything better." Donna wiped away the tears and quickly took a large drink from her beer bottle.

Donna's cell phone started to ring. She fished through her desk drawer to find it. After three rings, she answered. "Detective White."

"Donna?" Jen said weakly.

"Jen?" Donna asked. "Jen, what happened? Are you ok?"

"Donna, I fell down the stairs. Can you come and help me?" Her voice was faint.

"Yeah, I'm just doing some paperwork. I'll call for a paramedic team, and go with them, ok?"

"No. No paramedics," Jen delicately insisted.

"Jen, I have to. We gotta make sure you're ok."

Donna stood back as she observed. One paramedic sat next to Jen on the couch talking to her while another felt her pulse, and continued to monitor her vital signs. Jen's skin began to discolor as various bruises began to appear. Jen avoided eye contact while the male paramedic talked to her. She was visibly shaken up, but she was obviously more embarrassed than anything.

Donna decided now would be the best time to sneak away and let Liz know what happened. She left the room to make a quick, quiet phone call.

"Pennsylvania Ballet."

"Yes, hi. My name is Detective White. Is Elizabeth O'Kane available, please?" Donna spoke in a low and quiet tone.

"Miss O'Kane is in rehearsal right now. May I take a message?"

"This is an emergency, please pull her from rehearsal. My name is Detective Donna White; I am with the Philadelphia P. D. I promise it won't take but a minute of her time."

There was a deafening silence on the line as Donna waited and prayed that Jen wouldn't hear her.

"Hello?" Finally, Liz had answered.

"Hey Liz, it's Donna."

"Hey Donna! Why are you calling me here?"

Donna took a deep breath. "Look, Jen fell this afternoon. Down the stairs."

"Oh my God!" Liz exclaimed.

"She's okay. The paramedics have treated her, there are no major injuries. She's gonna be sore and hurting for a while. She was extremely embarrassed. She didn't want me to call the paramedics, let alone you. I had to let you know, though. She wouldn't tell you herself. Like I said, she's okay; I just wanted you to know."

"Thanks, darlin'. You're the best. Just make sure she lies down and is quiet for the rest of the afternoon. I should be out of here in about an hour and a half."

"You want me to stay till you get back?" Donna asked.

"Only if she wants you to. You know how prideful and stubborn Miss Jen can be."

"I sure do!" Donna replied. "Oh wait. Shit! I have a date tonight. Damn it! I won't be able to stay that long."

"That's fine. Like I said, just make sure she's good till I can get home." Liz assured her.

"Okay, will do!"

"Why did you ask me?!" Linda laughed and fell backwards on Donna's bed.

"Because you can at least tell me if it looks okay. You wouldn't lie to me...would you?"

Linda sat up and stared back at her.

The pair broke out into hysterical laughter.

"Okay, okay. Seriously." Donna said in between chuckled. "I need to know."

Linda wiped away a tear from laughing. "Okay fine. Whaddya got?"

"I figured I'd need three hours."

"Three hours?!"

"Well, yeah. One hour to shower, an hour to get ready and an hour to get there."

Linda broke out into laughter again. "An hour in the shower?! What the hell is wrong with you? Do you only bathe twice a year that you need to be in the shower that long?"

Donna laughed. "I want to impress this girl. I wanna shave good, and..."

Linda laughed even harder. "What the hell are you? A sasquatch that you need an hour to shave your hairy legs?!"

Both girls laughed and laughed.

"Shut up!" Donna teased, throwing a pillow at Linda. Linda simply laughed harder.

"Shit. This is great." Linda briefly paused. "Okay, dude. Seriously? An hour in the shower?" She started cracking up again.

"Well, just to be sure."

"Okay. Whatever you gotta do. So, then what?"

"My hair stuff. I have that down pat."

"Okay," Linda started. "And then what?"

"This is the hard part. I don't wear makeup. Except for weddings, funerals and first dates." Donna replied.

"Oh, that's good. At least it serves you for all the important shit."

"And, what few friends I have are either gay or married. I haven't been to a funeral in over a year. And first dates...well, you know all about that."

Linda chuckled. "Yeah, I do."

"Okay. So, first I use a face cream; oh, and I have concealer."

"What is that: a paper bag?" Linda roared in laughter.

Donna gave Linda a nasty look. "Bitch," she teased. "No. Okay, maybe my makeup isn't that bad. I have one eye shadow, one blush and one lipstick."

"And here I thought you had a ...plethora of colors."

Donna walked over and pushed Linda down on the bed. "Shut up!"

Linda continued to laugh.

"And then, this to wear." Donna turned around, grabbed two hangers and then held up a white blouse and a black skirt.

"Ummm hmmmm. I see. And how much action does this lovely outfit see?"

"It's used for the same purposes as my makeup."

Linda chuckled. "That's a surprise."

"I wanna look feminine and pretty."

Linda stood up and walked over to her. "You just need to be you. She should like you for you, not for what you are or aren't."

Donna skeptically looked at Linda.

"I mean it! You should just be yourself. If she's worth anything, she'll like you for you."

"Thanks," Donna sincerely replied.

"So relax and win her over tonight by just being yourself."

"Okay. I will." Donna smiled.

"So, what do you do?" The dreaded question. Fran had curly raven black hair. It was thick, beautiful and shiny. She could be a hair model. Her skin was perfect. She had make-up on, but it was very subtle. Just enough to emphasize all the right features. Clearly,

Fran was one of those naturally effortlessly beautiful women. Donna quickly became intimidated and insecure.

"I'm a cop. Actually, I'm a narcotics detective." Donna said hesitantly.

"Oh?" Fran seemed intrigued.

"Yeah. It keeps me on my toes; ya never know what's gonna happen." Donna paused for a moment.

Fran stared at her with deep, seduced interest.

Trying to break Fran's gaze on her, Donna quickly said, "especially with my friends."

Fran chuckled. "What do you mean?"

"My friends needed a cop, so I took the job."

There was an awkward moment of silence.

Donna continued. "Like today. My friend Jen fell down the stairs. She has MS. She called me to help. It's all about the connections." She feigned a chuckle.

"Oooh!" Fran said excitedly.

Donna then realized she had made herself out to sound like some kind of hero. "Oh, no. It's not as glamorous as they'd have you think," she stammered to correct the misconception she had just created. "It's long hours. It's either terribly boring or terribly straining. I mean, it's really pretty rare that you have a 'good' day."

"Oh, I'm sure."

Donna paused a moment. She sighed heavily.

As she did, Fran cocked her head and looked at her inquisitively with her deep, rich, infinite brown eyes.

"Look, Fran, I'm gonna be honest with you."

"Okay?"

"I'm a city cop. It's tough. It's tough on me and it's even tougher on anyone I date. It's stressful as hell, and it's lonely. I'm lonely."

Fran leaned in over the table. Softly she said, "truthfully, I don't think I could handle that kind of strain. Especially with all the traveling I do for work. Not being around and not knowing if you're okay would be too much. But, from all my traveling, I'm lonely too. So for tonight, let's just both not be lonely." She said.

Donna didn't say anything. She sighed heavily knowing that the potential was gone. Although she knew it would go nowhere, she decided to numb her pain – at least for tonight.

"Donna?!" Linda's voice was shaky.

"Linda what's wrong? What's going on?"

"Don...I...I've been fucking robbed!"

"What?! What the hell do you mean? Someone broke into your apartment? The shop? Are you okay? What's going on?"

"My shop, my tools. It's all gone. This is so fucked up!" Linda began to sob into the phone.

"I am on my way! I'll have some guys from Robbery come with me, okay? I'll be there as quick as I can."

Only Linda's crying could be heard.

"Hang on, Linda. I will be right there."

The guys from the robbery and theft department processed Linda's shop while she sat on the curb talking to Donna.

"It was Brittany. It had to be."

"Why?"

"She had made a pass at Liz. Liz and Steph told me about it. Just this morning, I told her to get out of the shop. That I was done with her and her bullshit. I didn't need her in my shop or my life. And then I come to work to find this." Linda struggled to speak through her tears.

"She still has the key?"

"I told her to get her shit out and leave the key. And this is what I got!" She began to cry even harder.

"If it's her, do you wanna press charges?"

Linda nodded. "Uh huh."

"Okay. Let the guys finish up here. Do you want to stay with me until we can get this sorted out?"

Linda looked over at her. "You'd let me stay?" Her eyes grew wide and bright.

"Of course! Dude, you're my best friend. If nothing else, I want you to be safe. You can stay with me as long as you need, alright?"

Linda put her arm around Donna and pulled her in close. "You are the best. Thank you." She wiped away her tears.

Linda hurriedly ate what little scraps remained on her plate.

"Dude! You'd think I didn't feed you or something." Donna quipped.

"You don't!" Linda teased. "Hey, I really wanted to thank you for taking me in and helping me with everything. There was no way I could have handled all this."

"It's my pleasure, Linda. You're a great friend and I wouldn't want to see anyone in that position, but especially not you."

"Well, thank you. I've got the new shop opening next week."

"Good." Donna replied. "Are you sure you don't want help tomorrow?"

"No, my brother Jerry is coming up in the morning. Since I don't have too much, I think he and I will be able to knock it out in no time."

"Well, you know where to find me."

"You're working tomorrow!"

Donna dropped her head and glared at Linda. "You know what I mean, wise ass!"

Linda laughed. "I do, thanks. You've done enough, though. Thank you."

"You're welcome. Now hurry up so we can go get some ice cream!" Donna teased.

"Alright, let's get out of here." Linda smiled.

"Donna!" His voice called out above the bustling morning rush in the office. She turned around to see John making his way towards her.

"Hey! What's up?" Donna fought her way through the sea of blue to get closer to him.

"How'd it go the other night?" John asked when they finally got close together.

"The usual," she said matter-of-factly.

His faced dropped. "Oh, man. I'm sorry." He put his arm around her. "Well, Beth wanted me to invite to our house for dinner tonight."

Donna smiled. "Thank you. That's a really generous offer. Especially with Beth's cooking. But, do I really need to come? I mean, I just went out yesterday with Linda, now this..."

"Oh come on. It's just us."

She paused for a moment. It wouldn't kill her to see Beth again, and to eat really good food for free. "Okay," Donna agreed.

"That's my girl." John smiled and winked at her. "Now, let's hurry up. They're about to start the briefing."

The pair quickly hustled over to the briefing room.

Donna sat on the cold, hard ground in front of the two head stones. "Hi, Mom. Hi, Dad." She said. "Nothing to report, really. Work is work. Dad, you know what it's like working with John." She tried to chuckle. "Taffy is being good. It's nice to have some company. I still don't have a girlfriend. I've got friends now, though. Real friends. Linda is my best friend. She's awesome. I love her like a sister. So, I guess I shouldn't complain, huh? Some people don't even have friendships like that."

She propped her right arm on her right leg. She rested her head on her right and wove her fingers through her curls. Donna took in a couple of deep breaths.

"This still sucks. Just so you both know. I hate this. It's not getting any easier. I don't care how much time has gone by. Do you guys have any ideas how many times a day I want to call you? Or how many times a day I think about you? Or how many times I think, Mom would like this or dad would love that? Do you have any idea what it's like to not celebrate mother's day or father's day or your anniversary or your birthdays? Don't even get me started on Thanksgiving and Christmas."

Once again, Donna felt tears cascading down her face. "It's so fucking lonely. I don't have a family."

She exhaled until she had no air left in her lungs. "I'm sorry. For everything hurtful thing I've ever said. For every selfish thing I ever did. For taking you out to dinner and not driving home with you. I'm sorry. I just wish that would make this all better. I'm just so sorry!"

Donna sat back in her chair. She took another drink from her beer while she watched Katie like a hawk.

"Ok, so how do you all know each other?" Katie asked eagerly.

"Well, Linda's been my mechanic since we moved here," Liz started. "I just happened to call her out of the phone book. She did such a great job on my truck, and we just hit it off."

Linda leaned over to Katie. She whispered in her ear. "So obviously, I met Jen through Liz."

Maria shifted in her chair. "And," she chimed in. "I was neighbors with Jen eons ago. She lived here for many years, and we had a great friendship. She moved away, but we stayed in touch. I was so thrilled when she moved back. She and Liz would come and visit. And after Liz met Linda, they introduced me."

"Now, here's where it gets interesting." Stephania said. "I've known Linda for...5 years? 6 years?"

"Yeah, something like that." Linda agreed.

"So anyway, one day these gals were all getting together for something...poker night?"

Donna glanced over at Steph; she shook her head.

Linda broke out into laughter. "Steph, when have we ever had a poker night? It was my annual Super Bowl party, dumbass!"

"Oh, that's right!"

"Linda invited me over, along with Liz, Jen, Donna and Maria. Well, I saw Maria and I instantly fell in love!"

Donna nodded her head. "Yup. And we could hardly watch the game the way you were swooning over her." Donna turned to Katie. "At first, I thought Steph was just drunk. Then I found out that's just how she really is!"

Steph shot Donna a dirty look.

"So, how did you come to the clutch?" Katie asked.

"Shit! How do I know you guys?" Donna probed the group.

"One name: Heather." Linda said flatly.

"Oh shit! How could I forget about her?" Donna paused and turned to Katie. "See, I was dating this girl for about 2 months. She was a client of Linda's. She got a really good job opportunity out in Chicago, so she just left."

"Taking pity on her as a homeless, loveless, friendless cop, we allowed Donna to stay in the group." Steph cracked.

"It was a short relationship, but Linda had gotten to know Donna best because of Heather. So kind of like Stephania, Linda brought her to hang out with us and she just stuck. The difference was that Donna didn't hit on any of us." Liz chuckled.

Donna laughed. "But I still gave you all my number."

"Well, yeah." Liz replied brightly. "We needed a super hero in this group and you were the best one for the job!"

Donna smiled. "Awe! Thanks, Liz."

Taffy lay perfectly still. She was quite content lying in the sun that cascaded through the large windows in the apartment.

Donna sat quietly sketching the peaceful image before her. Though she never considered herself an artist, Donna was very happy to lose herself in the process of drawing. For once, the silence brought her peace. This was one of the few rare moments where Donna could be completely serene without the aid of alcohol or women. This was the time her solitude brought her tranquility. Time was irrelevant. Noise was unnecessary. All that mattered was Taffy, the paper and Donna's pencil. This was the moment her soul had been longing for.

The phone rang. Donna rolled over; the numbers on the clock were too blurred to read. She grunted. She had an early morning ahead of her, why was someone calling her now? Wearily, Donna slapped her hand around on the nightstand until she found the phone. "Hullo?" Her voice was tired and scratchy.

"Donna," the voice on the other line whispered.

Donna thought she heard sniffling. "Hullo? Who is this?"

"Donna, it's Katie." Katie was whispering; she was barely audible.

"Katie?!" Donna sat up. "What the hell is going on?" She shouted into the phone. .

"Donna....Please be quiet. Please, I need your help. Can you come here?"

"Where's here?" She asked.

"Third and Chestnut."

"Third and Chestnut?! Why are you all the way down there?"

"I can't tell you. Go to room thirty one sixty. And please, get some back up and come in uniform." Katie hung up.

"Damn it!" Donna exclaimed. This was bad, she just knew it. Tiredly, she got up and got ready. She left as quickly as her weary feet would let her.

The lights from Donna's Mustang shined brightly on the dilapidated motel. Dark brown paint peeled off the front of the building. The neon sign flickered sporadically. The patrol car pulled in right behind her, bringing even more light on the rundown property.

Once Donna and two male uniformed officers walked in, it seemed almost as dark inside as it was out in the cold autumn night.

"You got a room thirty one sixty?" Donna asked the clerk. He was greasy and unkempt. He matched his environment well.

He pointed down the hall. "On the left," he grunted.

Donna slowly led the way down the dingy hall. No one dared to get near the dirty walls that were stained from decades of cigarette smoke. They eventually found room 3160.

Donna whispered to the male officers. "Look, this is a friend of mine. I appreciate you guys working with me on this. Just please let me lead, k?" The officers nodded.

She apprehensively moved her arm to knock on the door. "Shit. I wish I had a glove!" She whispered out loud to herself. Donna carefully knocked on the door. "Philadelphia police." She waited a moment, but heard nothing. "Police, open up!" Almost immediately, the door creaked open. There was a middle aged couple standing there.

"Can we help you, officer?" The man asked quietly.

"My name is Detective White, sir. I am with the Philadelphia Police Department. We received a complaint, so I need to investigate."

"A complaint? For here?" The wife asked in a high-pitched tone. "It's just us."

"I'm sure," Donna said shortly. "Listen, I received a call. So I have to investigate."

"Ma'am, please." The man pleaded. "We're just a middle-aged couple visiting the city. We have an early flight to catch. I promise there's nothing going on."

"I received a call, I must investigate." Donna said firmly. She leaned in and stared him in the eye. "If I find nothing, I will leave you folks alone. Until then, it is my duty to investigate the complaint."

"Fine," the man relented. He opened the door. The couple stepped back, and let them in.

Donna instantly began looking around the bedroom. Nothing seemed out of the ordinary. The couple walked uncomfortably close behind her.

"Do you see...?" The wife started to say.

Donna whipped around and was inches away from the woman's face. "Miss, why don't you and your husband sit over there in those chairs until I'm done?"

The couple reluctantly backed away. The male officers herded them out of her way.

After scanning the bedroom, Donna checked out the closet. There seemed to be quite a bit of luggage – more than a couple would typically have. "Wow. For just two people you sure did pack a lot. Any particular reason why?"

She glared at the couple who sat speechless just a few feet away.

Donna continued to investigate, but she was beginning to doubt Katie's distress call. As she made her way through the dingy room, she came upon a closed door. Light was shining through the bottom crack of the doorway.

Slowly, she placed her hand on the knob and opened it.

As the door opened, it revealed Katie. She was on the floor, duct-taped to the toilet bowl with an open Bible in front of her. Katie's cell phone and a pencil lay on her lap.

"Oh my God! Is that how you contacted me?" Donna whispered as she picked up Katie's belongings. She took a step forward, knelt down and began cutting through the duct tape to release her friend.

Katie was pale; her eyes were blood shot, and she was still crying. She sobbed so hard, she was struggling for breath.

"Are you ok?" Donna asked softly.

Katie could hardly muster the strength to nod yes.

"Do you want to press charges?" As she cut the tape off, Donna noticed there were hand marks on Katie's wrists, and a bruise was starting to come through on her jaw.

Katie still fought to catch one deep breath.

"Katie, honey. I need to know if you want to press charges."

Katie paused a moment, and weakly nodded yes.

Gently, Donna helped Katie stand up. She carefully guided her to a chair. "Sit here and I'll help you down to the car." Donna spoke softly and she kissed Katie on the forehead. "You're safe now. I'll get you back to Linda as soon as I can, ok?"

Donna walked back into the bed room with Katie's parents still sitting there, the two officers hovering over them. "Mr. and Mrs. Wolfe, you are under arrest for assault and kidnapping. I am going to read you your rights as provided by law.

"You have the right to remain silent."

"We know, we know!" Mr. Wolfe shouted.

"Well okay then. Take them away, boys."

The two male officers handcuffed them and guided them to their patrol car.

107

Donna went back to where Katie was seated. She offered her hand. Katie weakly grabbed it and slowly pulled herself up. Donna wrapper her arm around Katie's waist, allowing Katie to lean into her. Slow cautious step by cautious slow step, Donna helped her hobble to the front seat of her Mustang. She gently placed Katie in the passenger seat.

The drive seemed endless. Donna wanted to fly so she could get Katie home. Rain started coming down heavily, though, and the streets of Philadelphia seemed darker than usual.

They eventually made their way to Linda's apartment. Once again, Katie leaned on her as they carefully walked to the door. Donna knocked.

No answer.

Donna knocked again. "Linda, you in there? It's raining and I want Katie inside, warm and safe, as soon as possible."

Donna kept knocking, for several minutes. She thought she could hear Linda mumbling.

The door finally opened.

Linda stood in the door way. She stood unbalanced, keeping most of her weight on her right leg. A giant bruise surrounded her left eye. Other various scratches, cuts and bruises were scattered over her face, neck and arms.

"Holy shit!" Donna whispered. "Katie told me they got you too, but I didn't expect this!"

Gently, she nudged Katie forward. Katie and Linda awkwardly feel into each other, and held onto each other for dear life.

"Listen guys, I hate to interrupt you."

Linda and Katie pulled away from each other ever so slightly and they turned their attention to Donna.

"You both need medical attention. Are you both okay to get in my car and go to the hospital?"

Linda hesitated before she quietly said, "Yes."

"Okay. You guys both lean on me and we'll get you there."

Donna wedged herself in between Linda and Katie so they could both lean on her. Slowly but carefully they hobbled through the rain to the car. Donna was very cautious getting both of them seated.

She drove quickly to the hospital, not wanting them to lose any more time for medical treatment.

Once Linda and Katie were situated in the hospital and getting care and attention, Donna quietly slipped away and went back to her car.

Beyond exhausted, she returned to the precinct. She went to the lounge and tried to sleep on the couch for a little while before she had to get going again.

John woke her up. "What the hell are you doing here?" He asked.

"Oh. Katie needed help. Long story," Donna said through her groggy haze.

"Everything okay?"

"She and Linda are coming down later to make statements. I'll explain later." She said as she rubbed her eyes and tried to sit up. "What's our plan for today?"

"That dealer in the abandoned Rite-Way parking lot." John said.

"Oh, that guy on Twentieth and East Erie?"

"Yeah. And you're gonna buy." John said.

"Okay," Donna yawned. "I'll go change into my street clothes." She slowly stood up. "Oh hey," she said as she rubbed her eyes. "Can we stop on the way and get a Redbull or something? I am wiped out."

"Sure." John chuckled.

She studied his face as best she could. She had to remember every possible detail.

"Yeah, I got the cash." Donna said. She tried to play it cool, but her exhaustion was killing her. Try as she might, she couldn't concentrate; she just didn't feel sharp.

The dealer didn't look happy. "What's the madda witchoo?" he barked out.

"N...nothing," Donna stepped back out of fear.

"Ain'tchoo did this befo'?"

"Yeah, but..." she and looked down. She began to twitch and fidget, hoping to save her cover. "Normally my girlfriend gets this shit. She's got her friends. But...she's away." She stepped forward. "Look at me!" She decided to use her fatigue in her favor. "I need my stuff, man. Can't you see I'm crashing hard?! I gotta get fucking high!"

He cynically stared at her. "You a narc?" He asked.

"Me? Hell no!" Donna insisted. "I just want my stuff."

"I don't like this." He shifted his weight and crossed his arms. "How'd you get my name?"

"Word of mouth." She said quietly. She was struggling to come up with something. She needed to end this soon. "My friends, I swear."

Donna's mind began to wander. She looked farther out in the distance. She could see that John was behind the guy, probably about 50 feet. Thankfully, the dealer didn't notice.

"What the hell is wrong witchoo?!" He shouted at her.

Jolted back into reality, Donna struggled to find words. "My girlfriend's..."

"Gimme a name!" He demanded.

"Uh....uh...." Donna was sinking. Her eyes began to dart around, looking for help – looking for a way out. She noticed John had turned and was walking away. He was looking for others. She knew that having his back towards this guy was a mistake.

The dealer saw Donna was looking behind him. He turned around. He quickly pulled a gun out from under his pant leg. In somewhat of a crouched position, he shot. Donna ran and jumped on him, but it was too late. The gun had fired and the bullet flew towards his target. Donna looked up just as John fell to the ground.

From underneath her, the dealer curled up onto his hands and knees. She latched her hands around his neck. He stood up and pushed back, throwing Donna off of him. . She fell hard on the pavement. Lying on the ground, Donna couldn't see him, but she could hear his footsteps as he ran away. It was a minute before she could even try to get up.

She limped over to the car as quickly as she could. "Officer down! Officer down! I need all units and a paramedic at Twentieth and East Erie now! The abandoned Rite-Way parking lot. All available units and medics now!" She screamed into the receiver.

She ran painfully and awkwardly over to John. She threw her jacket off and applied pressure to the wound on his lower back. He was bleeding badly. Save him! Please let him be okay! She prayed. She didn't know to whom, but she prayed. She couldn't lose John.

Beth walked in and found Donna kneeling at John's bed crying. "Donna..." she said weakly.

She picked her head up out from her hands. She rose to her feet as best she could and the two women embraced.

"He's stable, but still critical. They stopped the bleeding as you can see. He's got an IV and they have him on oxygen." Donna began to explain, hoping that at least some of it would absorb. "They want to get him stronger before they do more. The bullet is still in him, but they're not completely sure where."

Beth began to sob.

Donna rubbed her arm. "Wherever it is, they said it's ok for a short while."

Beth could hardly hold herself up. She fell onto Donna; they held each other and cried.

"I studied this asshole's face. The sketch artist is already working on it, and we have a street name. We're going to get him. I swear it, Beth."

"Doylestown Police, Precinct 6. This is Officer Racanelli."

What are the chances? Donna pondered. Finally, she spoke. "Brynn?"

"Yes?" Brynn was unsure of the voice on the other side.

"Brynn, this is Donna White. John Crenshaw's partner…"

"Oh!" Brynn paused. "Hey Donna! How's John?"

"Not good. He was shot yesterday. He's in the hospital – at Penn Presby. He's stable right now, but still."

"Oh no!"

"Yeah, it's bad. Look. Today, I went around with the sketches we have from my description. I got one lead and I need your help. There was a Septa worker at the Market East Station. Says she sees this guy every day like clockwork. He arrives at Market East on the R5 that comes in around quarter to seven, and takes the 5:20 home. Pays in cash every time. I can't be sure he takes the R5 all the way to Doylestown, but I have to try. I have a street name, but no real name. John and I were on the bust. We only knew this ass as 'Big Boy.'"

"Big Boy?" Brynn asked with a hint of doubt in her tone.

"Stupid I know. It sounds like something out of a bad movie, but, that's what he called himself."

"Okay. You want to fax over your sketch and I'll see what I can find?"

"Please, Brynn. This guy is not gonna go back to where I know him to hang out. I need every resource I can get. I have to find this prick."

"I understand. I'll see what I can do."

"Thanks, Brynn."

"Donna!" John's scratchy voice tried to call out as she walked through the door.

"Hey Johnny!" Donna said softly. "I'm glad to see you're awake. What's the news?"

"Well," he struggled for his words. "Ya know how much alike we are? How we always said we're like twins?"

"Yeah?" Donna said in utter confusion.

"Now, we really will be! Gotta lose my kidney."

"Oh dammit, John!"

"No, no. It's okay," he tried to reassure her. "The doctors are convinced that my other kidney is in perfect shape. I should be fine. You should know about that."

"Yeah, but John..."

"They're removing it tomorrow, Don. It'll be a long time healing, but they gave me a great prognosis."

"I called Brynn today." Donna said trying to avoid the subject. "We found a lead, and it may tie us to Doylestown. Brynn's gonna help us catch this bastard."

"I'll tell you what." John's voice was growing weak. "I'll focus on getting through this, and you focus on getting him in jail."

The tears welled up in Donna's eyes. "Deal." She whispered. She held onto his hand, out of fear that it would be the last time she could ever touch him.

"Hi Donna, it's Brynn."

She didn't want to answer, but she couldn't let this wait on account of her lack of social skills. As Donna picked up, the answering machine made a horrible screech. "Hullo?"

"Donna?"

"Yeah. Hey Brynn. What's going on?"

"Just an up-date. I just wanted to know how John is."

"He came out of surgery about..." Donna had to look over at the clock, she had lost track of time. "Three, maybe three and a half hours ago. Everything went ok. He's stable, I guess. Now they just have to see how he'll do with just one kidney. They're gonna keep him there for a while and constantly monitor his kidney function. So, I guess that's good."

"Yeah," Brynn said optimistically.

"What's new? Any leads?"

"Well, yeah, actually. You're lucky. Your guy does come out of Doylestown. Rather unusual place for a scumbag, but we're working on it."

"Cool, thanks!" Donna said. She paused for a moment. She had nothing else to say. She was happy to hear the good news, but had no desire to spend any more time on the phone. "Uhhh...look, I gotta go."

"Oh, okay." Brynn said.

"Ummm...I'll call you in a day or two, or something."

"Okay," Brynn brightly replied. "I'll catch ya later."

The dial tone played into her ear for several seconds. After she hung up, Donna rolled over on her bed and smashed her pillow over her head.

Beth was sitting faithfully by her resting husband's side.

"Hey," Donna whispered as she walked into the room.

"Hi Donna." Beth replied.

Beth slowly rose and the two hugged.

Beth stepped back to look at her. "How is everything?" She asked.

"They stuck me with Coronado for the time being."

"Oh lord!" Beth chuckled.

Donna rubbed her eyes. "Maria has an article out in today's edition of her paper on this; she's hoping to get a positive response from the Hispanic community."

"That is so sweet. Please thank her for us," Beth said gently.

"I will." Donna briefly paused. "I haven't spoken to Brynn in a couple of days, but they did have a lead. I need to find out if they've gotten anywhere yet. We're trying, Beth. We're checking every possible avenue."

"I know." Beth whispered as she put her arm around her.

"Here," Donna said through the tears that began racing down her face. She handed Beth an envelope. "It's a card for John, from all the girls."

"Thank you." Beth's voice was cracking as she, too, began to cry. "John will appreciate it."

"What do the doctors say?"

"Well so far, he seems to be okay. They want to keep him on the fluids. They say they will flush him out and help with the kidney."

"Yeah, I know all about that." Donna mumbled.

"He did have to receive a blood transfusion last night, but now he seems stronger. It's still going to be some time, but they are optimistic."

"I hope so." Donna said.

Donna walked in and saw the light on her answering machine blinking. "Ugh!" She cried out. Who called her? She didn't want to talk to anyone. She had just come from seeing John. All she wanted to do was curl up on the couch and be a blob. With great hesitancy, she walked over to the machine and pressed the play button.

"Hey Donna, it's Brynn. I just wanted to let you know that we do have a positive ID on your guy. We have a warrant pending. We're hoping to get out to his place on Thursday or Friday. I'll keep you posted. Call me if you need anything. Talk to you soon."

"Okay, that's not so bad." Donna said to herself. She grabbed the phone and dialed the precinct.

"Narcotics, this is Detective Murphy."

"Murphy? Hey, it's White."

"Hey. What can I do for you?"

"Listen, Doylestown is getting a warrant for the guy that shot Crenshaw. I'm gonna go up with them. Hopefully Thursday or Friday. I'll let you know as soon as I know. I just wanted warn you ahead of time."

"That's great. It'll be good to get him off the streets. Thanks for letting me know."

"Yeah. Talk to you later." Donna hung up.

She was overcome with emotion. Images of John in the hospital, her parents' car accident, Linda and Katie being brutally attacked...all of the pain she had ever felt consumed her. Knowing that she was so close to getting the man who nearly killed John brought her joy, fear and sadness. She tried to take in a deep breath and compose herself. Taffy walked right up to her and began rubbing herself against Donna's leg. "Hey kid," she sniffled. She picked Taffy up and held her tightly. Donna closed her eyes, and just relished feeling Taffy's soft fur against her face.

Donna was well planted on her couch. She let her mind wander. The images on the television screen became blurry. She was focused solely on the giant bowl of ice cream she was devouring.

She was numb, but that was at least better than feeling the pain of John's situation.

Once the ice cream was gone, she slowly came back to reality and the television became clearer again. She glanced over at the clock. 10:52. "Shit," she said out loud. She needed to get some sleep. Tomorrow was going to be a big day. Good, bad or indifferent, it was going to be a life changing day.

In the middle of a normal suburban street was a dilapidated shack of a house. An old Ford pickup truck lay dying on three wheels in the front yard. A sleek black Honda Civic complete with black tinted windows and a large black wing on the back sat in the driveway, just in front of the door.

"It's kind of weird having someone from Philly PD here with us. Normally, you'd have no jurisdiction here. With John's shooting, though..." Brynn said.

Brynn was cuter than John or Beth had ever led Donna to believe. She stood about 5'4". She had thick, beautiful brown hair that she pulled into a tight ponytail. Her eyes were large, deep brown eyes with a softness to them that Donna had never seen before. She was very much in shape, and her uniform hugged her curves perfectly.

"Yeah, I know. I'm glad I can be here. To be a part of this and to see this ass-wipe's face again." Donna replied.

"Okay." Brynn said as she took a deep breath. "Let's do this."

The group of officers all walked up and spread out around the front door to the disheveled little house.

Brynn knocked on the weathered wooden front door. "Doylestown police, open up!" She called out. Donna was surprised at how big her voice sounded.

There was no response at the door.

One of the male officers proceeded to kick open the door. One by one, each officer, Donna included, crept into the house with their guns drawn. Quickly and quietly, they spread out throughout the little house and began looking around.

Donna and Brynn stuck together. They made their way through the dark, dirty house into the bedroom.

"We'll go through the furniture later. Let's get him, and then search the place for paraphernalia." Brynn whispered.

Donna just nodded her head.

There was a small closet in the corner of the room. In perfect synchronicity, the two women crept over to the closet. Brynn quietly grabbed the knob and carefully opened the door.

Lying on the floor with his gun pointed upwards, at no particular target, was the dealer. The same man who had boldly shot at John now cowered in a closet.

"Drop the gun!" Brynn screamed. "Drop it now!"

Looking up at two pistol barrels, he knew he had no chance. He put the gun down, and pushed it towards the two cops. He began to get up.

"Freeze!" both women shouted. He dropped to the floor immediately. Donna and Brynn reached down, each grabbed an arm and pulled him up.

"Is this him?" Brynn asked.

Donna looked at his face. Instantly she knew. "Yes."

The dealer looked up and saw her. "You!" He cried out. "I knew you was a cop!" He began cursing and screaming.

Brynn handcuffed him and handed him off to one of the male officers. "Hold him in the car." She commanded.

Brynn and Donna both took a deep sigh. They looked at each other. A look of content sat in Brynn's eyes. Donna sighed out of relief, but then tears began to build up.

"Hey, we got him." Brynn reassured her. "It's done. It's over."

"I know," Donna said weakly. "I'm glad. I just wish John could be here and..."

"I know." Brynn whispered with a soft smile. She unexpectedly embraced Donna. They paused for a moment.

Brynn said, "okay. Let's see what this asshole has so we can really nail him."

All the remaining officers began searching the house. Opening all the cabinets, drawers, dressers, closets, turning over the bed. Anything and everything they could fathom was fair game.

When they were done, they had ten thousand dollars in cash, and apparatus for smoking crack, a tube for snorting coke, and several one-gram bags of cocaine. All of the evidence was catalogued and then placed in brown paper bags.

The officers all dispersed into the various vehicles. Donna's Mustang followed closely behind Brynn's patrol car back to the precinct.

Once things settled, Donna slipped away and called the hospital.

"Hello?" John said. He sounded almost back to normal. There was strength in his voice.

"Hey John, it's Donna."

"Hey!" He perked up. "What's going on? I got the card, thank you. And thanks to the girls."

"Sure, no problem." She answered. "Hey, I have some news."

"Oh yeah? What is it?"

"Well, John...We got him! We just nabbed the guy who shot you. We found so much shit in his house. We got him good."

"Good job, Don! I'm proud of you." John said lovingly.

"Thanks," Donna said fighting back the tears. "John, I'm sorry."

"Don't be. I don't want to hear it. I know what you're gonna say and it's bullshit. Don't even think it. You did your job and you did it well. That's one less scumbag walking the streets."

"Okay." She whimpered. "Thanks John. I'll come by tomorrow. I love you." She hung up. She wiped the tears away and turned back into Brynn's processing room.

"Hey, Donna. You can go if you want. We're just processing the stuff. Once we have our end taken care of, we'll get you in as a witness for John's shooting and we'll go from there." Brynn advised.

"Okay." Donna said. She started to walk away. She had only walked a few steps. Suddenly, Brynn ran up to catch her; she gently touched her shoulder.

"Uh....Donna?" She quietly asked.

"Yeah?"

"I was just wondering if you were doing anything tonight."

"Tonight? Oh, well one of my friends is premiering as the prima ballerina at the PA Ballet, but maybe..."

"Can I join you?" Brynn boldly asked.

"If you want, sure." She paused. She didn't expect this. She wanted Brynn to come, but she hadn't planned on making a date of it. She wracked her brain for ideas. "The show starts at eight. Can I pick up you up at...six?"

"Sounds like a date!" Brynn said. She winked at her and walked away.

Donna left the precinct with a huge smile on her face.

Donna's eyes slowly opened to the bright sunlight pouring into the bedroom. As her sight became clearer, she saw beautiful brown hair cascading down a pillow. Donna carefully slid herself closer to the gorgeous woman sleeping next to her.

Her breaths were slow and deep. She lay perfectly still. Not one twitch, she lay in perfect serenity.

She softly inhaled the sweetness of her hair. This could not be real. There would never be such an exquisite, perfect woman next to her.

Donna ever so softly caressed the back of her arm. Albeit a light touch, she felt real. She then gently placed her hand on the woman's side. Her hand rose and fell with her perfect breathing pattern.

There was only one thing left to do. She came in right behind her. Tenderly, she caressed her face. Her cheek, her jawline all felt...real. Donna decided to leave her hand on her face for just a moment...just to be sure.

Brynn grabbed Donna's hand ever so slightly, and put it down. She rolled over towards Donna. Donna propped her head up in her hand. Her blonde curls were all tangled and misdirected; they knotted themselves around her fingers.

"You're still here," Donna whispered quietly.

"Yes, honey, I am. Just like I have been every morning for the past...How long have we been living together now?"

"Ummm...Almost 2 months now, I think."

"And you still feel the need to ask me that every morning? Honey, I am not going anywhere. Yes, I am here again this morning. And I'll be here again tomorrow morning and the morning after that."

"You sure you're not getting tired of me? I mean, eight months of dating and now two months living together..."

"Are you kidding, Don?" Brynn asked.

"Yeah...Well, sorta."

"Honey, I love you. John and Beth were absolutely right about us! We're a good match; we both understand working hard and late...And besides, now our lonely cacti aren't lonely anymore!"

Donna laughed so hard, that tears began to form.

"Seriously Donna, why are you so afraid that I'm just not going to be here one day when you wake up?"

Donna sat in silence for a moment. Looking away from Brynn she said, "I look at Linda and Katie, Liz and Jen, Steph and Maria. They're different from me. They're all always so happy; they don't have the weird quirks I have..."

"Okay, that's it!" Brynn said firmly as she sat up. "Do you think it's all roses for them all the time? Seriously?

"Don't you think that Steph's eccentricity gets on Maria's nerves some times?

"I know for a fact that Liz hates the fact that Jen is so sick."

"We all do." Donna interrupted.

"Right! I do too. But think about the physical, mental and emotional strain that puts on Liz. I'm sure it drains her. As chipper as Liz can be, I can guarantee you that she has bad days. Days where the stress just gets the best of her."

Donna quietly said, "I never thought of that."

"And look at what Linda and Katie had to go through! Linda has a permanent limp because of that! Never mind the fact that Linda owns her own business which is extremely time consuming. And Katie decided to do a double residency, so I'm sure they never see each other." Brynn paused for a breath. "Honey, none of their relationships are perfect. They all have personality quirks. They all have stresses. We all do. That's just life.

"What you're seeing is their love and dedication to each other. Even on the worst of days, that love and dedication never goes away. And guess what. That's the same love and dedication I have for you." Brynn stopped.

Donna silently cried.

Brynn continued. "No matter what stresses or bullshit comes our way, I'll still be here. Just like they're all there for each other. That's what life and love are all about."

"Damn," Donna's voiced cracked. "How did I get so lucky?" With that, she grabbed Brynn, pulled her in close and kissed her on the cheek.

The Mechanic

by

Lauren Shiro

Dedication

I dedicate this book to my mother. You are my best friend and confidant. You have loved and accepted me when I didn't deserve it. Thank you for everything you've done. You're a tremendous blessing to anyone and everyone who knows you. I love you!

The Mechanic

Linda and Jerry stood hunched over the old truck's motor.

"Okay, tighten the wing nut on the cover of the air filter," Jerry said.

Linda did as she was told. "Okay, that's as tight as it goes." She replied. Her voice was almost as deep as her brother's.

"Okay, then you should be good to go." Jerry slowly unrolled himself from under the hood. "Good job, sis."

"Thanks." Linda said as she, too, uncurled.

"Kids, time for dinner!" Their mother called out from the back door.

"Coming!" Linda and Jerry called back in unison.

"So, are you gonna tell 'em *tonight*?" Jerry asked. This had become his daily question.

"What?! No!"

"Oh come on. You could be all like, 'yeah so I'm gay. Could you pass the rolls, Dad?'"

"Oh yeah. 'Cause that would go over well." Linda replied. "If Mom had her way, I'd be wearing pink dresses every day in my *mechanics* classes!"

"If you get in second, I'm telling!" Jerry said as he raced off.

Realizing what her brother had just said, Linda shot off and ran as hard as she could to beat her brother back to the house.

"So how was school?" Melanie addressed her two children.

"Okay." Both Linda and Jerry said in unison.

"Do you have any homework?" She asked innocuously.

"Nah." Linda and Jerry both dismissed her question.

"But Linda does have something to tell you." Jerry winked at his sister.

Linda's face dropped. How could Jerry have set her up like this? She was mortified.

"What's that, honey?" Melanie asked.

"Oh! Uhhh... I... I just got... uhhh... an A on my English test." Linda glared at Jerry.

"Oh, that's wonderful!" Melanie said in delight.

"How are you two doing in your mechanics classes?" Their father, Chuck, asked.

"Good, good." Both kids nodded their heads.

"Linda seems to really be *coming out* as the best in her class." Jerry teased.

Linda's eyes were fixated on her brother

"That's wonderful." Chuck said proudly.

"Linda, don't you and Erica Wallace have a party or something coming up? A date of sorts?" Jerry pushed even harder.

Linda turned and told him to hush through her gritted teeth.

"Is that true, honey?" Melanie asked.

"No. I can't go. I have a history paper to write."

"That is so gay." Jerry retorted.

Linda whipped around. "Jerry!" She shouted.

"Alright you two. What's going on?" Their father bellowed.

"Go on. Tell 'em, sis."

Linda took a deep breath. She looked back and forth at both of her parents. She started to fell nauseas and light headed.

"Is something wrong, honey?" Melanie placed her hand on Linda's arm.

Linda swallowed hard. She tried to speak, but not even a sound came out.

"Honey?" Melanie asked again.

"Oh come on!" Jerry shouted. "She's gay, mom! Linda is gay. She's been too afraid to tell you, but she's gay. She likes girls."

Melanie turned and looked at her. "Is that true, honey?"

Tears cascaded down Linda's cheeks like small waterfalls. Still unable to speak, Linda pushed her chair back and ran upstairs to her bedroom.

Only a small, thin wall separated Linda from her parents. Tears still raced down her face, hours later. She cried silently while listening to her parents.

"Should we talk about this with her tomorrow or act like nothing ever happened?" Melanie asked.

"I don't know. Do you even think it's true?"

"Oh come on, Chuck. We both know it is. We've been speculating about this for years."

"We have, but maybe she's just one of those straight girls with an edge to her."

"Perhaps. But I don't think she would be nearly as upset as she was if that were true."

"Maybe she was upset because her brother humiliated her." Chuck said.

"I guess. I don't know. I just wish she would have been able to tell us on her terms."

"Agreed. But it's done. There's nothing we can do about it now."

"Well, I will speak to him again in the morning."

"Alright then. Good night." Chuck's voice was the last thing Linda heard.

"He told my parents last night." Linda whispered. She felt her eyes fill up with tears yet again.

Tina leaned in. "He did?!" Her dark blue eyes were large as she watched Linda in horror.

"It was so fucked up. He tried to hint at it, but neither of my folks was getting it. Dad finally asked and Jerry just blurted it all out." Linda discreetly wiped her tears away.

"Holy shit! What did you do?" Tina pushed her sandy brown hair back behind her ear.

"Nothing. I fucking ran away."

"I can't believe Jerry told your parents you were gay." Tina spoke just loud enough that Mike Harris heard her just as he walked by their table.

He stopped walking. Holding his lunch tray, he turned to Linda. "You're gay?!" He asked.

Linda clenched her jaw. "Shut up."

"You're gay?!" He asked a little louder.

"I said, shut up!" Linda stood up.

"You're gay?!" It seemed his voice carried through the entire cafeteria.

Linda pushed his tray up, spilling food all over him.

Mike folded in at his waist and began shuffling backwards. Linda was slapping his arms as hard and as quickly as she could. After a few steps, she stopped; she pushed her knee up right into his groin. Mike doubled over in pain. He dropped to his knees, his back against the cafeteria wall.

A small crowd of kids circled around them, watching the school's biggest bully get beat up by a girl.

Linda punched him repeatedly in the arms and stomach. As she heard the crowd grow and become more rowdy, she punched him once in his right eye, turned and walked away.

"It's fine, really, honey. It's just that...well, your father and I would prefer if you didn't...flaunt it. We don't mind, we just don't want to see it. Just don't bring girls home, that's all." Melanie stopped for a few moments. "And look at you! Such a pretty girl. That's what your name means: beautiful. You *are* beautiful. You just can't see it. It's all hidden in how you dress. Why don't you look more feminine? Grow out your hair, put on some make up. Dress and act like a lady. You should! After all isn't the point that you like girls and they like girls? If a girl looks like a boy, what's the point?"

Linda shook her head and buried her face in her hands. This may have been worse than dinner last night. She took in several deep breaths. "I don't know, Mom."

"Well I do. You have spent too much time around boys. You played soccer with boys, now you're taking mechanics classes with boys. We need to get you looking and acting like a girl again. Why don't we go shopping this weekend and buy you some pretty new dresses?"

Linda used every ounce of strength to not scream, run away, or say something terribly sarcastic. "Mom, I..." What to say and how to say it? Linda was fishing for some diplomatic way of telling her mother no. "I..."

"What honey?" Her mother looked at her inquisitively.

"I appreciate it. I do. It's just...This is me. This is what I like; it's who I am. This is how I'm comfortable."

"So, you don't even want to try to dress and act more like a girl?"

Linda sighed. "Not really. I just...I don't know. This is comfortable. This is...me." She said, looking down at herself.

Melanie's posture straightened and her lips pursed. "Well, I see. So that's how you're going to be about it." She paused for a few moments. "This is not what your father and I want for you, you know. You could be very happy if you would just act like a girl. Maybe one day you wouldn't feel that way anymore and date a nice boy on the football team."

"Mom!" Linda shouted. "I don't want to date a boy on the football team. I don't want to dress like I girl. I just want to be who I am. This is my life, not yours."

"You're right. It isn't. Just don't expect any support from either your father or me!" Melanie turned around and walked out of the room.

Linda fought back the tears. This is exactly why she didn't want to come out to her parents. Not yet anyway. But it was too late. The damage was done, and there was no reprieve in sight.

"Linda!" Bob called out as Linda was walking to her car.

Linda turned around.

Bob was a short, stocky, bald man. His dark blue overall suit was tight around his rotund belly. He had dark, gentle brown eyes. He slowly waddled his way over to Linda. "I just wanted to wish you luck." He looked down at the ground. "I hate to see you go. You're a great gal and a great mechanic." Slowly, his eyes made their way up to meet hers. "I've really enjoyed working with you for the past six years. You went from an eager student to a competent mechanic."

Linda smiled. "Thanks."

"There's no doubt in my mind that you'll do well. Opening up your own shop is a big step. It'll be scary and stressful at times. But you've got what it takes." Bob began tearing up. "Just...uhhh...do me a favor and keep in touch, okay?" He smiled weakly.

Linda smiled back. "You bet!" She stepped forward and embraced him. "I wouldn't be able to do this if it wasn't for you. You taught me, you encouraged me, you supported me."

"Remember when all the boys were making fun of me being a girl in their class?"

"Yeah," Bob whispered as a tear rolled down his round cheek.

"And you stuck up for me. I'll never forget that." Linda was now teary eyed too. "You've been like a father to me these last couple of years, especially after everything that happened at home. I can't thank you enough for that." Linda paused. "I'll stay in touch if you stay in touch." Linda winked.

"Deal!" Bob hugged her one last time. "Be good, kid. I'll catch ya later."

"Yeah." Linda smiled at him for a moment, hanging on to this bittersweet moment. Slowly, she turned and walked towards the El Camino.

Linda looked over her shoulder as she merged onto 76. The right lane was clear as she drove on. She just started to pick up speed when she was suddenly hit from behind. Her car lurched forward, throwing her into the steering wheel and then back again. She inhaled and exhaled deeply after a moment. She put on her hazard signals and limped her car to the shoulder.

"Get out of the way, you fucking dyke!" A well-dressed man in a luxury sedan shouted as he drove by. Linda could see that his bumper now wore the green paint of her car; his headlights were cracked as well.

Linda stood by her car on the shoulder. Car after car whizzed by her, not paying any attention to her distressed vehicle.

Linda fought back the tears as she stood in solitude. She gripped her hair by the roots as she looked at the damage. She tried to settle her breathing, but there was such a weight on her chest. All she could manage were frequent, shallow breaths. She walked back to her car. She cautiously opened the door and pulled her cell phone. She slammed the door shut and hastily scrolled through her contacts. She dialed the number.

"Hey, Jerr?"

"Hey Linda. What's up. You okay?"

Linda still fought her tears. "No. I just got hit."

"What?!"

"I got rear-ended by a guy. He didn't stop. My car is ruined and..."

"Are you okay? Did you get hurt?"

"I think so. I don't know."

"Okay. Are you safe?"

"I guess. I'm on the shoulder, just passed the on ramp."

"You on your way home from work?"

"Yeah," Linda sniffled.

"Okay. Stay there. I'll come down and get you. Get in the car. Did you call the police yet?"

"No, not yet."

"You should call them. Let them know what happened."

"But, I let my insurance lapse...I was gonna pay that tonight so nothing happens..."

Jerry sighed heavily into the phone. "Breathe deep, sis. I know you're upset, but you're rambling. Don't worry about it; just tell them you're a disabled vehicle or something. You need to be safe until I get there."

Linda was too nervous. She was afraid of what the cops might say or do. "I'll figure something out. Maybe I'll just go home."

"Can you make it? How bad is it?"

"I...don't think it's that bad. The wheel wells are intact, so I should be able to get home."

"Linda, I don't know..."

"No, Jerr. It's fine. I'll just go home." Linda wiped the last tear off her face. "I'll stop by your shop in the morning."

"Just be safe." Jerry hung up.

Linda got back into her car. She watched every car until she could finally hobble her car onto the highway. She kept her hazards on and drove home very slowly.

Jerry hovered around the back bumper of Linda's El Camino. "So, tell me again what happened."

Linda paced around the garage, staring at the floor. "I was merging onto 76. I had just gotten into the right lane. It was clear when I came up the on ramp. Next thing I know, I get hit from behind. So I pull over and this dick in a Lexus goes flying past me and he yells, 'get outta the way, you fucking dyke!' Like, what the fuck, dude?"

"I've told you this before. You gotta be careful about putting that pride shit on your car."

Linda walked over to her brother. "Jerr, it's a fucking window cling. I wouldn't put bumper stickers on a goddamn 1960 El Camino, I know better than that! And that window cling is small! It's not like my car is pimped out pride or anything."

"Yeah, but still. You never know how people are gonna react...even to the small stuff."

"I guess. Whatever. It's fucked up and it's stupid and now my fucking car is ruined." Linda walked a few steps away.

"It's not that bad. I can fix that. I don't think it's gonna take much. Give me like...two days."

"That's great, but what am I gonna drive to and from work until then?"

Jerry walked over to Linda. "My car," he said as he dropped his keys into her unsuspecting hands.

"What about you?"

"I'm borrowing Mom's car."

"Oh great!" Linda turned away.

"She doesn't know."

Linda turned back and looked at him. "What do you mean?"

"I told Mom I needed to do some work on her car. So I have it for a couple of days and you can use mine."

131

Linda looked at him.

"It's cool. I promise."

"Okay," Linda said warily. "I gotta go open my shop. We're good for now?"

"Yeah. I'll call you this afternoon."

"Okay. Thanks, big brother." She smiled.

"No problem, Quasimodo." He winked.

Linda jokingly elbowed him in the gut before walking away.

Linda held the old family photo. She couldn't believe how young her parents looked. They hardly looked old enough to have children! Their faces hadn't changed, just aged. Well, at least as best as she could recall.

Jerry looked the same. He had thick, rich chocolate brown hair and deep brown eyes. He and his sister both shared their father's tall, lean, lanky physique. He had thin, sharp features and high cheek bones. His smile was wide. She chuckled looking at him.

Linda was sitting on the floor. She held Bonnie, the family's Golden Retriever, who was only a young pup in the picture.

They looked like a normal, average family. Everyone looked so young and happy.

A single tear escaped from her eye and slowly rolled down her cheek. How she wished they could be a real family again. A family where they were all free to be themselves...like they used to be. A family among whom she could feel safe. A family. An open, honest family. Linda sighed heavily remembering the good old days.

"You know I'll never forgive myself, right?" Jerry asked. His attention was focused on the lumber beams, though he spoke to his sister.

"It's alright." Linda shrugged. "It is what it is. Besides that was what...four years ago?"

Jerry pulled out a beam and inspected it. "Yeah. But it's been four years of tension and bullshit."

"Whatever dude. Mom would have reacted this way no matter what. She knew it. I heard her say it that night. She knew; she just didn't want to admit it. And now that she knows she can't 'undo' it, she would rather live in some kind of fantasy world where I am the girly daughter she always wanted."

"But you shouldn't have to be someone you're not."

"You're right. And that's why I only come over for Thanksgiving and Christmas. I can put up with the façade for holidays, but not every day."

"Mom doesn't even ask about you or anything when you're not there." Jerry said in a defeated tone.

"I think she would prefer it if I didn't exist. I guess it's better to have no daughter rather than a gay one."

Jerry turned and looked at her. "You know that's not true."

"I don't know," Linda replied. Trying to distract herself, Linda began inspecting the lumber as well.

"I wish dad would just fucking say something. He and I have talked about it before. He thinks she's overreacting, but he won't do anything about it."

"But that's dad. That's just the way he is. He doesn't like confrontation."

"Yeah well, he should still stand up for what he believes in."

Linda huffed. "Let's just get this stuff and get out of here."

"Okay. So you need three new boards. And you wanted to strip the paint off, right?"

"Yeah. I think it looks dumb that the deck is green. So I wanna strip it and then refinish it."

"Okay. I'll go grab you a gallon of paint thinner while you get the boards."

"Excuse me?!" Linda said as she gently elbowed him in the ribs. "I think not! *I* will go get the paint thinner and you can grab the boards."

"Fine!" Jerry teased. "Are we going right back to your place?"

"Yeah. I figured I'd stop at Wawa and get us a couple of drinks and a snack or something."

"That's cool. While you're doing that, I can get started on taking out those warped boards and get everything ready to put in the new ones."

"Okay, sounds good. Lemme go get the paint thinner and I'll meet you back here for check out."

"Don't even bother." Jerry said. I got the boards. I'll just meet you back at your house."

"Oh, okay." Linda said. "Meet ya back there, then." She walked off to somehow find paint thinner in the giant home improvement store.

Linda walked towards the back of the store. She turned herself sideways so she wouldn't hit the man in the aisle when she walked by.

THE MECHANIC

He was a man who was probably in his mid-late forties. He was in a regular business suit. Linda wouldn't have even noticed him had she not seen and felt him glare at her. Her pace quickened. She grabbed some bottles of soda, paid for them and scurried out the door.

As she walked back to her car, something grabber her attention. She stopped and stepped back. A tan luxury sedan sat just a few spots away from her car. There was nothing spectacular let alone special about this car. Except for one obvious trait. Dark hunter green paint was splattered all over the front bumper of this car. A shade of green that exactly matched her car.

Linda looked from her El Camino back to this sedan several times. The patterns matched.

Wasting no time, Linda began to think. Keying his car or slashing his tires was ineffective and juvenile. No. If she was going to do this, it had to be something good.

She ran to the back of her car. She began to quickly and frantically look through the various items in the bed of the car. She haphazardly looked until she found it. She grabbed the can, her funnel, and she ran back to the sedan. She tried to be as quick and discreet as possible, though it's difficult to hide pouring paint thinner into a car's gas tank. She held the can almost completely upside down. Some paint thinner spilled and ran down the side of the car. She had poured nearly the entire contents when she feared she had taken too long. She closed the gas cap and door. She picked up the can and hastily placed it back in her car. She got into the car and drove away.

After a few blocks, Linda slowed down. She finally remembered to breathe. She didn't know whether to laugh or cry. She felt a tremendous amount of pride and satisfaction. There was a touch of guilt, too. The satisfaction was so much greater, though.

Linda strolled through the street, trying to take it all in. The Philadelphia Pride Parade seemed huge this year. There were drag kings and queens all over. Rainbow balloons were tied to pretty much everything. People. Lots of people. People of every color, every orientation, and every type filled the streets. Linda's ears were bombarded with sounds of music, voices, street sounds, and car horns. It was an overwhelming experience.

As she meandered through the crowds, she looked in booth after booth. Politicians and political booths were mixed in with booths from local companies, radio stations and organizations. She walked past the HRC booth, and had to stop. An absolutely beautiful woman stood inside, talking to the Human Rights Campaign representatives. Curious, Linda made her way over to the booth.

"I don't know if it would be a problem with my contract or not. I would just like to help out." The gorgeous lady said to one of the male reps.

"We appreciate your offer. I would advise you to speak to your agent and see what they say. And we can certainly look into opportunities for you as well."

"Here's my card," the exotic woman said as she presented a business card. "Please feel free to contact me any time."

"Thank you so much for your offer." He replied. "We will certainly see what we can do."

Just then a woman with HRC walked up to Linda. "Hi there. How can I help you?"

"I'm not sure. I just figured I would stop by and see what you guys had going on."

"Well, specifically for Philadelphia and Pennsylvania in general, we are fighting to pass laws that would protect members of the LGBT community from getting fired based on their gender and sexuality expressions."

Linda looked at her, not quite sure she understood.

"Take yourself for example. Is that how you normally dress? Is that what you would wear to work?"

Linda looked down at herself. She was so thin, she lacked any real curves. She wore a large, shapeless tee-shirt and jeans. Her chest was nearly invisible under the oversized shirt. Her plain light blue jeans sat loosely on her frame. "Well sorta. I wouldn't necessarily wear this to work."

"Did you know that you could be fired from your job for dressing in such a gender neutral or even more masculine manner?"

"That would be pretty near impossible." Linda replied.

The stunning woman stopped, turned and listened to Linda's conversation.

The HRC woman seemed rather perturbed by Linda's answer. "And why do you say that?" She asked with a bit of a snarl.

"'Cause I own my own shop. I don't think I would fire myself over my clothes." She laughed.

"Well, not everyone has that luxury and they could potentially be fired for dressing in a way that is comfortable to them but does not necessarily fall into typical gender-specific attire." The woman lashed back.

"What kind of shop do you own?" The male rep who had been talking to the beautiful woman now asked Linda.

"Car shop. I'm a mechanic."

135

"Is your shop LGBT exclusive?" He asked.

"No." Linda answered almost apprehensively.

"But you are LGBT friendly?" The female rep said.

"Well, yeah. I have your sticker on my door and stuff."

"Oh you do?" The male rep asked. "That is probably one of the best ways to help us in our political fights. If you show that you support us, and your clients can see that, you are helping to spread awareness and political change."

"What else can I do? I mean giving you guys money is fine, but are there other ways or other things I can be doing to help?" Linda asked.

"Well, this nice young lady just gave us her card. She's a model and said she would love to do some shoots to support the HRC."

Linda turned to the beautiful young woman. "You are?"

"Yes." She looked at Linda intensely.

"Ya know, a lot of my clients drive classics and hot rods. We should have you shoot with some of our cars."

The young, exquisite lady pondered for a moment. "How many is a lot? How many classic cars are we talking about? A dozen? More? Less?"

"I have one and I think I have at least twenty five clients with classics. Why?"

"Well because, if you have that many cars, we could actually shoot a calendar. Me with your clients' cars. And we could sell those calendars and then donate the proceeds to HRC."

"What a great idea! That's awesome!" Linda briefly paused. "I'm Linda." She extended out her hand.

"Stephania." The beauty replied.

"See. This is great! You are both using your talents to help support us so that we can ensure you have equal and protected rights." The male rep said.

"This was rather serendipitous." Stephania said.

"Uhhh...yeah!" Linda agreed.

"Here's my card." Stephania said, handing Linda a business card. "Give me a call some time and we'll see what we can do."

Linda smiled. "Sounds great!" Linda tucked Stephania's business card into her wallet. She smiled to her and the HRC reps and then continued to take in the pride parade.

Linda curled up under her blue chenille blanket. She settled in on the couch and turned on the television. The Cosby Show had just started. She put her beer on the coffee table and grabbed a hand full of potato chips.

The phone rang. Linda reached over. "Hello?"

"Hey!" It was Jerry. "Whatchya doing?"

"Watching the Cosby Show. Why?"

"Geez!" He laughed. "What the hell is your deal with all things eighties?"

"What?"

"I will never understand your obsession with the eighties."

"Don't be a hater!" Linda teased. "So, what's up?"

"Not much. Just got done at the shop."

"Wow, you're working late. What are you doing?"

"Oh just a full frame-off resto."

"Nice! On what?"

"Only a 1968 Camaro SS." Jerry said slyly.

"Sweet!"

"Yeah. It's in rough shape; it's gonna take a while to get it all done."

"Really? That bad?"

"Yeah. You should stop in some time and take a look."

"Yeah. I'd love to see where it's at and how it ends up." Linda said.

"It's a long road, but it'll be great when it's done." Jerry paused momentarily. "Hey. The engine needs to be completely rebuilt. I was wondering if you'd want in on it. I'll split the money right down the middle with you."

"Yeah!" Linda shouted. "That would be awesome. Thanks!"

"No prob. Catch ya later."

"Bye." Linda hung up. She smiled with excitement. It would be fun to work on a project with Jerry. She had a great feeling about this.

Eager and content, she refocused her attention to the television.

"Hello?" Her voice was as unique as her.

"Hi, Stephania?" Linda asked even though she knew the answer.

"Yes. Who is this?"

"This is Linda Scott. I own a garage. We met at the HRC booth at pride."

"Oh that's right! Hi! How are you? I am so glad you called. I am having a terrible day!"

"You are? I'm sorry. What happened?"

"I got turned down for a job with a major fashion company. They said I wasn't pretty enough. Can you believe that?! How could they say that to me? Do you think I'm not pretty enough?"

"What?! Oh no! Not at all! I think you're beautiful."

"You do?"

"Yeah!"

"Do you think I'm pretty enough to date?"

Linda shook her head in wonder. *Dear God, what had she gotten herself into?* "Uhhh...yeah."

"You hesitated. Why did you hesitate?"

"Well, you're just not my type, that's all."

"Not your type?! What do you mean I'm not your type? What? Why? Is it because I'm mixed?"

"What?! No! Not at all!"

"Well why, then?"

"Honestly? You're too...tall." Linda chuckled. "I like short girls."

"You do?" Stephania asked cynically.

"Yeah. I've always been tall and I just think it's...weird to be with someone my height or taller."

"So you would like me better if I was short?"

"I like you for you. I just date short girls. Is that okay?"

Stephania laughed. "I think so. So, now, why did you call me?"

"Oh! I don't..." Linda struggled to remember. "Oh yeah! The shoot!"

Both women laughed.

"So, I have fourteen cars definitely lined up. I just wanted to know what your schedule looked like and where I can find a good photographer."

"Oh, I know a great guy! He would do an excellent job. I will call him. And scheduling...Let me look. I think I have some openings in August. Will that work for you?"

"I think that my clients and I are way more open and flexible than you are. You tell me what works for you and we should be fine." Linda replied.

"Let me look and ask my photographer. Can I call you back?"

"Of course! Call me back once you know and we'll get it all set up."

"Deal!" Steph exclaimed.

"Okay. Talk to you soon." Linda said.

Linda leaned on the wall outside the garage, smoking a cigarette. A giant truck pulled into her driveway. This was no ordinary truck. It was an old Chevy. Probably from the seventies, Linda guessed. It boasted a beautiful black with red metal flake paint job. It sat up high: lifted with large tires. The engine rumbled loudly. It was a beautiful sound.

A very tall redhead jumped out the beast and walked over to her. "Excuse me," she started. She had a very thick southern accent. "I just called a little while ago. Is the mechanic inside?"

"Nope." Linda felt a smirk come across her face.

"Well, do you know where I'd find him?" The woman asked.

"You're looking at her." Linda said with a smile.

"Oh dear lord! I am so sorry! I didn't mean…"

"It's cool." Linda extended out her hand. "I'm Linda."

She shook her hand, "Liz."

"Nice to meet you Liz. Nice truck. Very nice truck."

"Thank you. It was my daddy's, but he gave it to me when I graduated from college."

"Wow! That's one hell of a present." Linda said, impressed.

"It sure is. It was always his dream to have a nice truck, but he's a farmer. So it's not really helpful for him to have a show truck. So I've done my best to trick it out and maintain it for him."

"From here, it looks like you've done a great job." Linda said. "Pull 'er right in and I'll take a look."

"Hey Linda?"

"Yeah?"

"It's Steph."

Linda had to think for a moment. "Oh, Stephania! How are you?"

"Good. How are you?"

"Fine, thanks. What's up?"

"Listen, my mechanic just got laid off. The garage she's been working for is closing and she needs a job. She's been great with my car. I know how busy you've been. Any chance you'd want to take on another mechanic?"

Linda remained quiet. She really didn't like the idea of bringing in anyone new, especially someone she didn't know. She was apprehensive about the idea. It really didn't sit well with her. She simply wasn't comfortable.

But this was Steph. She was eccentric, but she wasn't a bad person. She was a friend. She would never hurt Linda. She had introduced Linda to other friends of hers and they all seemed to be decent people. She obviously did good work if Stephania said so. How bad could it be? Linda was probably just being territorial.

"Sure. Yeah. Have her come by so I can meet her and show her around."

"You are the best! Thank you! You won't regret it!"

"Okay," Linda smiled.

"Oh, and one more thing!"

"Yeah?"

"She's hot!" Stephania giggled and hung up.

Linda laughed as she hung up her phone. She shook her head. Stephania was one very interesting character.

Linda took a long drag of her cigarette as she walked. She looked up. The sky was a jet black blanket with the stars as little shining decorations. A three quarter moon sat like a full, round, content Buddha belly. The Philadelphia skyline was a lighted mountain range, poking the sky at various heights.

She exhaled her smoke and watched it swirl up into the night. Linda suddenly felt so small. The buildings around her stood at unfathomable heights. The sky was so much larger than the small portion she could see. The universe was so much greater than the few stars she saw.

Linda wondered what was out there. What waited out there in the giant world...in the infinite universe? How much didn't she know? How much of the great world was she missing? How much more was there than she could ever imagine? Was her life of any meaning? Was there more to her than she even knew? Could she possibly have some kind of an impact on such a giant world when she was just so small? What did it all mean, if anything?

Knowing that she would never really know, she took another hit off her cigarette and kept walking.

Linda smashed the cigarette under her foot. When she looked up, she saw a tall, thin, platinum blonde approaching her. This girl had long legs – very long, sexy legs. She was slender, but still boasted feminine curves. She was very attractive, to say the least.

"Linda?" She asked as she got closer.

"Yeah."

"Hi, I'm Brittany! I'm Stephania's mechanic. She told me to come down here and meet you."

Linda smiled. "Hi," she shook her hand. "It's nice to meet you."

Brittany's handshake was weak and delicate. For a mechanic, she was quite feminine. Even her hands were relatively clean. Linda thought that was unusual, but she let it go.

"This is a nice shop." Brittany said.

"Thanks."

"This is all yours?!"

"Yeah. I opened it on my own. It's been just me all this time. I am getting really busy, so it wouldn't be bad to have an extra set of hands to keep up with the work."

Brittany slightly leaned in. "What do you do? Do you 'specialize' in anything?"

"I pretty much do it all. I work on quite a few classic and antique cars. Those have always been my passion. But you still get the occasional station wagon."

Brittany laughed. "You can't avoid those, no matter what you do!"

Linda also chuckled. "Yeah, right?"

"Is there anything that you don't do?"

"When it comes to body work, I don't do a hell of a lot of that. My brother has his own body shop, so I send folks over there when they need it."

"Oh cool! A family affair. I like it." Brittany's smile was intoxicating.

Linda caught herself getting pulled in by Brittany's dark brown eyes and brilliant smile.

Brittany began walking around. "So, you have two bays?"

"Yup. Two bays. Two lifts, dymo...you've got everything you need here. I would say to bring your own tools, though. Always better to have more."

"Well, of course. I wouldn't go stealing your stuff!" Brittany laughed lightly.

The longer Linda spent with her, the better she felt about the change. "Good to know." She chuckled. "Do you have any questions?"

"No, I don't think so. You're sure you're okay with this?"

"Yeah. If you're a friend of Steph's and you do good work, I know you're good."

Brittany's smile grew even more. "Thanks. So...when can I start?"

Linda thought for a moment. "Monday?"

"Monday sounds great. Thanks! See you then!" Brittany shook her hand one more time and winked at Linda before walking away.

Linda replaced the throttle plate on to the carburetor.

Liz sat a few feet away on the floor just under the bay door. "You know, I have really felt out of sorts in such a large city. You've become my first real friend."

"Awe. Well thanks. I'm sorry you don't feel at home here. It's a big adjustment from country living to city life."

"We lived out in Los Angeles before coming here. But I'm not dancing here. It's weird. I think it wouldn't be so bad if I was dancing."

"How come you aren't?" Linda's eye peeked up quickly and then dropped back down to inside the carburetor.

"Jen has MS. She wanted to come back here to be closer to her family. And I want to be home for her, in case something happens."

Linda turned and looked at Liz with a puzzled expression. "Wait. Who's Jen?"

"Oh, my girlfriend."

"You stopped dancing so you could help a friend? Wow. You're one hell of a friend!"

"Oh no, I mean like girlfriend girlfriend. Partner. Wife. Whatever you want to call it."

Linda's expression reflected her even greater confusion. "You're gay?"

"Yeah. Sort of. I think." Liz paused. "Yes. Yes I'm gay."

"I'm actually kind of surprised." Linda said.

"How come?"

"Well, you just don't strike me as the type."

"How would you know?" Liz innocently asked.

Linda chuckled. "I am too."

"You are?!" Liz's eyes grew wide with surprise. "Oh. So...?"

"You just don't set off my 'gaydar,' if you know what I mean." Linda laughed.

"Okay?" Liz's tone indicated her confusion.

"You know – when you can just tell a person is just by looking at them.

"People have always picked up on it with me. Hell, my parents knew when I was little. My mom didn't want to accept that her one and only little girl was a dyke, but she knew.

142

"It's just something I've always known about myself, too. So, I've just always known. I know I'm gay, I act gay, I consider myself gay. I don't know. It's just a way I identify myself."

"Oh, okay!" Liz responded brightly.

"So, do you think of yourself as gay?" Linda shyly asked Liz.

"Hell yeah! I'm a rootin' tootin', lady-lovin', pick-up truck driving lesbian! Yee haw!" Liz said loudly before falling into laughter. After a few moments, she composed herself and her tone quieted. "To tell you the truth, I never really thought about it, Lin. I just know that I love her and she loves me. If that makes me gay, then so be it."

"It's great that you have that. You're really lucky."

"Yeah. She's great."

"No, well yeah. It's great that she's great, but I also mean what you have. You have a home with someone you love and they love you back. You have a life, a family. It's nice. I hope to have that someday."

"You don't have a girlfriend?" Liz asked gently.

"Nah." Linda dismissed.

"Well, why not?"

"I don't know. Lots of reasons, I guess." Linda sighed. She hated talking about personal issues. She quickly ducked her head back under the hood to avoid eye contact. She worked quietly and then quickly changed the subject. "There. Your timing is all set. You should be good to go for a while."

"You got any plans for Memorial Day?" Linda asked from under the truck.

Liz sat in a contorted position on the floor. "Why yes we do! We are going to have a barbecue at our house. Jen's brother, Adam, will be there. And her friend Maria is coming. Just a small get together. You?"

Linda turned her ratchet. "Nah, nothing really. I'll probably just stay home, drink a couple of beers."

"Why don't you come over?" Liz asked brightly.

"Thanks. I just...I don't...I don't normally mix business with pleasure. It's gotten me into trouble in the past."

"Well, I...you're the only friend I have out here right now, Lin." Liz sadly stated. "I would love to have you there."

Linda slid out from under the truck. She swiped sweat off her forehead and smeared oil in its place. "Oh, don't kill me with that pitiful me stuff." She smiled.

"Well, it's true! And I really would like to have you there." Liz's face displayed a rather pathetic look.

"Oh, alright. I'll go. On one condition. You're not going to try to hook me up with anyone, are you? Are there going to be any single lesbians that you're going to play match-maker with me and them? 'Cause I won't go if you try to hook me up with some lonely, single lesbian."

"Maria is single, but I didn't plan on getting you two together."

"You didn't? Okay, good." Linda smiled. "Write down your address for me, and what time?"

"One o'clock."

"Okay, I'll be there." Linda smiled.

Brittany strolled over to Linda as she put her tools away. Linda looked up to find Brittany standing very close to her. "Whoa! Hey. What's up? You need something?"

Like lion stalking and closing in on its prey, Brittany inched in closer and closer until Linda backed into the wall. "No. I want something," she said in a seductive tone.

She didn't even wait for Linda to respond. She forcefully kissed her. Her tongue skipped over Linda's lips. Her kiss was full of passion and desire.

Linda was tense at first, but she quickly melted into Britt's kiss. She felt her entire body heat up and beg for more.

After several intense moments, Britt finally pulled away and smiled. "So, can I have you?"

Linda stood dumbstruck. "I...uhhhh..." As much as she enjoyed Brittany's kiss, she really had no inclination to date anyone and certainly not mix business with pleasure.

"You know you liked it. You know you want me. Come on," Brittany implored her. "Take me out tomorrow night. I'll be the best girlfriend and the best co-worker you've ever had. You won't regret it." She kissed Linda again.

"See you tomorrow." Brittany winked and casually walked away.

The parking lot of Linda's shop was filled with classic and muscle cars, and what seemed to be an infinitely large number of people.

Liz stood behind everyone next to Linda. "This is so cool!" She whispered.

Linda chuckled. "Yeah."

"So you do this every year?" Liz asked in awe.

"Yup. This is...our third year in a row, I think."

"That is so cool!" Liz exclaimed.

Heather, with her rich, chocolate brown bouncing hair, walked over to Linda. "Hey," she said quietly.

"Oh hey Heather! How are you?"

"Good. You guys haven't started yet, have you?"

"Nah. They're still getting Steph all put together." Linda teased. "You know what a process that is!"

"I do! Oh good, I am so glad it's okay that I'm late!" Heather laughed.

"Yeah," Linda laughed with her.

Linda could feel Liz watch them. "Oh, I'm sorry. Liz, this is Heather. She owns that MG over there." She pointed to a car that was merely a blip in amongst the giant crowd.

"Heather, this is Liz. She owns that jacked up Chevy truck."

"Oh, I love that one! So unique. What a great ride." Heather's tone was sickeningly sweet. She could be rather fake at times, and this seemed to be one of those times.

Linda watched as Liz shook her hand, saying nothing in response.

"Well, I have someone I want you to meet." Heather said turning to Linda.

She reached out and pulled over a blonde woman who wasn't paying attention.

The blonde pushed her curls out of her face.

"Linda, this is my girlfriend, Donna. She's a cop." Heather bragged.

"Hey," Linda said extending her hand. Donna's grip was firm, honest, real.

"Hi." Donna answered.

The two looked at each other for a moment. There seemed to be some kind of connection or silent understanding between them.

"Honey, Linda is the one who owns this shop." Heather leaned over and whispered in Donna's ear.

"Oh hey." Donna said again, still gripping Linda's hand.

Linda turned. "This is Liz." She said, finally breaking Donna's hold.

"Hi!" Liz said with her bright, strong drawl.

"Hi." Donna said as she shook Liz's hand.

Chris, the photographer sounded off his bull horn. "Okay, everyone. Quiet on the set! We're shooting with the Camaro first. Everyone to their positions!"

Linda tapped Liz on the shoulder and pointed in the direction of the shoot. All four women then turned their attention to Stephania as she began to pose with the Camaro.

Linda put her ratchet in her toolbox and closed it. "Wanna go grab some Chinese?"

"I guess we could." Brittany replied.

"You don't want Chinese? What were you thinking of getting?"

"Oh, I don't know. I'm just so sick of eating out or ordering in."

"Okay. Well, it's seven o'clock. We both just got done with a long day. Our hands are absolutely disgusting, but you want to cook."

"Well…"

"Oh! I see, you want *me* to cook."

"Oh please! Would you? Would you? Would you?"

Linda sighed. "I'm tired, babe. I'd really like to be able to just crash when we get home."

Brittany smiled.

"What?"

"I love that you said, 'when *we* get *home.*' When can we really make it our home?"

"Oh Jesus. Britt, come on! We're not doing this now." Linda turned and began pacing the garage floor.

"Why not, kitten? We have a great relationship, we have a great garage and we work well together. It's perfect. This is the only missing piece."

Linda pulled her hair. "No. Not now."

"But, kitten!" Brittany's voice began to break.

"Not yet." Linda said. "I'm not saying no forever. Just not yet. I'm not ready yet."

"Okay." Brittany sighed heavily. "Now about dinner…"

"Fine!" Linda snapped. "Fine. I will cook."

"Thank you, kitten." Brittany sang.

Linda sat in the dark shop. The only light coming in was the light from the lamppost outside. It was enough light. She should have been done hours ago, while it was still light out. But nothing was adding up. Quite literally.

The cash register and her cash in hand did not add up. Not even close. How could that be? It was one thing if they were off by a few cents…or even a few dollars. But to be short by over two hundred dollars didn't make sense. Linda tried adding the two hundred thirty five dollars to the total of credit card slips. That didn't match up. She tried subtracting it from the total of credit cards. That didn't match up. The credit cards matched the register, only the cash didn't.

So where had this money gone? Two hundred thirty five dollars. Missing. Just missing. Was it a mistake? Did that get entered by accident? Had there even been a transaction for that? Linda shuffled through her work slips. There it was. A tire job Brittany had done. Two hundred thirty five dollars and sixty cents. So where was it? Why couldn't she find it? Where would it possibly have gone? What happened?

There was nothing she could do about it now. She would just have to ask Britt in the morning. Shaking her head in confusion, frustration and despair, Linda put everything in the safe and locked up the shop. She was off to go enjoy the quiet company of solitude in her own house for the rest of the evening.

Linda came back to the front of the shop after throwing out the garbage into the dumpster. As she approached the shop, she could see someone peering into the front door. Linda walked closer. The woman turned around and began to walk away.

"Hey!" Linda called out.

The woman stopped when she heard Linda's voice call out; she spun around. "Oh hey." She said nervously.

Linda walked up to her. The woman's face was familiar. Her curly blonde hair was a dead giveaway. "Donna, right? Heather's girlfriend. The cop."

"Yup, that's me. Well, except for the part about being Heather's girlfriend." Donna spoke quickly and nervously.

"Oh man, I'm sorry. I didn't mean..."

"No, that's okay. Seriously. I didn't expect you to know. I..." Donna's voice trailed off.

Linda took a small, guarded step forward. "So, what's up? What can I do for you?"

"Well...ummm...that's actually why I'm here."

Linda looked at Donna, perplexed.

"I...was just wondering if we could grab beers together some time."

Linda stepped back with her arms up. "Are you asking me out on a date?"

"No!" Donna shouted. "No. I'm sorry. I didn't mean it like you're not attractive. You are. I'm just not...I don't even know what I mean." Donna took a deep breath. "No. I wasn't asking you out. I just...I like you. I don't know. I just felt like we connected that time. I don't have many friends, and I like you and so I thought maybe we could hang out. As friends. I don't have many friends and..."

"Okay, I think I got that part down." Linda said with a light chuckle. "Sure, we can hang out. Is that gonna be a problem with Heather, though? I don't want to get caught in the middle of some shit between you guys."

"No. She's going to Chicago. Shit, no. Now she's already in Chicago. She's gone. And I'm all alone and..." Donna's eyes filled with tears.

"Dude, what did she do to you?!" Linda stepped forward again.

"I loved her. I was about to tell her I loved her and then she told me she was moving. She said there was nothing between us and that I suck in bed and I knew that we weren't going anywhere and that this was nothing and..." Donna rambled. "My parents are dead and I work a lot and I have no friends..." Tears rolled down her face while she blubbered endlessly.

"Whoa! Jesus. I'm sorry, man. That is not right. I am sorry." Linda tenderly embraced Donna.

Donna cried even harder in Linda's arms.

"Thanks for inviting me." Donna said to Linda.

"Yeah, any time." Linda leaned over to Donna. "You remember Liz and Steph from the shoot, right?"

Donna nodded.

"Okay. Jen, the one sitting next to Liz, is her girlfriend. Maria, over there, is an old friend of Jen's and she and Steph began dating recently. Got it?"

"Got it. I think." Donna replied.

Linda chuckled.

Liz sat up and looked at everyone. "This is nice. I like this." She smiled.

"It is always good to be in the company of family," Maria agreed.

Stephania moved her chair in even closer to Maria and she rested her head on Maria's shoulder. "Yes. Family." She said softly.

"Hi ladies. What can I get you for drinks?" A young waiter asked the group.

"An apple-tini!" Steph shouted out.

"A Corona, please." Maria looked up at the young man.

"I'll just have a Bud," Linda said.

"Make that two, please." Donna requested.

"I'll just have water." Liz said.

"Can I also have a water, but could you put lemon in mine?" Jen asked.

"Certainly!" The young man flashed a smile and quickly disappeared into the restaurant.

"This is going to be a good night." Maria said, nodding and smiling at them all.

Linda sat on Donna's bed. "Why did you ask me?!" She laughed and fell backwards with her head landing perfectly on one of Donna's pillows.

"Because you can at least tell me if it looks okay. You wouldn't lie to me...would you?!"

Linda sat up and stared intensely back at Donna.

The pair broke out into hysterical laughter.

"Okay, okay. Seriously." Donna said in between chuckled. "I need to know."

Linda wiped away a tear from laughing. "Okay fine." She took in a deep breath to try to stop herself from laughing. "Whaddya got?"

Donna looked right at her, and in all seriousness said, "I figured I'd need three hours."

Linda's eyes grew wide with surprise. "Three hours?!"

"Well, yeah. One hour to shower, an hour to get ready and an hour to get there." Donna said matter-of-factly.

Linda could no longer contain her chuckles and she broke out into hysterical laughter again. "An hour in the shower?! What the hell is wrong with you? Do you only bathe twice a year that you need to be in the shower that long?"

Donna smiled and laughed a small laugh. "I want to impress this girl. I wanna shave good, and..."

Linda snorted. "What the hell are you? A sasquatch that you need an hour to shave your hairy legs?!"

They were both roaring with laughter.

Donna grabbed a pillow. "Shut up!" She teased as she threw the pillow at Linda.

Linda simply laughed harder. "Oh shit! This is great." Linda tried to compose herself. "Okay, dude. Seriously? An hour in the shower?" She couldn't help it, she started cracking up again.

"Well, just to be sure." Donna tried to defend herself.

"Okay. Whatever you gotta do." Again, Linda inhaled deeply. "So, then what?"

"My hair stuff. I have that down pat."

"Okay," Linda started. "And then what?"

"This is the hard part. Makeup. I don't wear makeup. Except for weddings, funerals and first dates." Donna replied.

Linda smirked. "Oh, that's good. At least it serves you for all the important shit."

"And, what few friends I have are either gay or married. I haven't been to a funeral in over a year. And first dates...well, you know all about that."

Linda chuckled. "Yeah, I do."

"Okay." Donna turned away and began pacing. She was clearly talking herself through the steps. "So, first I use a face cream; oh, and I have concealer."

"What's that: a paper bag?" Linda's laughter bellowed throughout the room.

Donna gave Linda a nasty look. "Bitch," she teased. After a brief pause, she started again. "No. Okay, maybe my makeup isn't that bad. I have one eye shadow, one blush and one lipstick."

"And here I thought you had a ...plethora of colors." Linda teased.

Donna walked over and pushed Linda down on the bed. "Shut up!"

Linda continued to laugh.

Donna walked into her closet. "And then, this to wear." She grabbed two hangers, turned around and then held up a white blouse and a black skirt.

Linda tried to mask her level of disbelief. "Ummm hmmmm. I see. And how much action does this lovely outfit see?"

"It's used for the same purposes as my makeup."

Linda chuckled. "That's a surprise."

"Linda! I wanna look feminine and pretty!" Donna pleaded.

Linda stood up and walked over to her. "Dude! You just need to be you. She should like you for you, not for what you are or aren't."

Donna looked skeptically at her.

"I mean it! You should just be yourself. If she's worth anything, she'll like you for you."

"Thanks," Donna sincerely replied.

Linda put her hand on Donna's arm. "So relax and win her over tonight by just being yourself."

Donna took in a deep breath. "Okay. I will." She smiled.

Linda grabbed the shop phone. "Classic Car Care."

"Linda?"

"Yes?"

"Hey, it's Mark Thompson."

"Hi Mark. What's going on?"

"I brought the car in the other day and Brittany worked on it, but it's still doing the same thing."

"Is it *any* better?"

"No. It's the same. It's like she didn't do anything."

"Hmmm. Okay. What did she say was wrong?"

"The tie rods."

"Really? Okay. Bring it right down. I'll take a look."

"Thanks Linda."

Linda hung up the phone. She sat down to finish up writing out some of her work order slips. She tried to focus on the papers before her, but she was so perplexed as to how Mark could still be having problems with his tie rods. It should have been an easy fix. How could Britt not complete a tie rod job? Was it more than that? Maybe there was something she had missed. It had to have been. Brittany wouldn't have done a hack job. Especially on something so simple and especially for such a good client. There had to be more to it.

As she slowly wrote out the slips, Mark's car pulled in. Linda got up and met him outside.

"Hey," she said as she walked over to him. "I'm gonna get it right up on the lift and see what we've got going on. Okay?"

"Okay. Thanks, Linda."

Just in slowly moving the care onto the lift, she could feel it in the steering. The tie rods were shot. She carefully pulled the sedan onto the lift.

Linda sent the lift upwards. It had only just begun to rise when she could see the tie rods were in horrible condition. She stopped the lift and walked underneath.

The front left tie rod had never been replaced. It was old and in horrendous condition. The front right had a new tie rod, but it looked as though it was coming loose. What the hell had happened? What was Brittany thinking?

Linda inspected the rest of the car from underneath, but she couldn't find any other obvious issues.

She came back out to Mark. "Well, you're right. It is the tie rods. I'm not quite sure what happened, but I'll get it fixed. Do you have some time for me to fix it now?"

"Sure. But how much more is this going to cost. I mean, I just paid the other day…"

"Nothing, Mark. This was a mistake on our end. You shouldn't have to pay twice for a job that wasn't done right the first time.

"You've always been a good customer. I don't want to rip you off. I just want to get your car fixed. Okay?"

A smile of relief washed across Mark's face. "Thanks Linda. I appreciate that."

Linda shook his hand and immediately went back in to fix his car.

"How have you been?" Liz asked.

"Not bad. Pretty busy. How's Jen?" Linda asked as she removed the old brake drum of Liz's truck.

"She seems to be doing well. She is in remission right now. She has that relapsing/remitting kind of MS."

"Uh huh." Linda grunted.

"So anyway, she's been pretty stable."

"That's good. What are your plans from here on out?" Linda strained to speak as she lifted the heavy new brake drum and placed it on the truck.

"I don't know. We don't really have one. We've just been taking it day by day."

"Okay."

"Why, Lin?" Liz looked at her. "What's up?"

"Hang on." Linda got up. She took a moment to walk over to her small, crowded desk. She fumbled through some papers and eventually grabbed a tiny newspaper clipping. "Here." She said handing it to Liz.

"What's this?" Liz asked.

"I just saw this in the Philadelphia Inquirer the other day. I thought it might interest you." Linda shifted her weight and leaned in closer to Liz. "Are you and Jen in a place where you can go back to dancing full time?"

"I think so. I want to ask her first, but to audition and to be a part of a company again would be amazing. I don't have to be a principle dancer. I just wanna dance!"

Linda chuckled. "I hope you can." She smiled.

Linda had just gotten out of the shower. She was headed towards her couch when there was a knock on her door. Linda walked over and opened the door.

Liz and Stephania looked worried.

"Can we talk?" Stephania asked.

"Sure... yeah. Come on in." Linda stepped back so they could come in. "What's going on, guys?"

Liz and Steph looked at each other before they sat down on the couch.

"Well, umm..." Liz started.

"No, let me tell her. It's my fault."

Linda turned and looked at Steph intensely.

"Linda, it's about Britt." Stephania said.

"Britt?! What's wrong?"

"She's fine. She..." Stephania was clearly at a loss for words. "She's not who you think, Linda. If I had known what I know now, I never would have introduced you."

Linda's eyes went back and forth between Liz and Steph.

Liz looked down at the floor. "She made a pass at me, Lin." She said quietly.

"Made a pass at you? She fucking fondled you!" Stephania cried out.

"What?!" Linda asked in utter shock.

"She did," Liz said dolefully. "She's been trying to get me down there when you're not around.

"I called this morning to have you check my brake line. She told me you'd be in. So, I went down there thinking you'd be there. And you weren't. She said you had gone home sick. I told her to just leave a message for you to call me when you felt better. She told me that she didn't want me to have a wasted trip. I told her it was no big deal. She insisted that she could do it.

"I told her I didn't mind. I tried to be polite and explain to her that I really only wanted you to work on the truck. And I don't know...during the whole thing she kept moving around. She somehow cornered me."

Linda's face dropped, expressing her sheer shock.

"And then she kissed me and she started to grab me and..." Liz's words hung heavily in the room.

"Liz got out," Stephania said quietly. "She got out okay and then she called me." Steph took a deep breath. "She told me what happened. I called Britt just to see if she would say anything. She acted all nonchalant on the phone with me. She said there was nobody there and that it was pretty much dead." She rubbed her forehead with her hand. "She did tell me, though, that she has a thing for Liz and that she really wanted to...well, you know." Stephania sat up. "When I asked her about you, she said what you didn't know wouldn't hurt you." Steph slowly rolled her head to the side to look at Linda.

Linda bit her lip, trying not to cry.

"I'm so sorry, Lin." Liz said.

"No, *I'm* sorry." Stephania said. "I am so sorry I ever introduced her for you, your shop, everything. This is all my fault. I am so, so sorry. I would never have done this if I had known she was like this. Please forgive me, Linda."

Linda stood like a statue in her own living room. Tears flowed freely from her eyes.

"Lin?" Liz asked as she stood up.

The silence was stifling.

Both Liz and Stephania walked over to Linda and hugged her.

Linda stared at the ceiling. Despite her exhaustion, sleep would not come to her.

How could Brittany have done this? Linda had trusted her with her shop and her love. Was anyone trustworthy anymore? Why did this happen? Why would she do this to Liz and Linda? How could she? Were emotions irrelevant to her? Was loyalty even in her vocabulary?

Linda wanted to scream. She wanted to cry. She wanted to curl up in a ball and simply disappear.

The sunlight that had only been peeking in now began to pour in. Linda slowly rolled onto her side. The clock read 8:06. She stared at the clock until the numbers became blurry.

She knew what she needed to do, but she feared doing it. She told herself repeatedly that she needed to do it. She also told herself repeatedly how fearful she really was. The conversation circled around and around until somehow, she mustered up the courage. Linda reached over for her phone and dialed Brittany.

It rang a few times before she finally answered. "Hey!" She said brightly.

Linda's heart was racing. She felt hot and nauseated, and she hesitated. "Hey, Britt. Listen... we need to talk."

"Okay? What's up?"

Linda sighed heavily. "Listen, I...I don't even know what to say or how to say it." Linda searched desperately for the words.

Brittany interrupted her thoughts. "What's wrong, kitten?"

"I'm not your kitten." Linda paused. "I'm not your anything anymore."

"Linda, what are you saying?"

Linda took in another deep breath, and yet, she somehow felt depleted of air. "It's done. It's over. There's been too much bullshit going on. The drawer not matching up, jobs done half-assed. And...I know what happened with Liz yesterday."

"I don't know what you're talking about." Brittany was getting loud and defensive.

"Please don't. I can't..."

"Linda, what are you talking about?" Britt's tone dropped and indicated her anger.

Linda sighed. "I don't know what's worse: that you would hurt my friend like that or that me and my emotions aren't important to you."

"Linda, what the hell are you talking about?!"

"Brittany, stop. Please just stop!"

"I didn't do anything. Not with Liz, nothing. I don't know where you would come up with something like that. She's not even that attractive. If I was going to cheat on you, it certainly wouldn't be with her!"

"Just stop with the lies, already!" Linda shouted into the phone. "I know what's going on and I'm done! I'm done with you, your lies, your selfishness...all of it! I'm done. I want you out of my shop and out of my life. Just go. Leave your key at the shop and get out. I don't ever want to see or hear from you again!"

The dial tone was thunderous in Linda's ear. She sat in bed with her heart still racing. Her hands were shaking. Wave after wave of nausea overwhelmed her. Linda felt sad, angry and confused all at the same time.

Linda was floored by the sight before her. The front door of the shop was wide open. The windows had been smashed from the inside out. Tools and equipment were tossed around like a tornado had ripped through the shop. Linda's desk had been flipped over. The cash register lay in pieces, and what was left of the drawer was devoid of any money. Graffiti was sprayed everywhere. The bay doors were folded like accordions.

The picture before her resembled that of a devastated city after a natural disaster.

This couldn't be happening. Fear, hurt and anger consumed her. Somehow, she was able to get her phone and call.

"Donna?!" Linda fought to maintain her composure, but her voice was shaky.

"Linda what's wrong? What's going on?"

"Don...I..." Linda couldn't even describe the scene. After several tearful moments, she said, "I've been fucking robbed!"

"What?! What the hell do you mean? Someone broke into your shop? Are you okay? What's going on?"

"My shop, my tools. It's gone. It's all gone. This is so fucked up!" Linda began to sob heavily into the phone.

"I am on my way! I'll have some guys from Robbery come with me, okay? I'll be there as quick as I can."

Linda could only cry at this point.

"Hang on, Linda. I will be right there."

Linda collapsed into a ball. Her tears formed a small puddle on the shop floor.

The guys from the robbery and theft department processed Linda's shop while she sat on the curb talking to Donna.

Linda battled to breathe. She cupped her hands around her face, unable to look at the painful scene that sat just a few feet away. "It was Brittany. It had to be."

Donna leaned in closer. "Why?"

Linda shook her head and swallowed. "She had made a pass at Liz." Linda inhaled deeply. "Liz and Steph told me about it. Just this morning, I told her to get out of the shop. I told her that I was done with her and her bullshit. I didn't need her in my shop or my life." Linda's tears began flowing again. "And then I come to work to find this!"

"She still has the key?!"

"I told her to get her shit out and leave the key. I never expected her to do anything. I knew she'd be pissed, but I thought I could trust her enough to just leave the key and go.

"I tried so hard. I tried so hard to make her happy and to do things the right way. Even today, I tried to be respectful. And this is what I got in return!" Linda's breaths became quick and shallow. Tears raced down her cheeks.

"If it's her, do you wanna press charges?" Donna placed her hand on Linda's knee.

Linda nodded. "Uh huh," she sniffled.

"Okay. Let the guys finish up here. It shouldn't take too much longer. But the more they do and the more they get, the better your case will be." Donna paused for a few moments. "Hey, Linda. Does she have a key to your place?"

"What?"

"Does she have a key or any other kind of access to your place?"

"Yeah." Linda sniffled.

Donna pressed her lips. "Hmmm. Do you want to stay with me until we can get this sorted out?" She gently asked. "You'd be safe; she wouldn't know where you are. She wouldn't be able to bother you anymore. You can hang out as long as you need. Get your shop up and running again, find a new place somewhere where she can't find you…"

Linda looked over at Donna. Her eyes lit up despite the tears. "You'd let me stay?"

"Of course! You're my best friend. If nothing else, I want you to be safe. You can stay with me as long as you need, alright?"

Linda put her arm around Donna and pulled her in close. "You are the best. Thank you." She wiped away her tears.

Linda and Donna sat on the couch, thoroughly engrossed in the Philadelphia Eagles game on television. They both cheered as they watched their team score yet another touchdown.

"This is awesome," Linda mumbled.

Donna turned and looked at her. "Huh?"

Linda looked back at Donna. "This. This is awesome. I like this. I haven't had anyone else I could watch football games with besides my brother for…a long time."

"At least have him." Donna muttered.

"Yeah," Linda whispered. "He's all I've had for years."

"Really?!" Donna sat up in surprise.

"Yeah. You knew that. I told you about my parents." Linda said.

"No." Donna replied, completely puzzled.

"I didn't? I thought I had."

"My parents were…okay about me coming out. They kind of expected it. But, my mother wasn't too happy when I told her I wouldn't start dressing or acting like a girl."

Donna's expression twisted.

"She wanted a girl. Not a nearly androgynous tom boy like me. She would have been okay with me being gay if I suddenly turned into a fem."

"Oh," Donna whispered.

"So ever since then, things have been strained at best. I don't see my family outside of major holidays."

"And they're close?"

"They live over by Passyunk Park."

"Oh!" Donna said in shock.

"Yeah." Linda choked up for a minute. "So," she sighed. "I really only have Jerry."

"Sorry to hear that," Donna said softly.

"Yeah. Thanks. It sucks sometimes. I just wish...I was normal. That my family was normal. That I had what everybody else has."

"Well, if it's of any consolation, I don't have a family either. None at all. All I see are headstones when I visit my family on holidays."

"Yeah, no shit." Linda took a sip of her beer. "You *really* have it rough." Linda paused. "Were you 'normal' before they died?"

"Whaddya mean?"

"I don't know. Did you do things with them? Were you like a normal family? Did they care you were gay?"

"Yeah, we did stuff. I took them out to dinner for Father's Day the day they died.

"Did they care? I don't know. John told me they knew and they didn't care. But I'll never know for sure."

Linda shrugged. "Looks like we're both out a family."

"Yeah." Donna agreed.

"Tell you what." Linda said, putting down her beer.

"What?"

"We can be our own family. The family you once had and the family I don't have. We'll be each other's family. Shit, we see each other and talk to each other enough. You've let me stay here for the last fucking month because of Britt. If that isn't family, I don't know what is." Linda smiled.

"Yeah." Donna nodded her head. "Sounds good to me. Family. I like that."

Linda grabbed Donna's hand and squeezed it.

Linda hurriedly ate what little scraps remained on her plate.

"Dude! You'd think I didn't feed you or something." Donna quipped.

"You don't!" Linda teased. She scarfed some more food. "Hey, I really wanted to thank you for taking me in and helping me with everything. There was no way I could have handled all this." She said with a mouthful.

"It's my pleasure, Linda. You're a great friend and I wouldn't want to see anyone in that position, but especially not you."

"Well, thank you. I've got the new shop opening next week."

"Good." Donna replied. "Are you sure you don't want help tomorrow?"

"No, Jerry is coming up in the morning. Since I don't have too much, I think he and I will be able to knock it out in no time."

"Well, you know where to find me."

"You're working tomorrow!"

Donna dropped her head and glared at Linda. "You know what I mean, wise ass!"

Linda laughed. "I do, thanks. You've done enough. Thank you."

"You're welcome. Now, hurry up so we can go get some ice cream!" Donna teased.

"Alright, let's get out of here." Linda smiled. She tossed a couple of twenty dollar bills on the table and the pair quickly left, aimed in the direction of their favorite ice cream parlor.

Linda waited in the endless line. She shifted her weight. It was all she could do. All she wanted was to get her pizza and get out. It was taking longer to get her food than it had for her to drive out of her way for her favorite pizza parlor.

Suddenly, a cute little honey blonde walked hurriedly by trying to attend to all of her tables. Linda's attention was now completely focused on her. Her bright, flaxen hair darted from one table to another working efficiently and effectively. It was almost a game for Linda to try to keep her focus on the blonde as she moved about.

Linda felt a tap on her shoulder.

"It's your turn." The guy behind her in the line said.

"Oh, sorry." She walked up to the counter.

"I called in an order. Name is Linda."

A male college student behind the counter handed Linda a pie. She handed him the money and then took her pizza.

She wanted to see the blonde again, but she had disappeared into the sea of faces. Linda strained to find her whereabouts one last time before she went outside, but she could not find her.

The smell of cigarette smoke filled her nostrils as soon as Linda stepped out through the door. She looked over.

There was the little blonde cutie smoking.

Linda smiled.

The blonde was short: she was just five feet tall. Her shiny, sun colored hair was pulled back into a short pony tail. Her dark blue eyes reflected the stars in the night sky.

Both girls paused a moment and smiled sheepishly at each other.

"Hi," Linda said. Linda's voice sounded deep and raspy to herself. She hoped she didn't sound too awful to this girl.

"Hi, I'm Katie!" The little blonde spoke. Her voice was as cute and bubbly as she was.

"I'm Linda." Linda replied. She was fishing for something, anything clever to say, but nothing came to her. "Busy night, huh?" It was pathetic, but at least it started a conversation.

"Yeah," Katie answered. "Friday's always are. Hopefully I won't have to put up with this for much longer, though."

"Oh? How come?"

"I'm a third year vet student at U Penn. Next year is all my clinical rotations and being on-call, so I can't work here much longer. Thank God!" Katie chuckled.

Linda smiled. "Good for you. I hope..."

The young guy from behind the counter came out. "Katie, table four is ready to go." He darted back inside.

"I guess I gotta go." Katie said hesitantly.

"Wait!" Linda begged. Quickly, she grabbed a pen out of her pocket and leaned on the pizza box and wrote her number on a napkin. "Here's my number. If you ever get a free moment and want to... hang out, just...uhhh...call me...if you want to." She thought she must have sounded like a babbling idiot.

Katie's face lit up brighter than the moon that hung over her head. "Thanks!" She took the napkin, folded it, and put it in her pocket. She then disappeared quickly.

A number Linda didn't recognize came up on her phone. Leary of who it might be, she answered, "Classic Car Care."

"Linda?"

As soon as she heard the voice, she knew who it was. Her heart began to pound in her chest. She tried desperately to stay calm and cool. "Yes?"

"This is Katie, from Mario's Pizza."

"Oh hey." She hoped she sounded casual.

"Hi!" Katie said excitedly. "I was wondering if you'd want to get together or something."

Linda's heart was in her throat. "Well, sure...yeah." She choked on her words. "That would be great. What works for you?"

"Well, I have to work all this weekend, but I have next Saturday off. Is that alright?"

"Of course! I know you have a lot going on with work and school. Whatever works for you is fine for me."

"Thanks." Katie replied. "So next Saturday. Want to have dinner at the Culinary School at Walnut Hill?"

"Yeah. That sounds great. Where should I pick you up?"

"I have an apartment in Sansom Place East. Is that okay?"

"Sure. Is that the one on Chestnut?"

"Yeah. 3600 Chestnut."

"Oh, okay. I know exactly where that is. What time should I pick you up? Seven?"

"Yeah, that's perfect. Sounds like a date!" Katie exclaimed.

Linda's heart began to pound even harder. "Okay. See you then."

"Bye." Katie said. Her voice was mesmerizing to Linda.

Linda stood holding her phone, wearing a smile that would not go away.

Linda sat nervously across from Katie. She could feel her heart hammering within her chest. Her stomach raced back and forth from hunger to nausea. She could feel beads of sweat all over her body.

She couldn't believe Katie was there. She was so cute and bright. Linda had never met anyone like her before. She was smart. She was funny. She was...great.

The waitress came over with their fajitas.

Linda looked down at her plate. She began shaking her head.

"What?" Katie asked.

Linda laughed. "This is not good first date food."

"What do you mean?" Katie asked. As she did, she looked up and saw a clump of lettuce and sour cream fall out the back of Linda's fajita. Katie laughed.

"See?!" Linda said as she crunched down.

Both girls laughed.

"Well, I don't mind. I think you still look sexy." Katie winked.

Linda's heart skipped a beat; she could feel her cheeks flush with color. A surge of heat shot up her body and enveloped her face. She smiled and tried to contain her excitement.

After their tasty, though somewhat comical dinner, Katie and Linda were walking through University City District. The night was curiously warm with a cool, gentle breeze that kicked up every so often. The night was clear and the stars seemed brighter than usual.

As nervous as Linda was, holding Katie's hand somehow felt normal, comfortable, right. They strolled down the sidewalk. There was no world around them. Just a beautiful black sky with diamond stars...and each other.

As they walked in the crisp October night air, Katie's watch beeped, signaling that it was midnight.

"I should get back. I have class early in the morning."

"Ok," Linda said softly.

At Katie's building, they turned towards each other. They fidgeted awkwardly, waiting for the other to make the first move.

Finally, Linda leaned in, and gently kissed Katie. It was like nothing either one had ever experienced. It was soft and gentle. It was warm and intense. It sent a shock through both of their spines. It was an amazing feeling that neither wanted to end.

Linda looked at all the women around her. As the group of seven women sat around enjoying their dinner, the conversation flowed freely. Katie definitely fit in with the rest of the crowd.

"Well, I think it's great that you're a vet student." Liz said.

"Thanks!" Katie replied with a big smile.

"Hey! Now you know someone who can care for your herd!" Stephania joked.

The table broke out into laughter.

"Herd?" Katie asked.

Linda slipped her hand under the table and rested it on Katie's knee.

"We have seven cats." Liz explained.

Katie looked at Linda and then back at Liz. "Seven?!" Her pitch rose up in utter shock.

"You see," Jen quietly explained. "I used to be the director of an all feline shelter in Florida."

"And in Seattle and L.A.!" Liz chimed in.

Jen continued. "Cats have always been my passion, and so I've taken in countless kitties over the years."

"Wow. That is amazing!" Katie said with great enthusiasm. "I'll be more than happy to help out with the troops. And maybe if you know any good rescue organizations here in the city, maybe we can work something out there too!"

Liz and Jen smiled at each other.

Liz looked over at Linda and winked at her: her sign that Katie was a keeper. "Well, I would just like to welcome Katie to our group! She seems like a great gal and a good match for Lin. So, here's to Katie!"

Jen interrupted. "Wait!" She jokingly slapped Liz's arm. "I can't believe you didn't say anything." Jen turned to address the table. "That's not all! *We* have an announcement to make. As of two o'clock this afternoon, my amazing woman is the new Prima Ballerina for the Pennsylvania Ballet!"

"Liz! Why didn't you tell us?!" Linda asked.

Liz simply blushed. "I forgot. I was so excited about meeting Katie..."

"You forgot? We all knew how important this was for you! I'm so glad you made it! Congratulations!" Linda raised her beer. "Here's to Katie *and* Liz!" Linda toasted.

Everyone raised their glasses and cheered.

Linda walked around the junk yard. An open cemetery for cars all in various stages of decomposition. Rusted parts and components lay all around.

Linda looked slowly and carefully, studying the various car carcasses surrounding her. Some were in better shape than others; others seemed more suited for the task at hand.

She meandered for an unknown length of time. Suddenly, out of the death and destruction appeared the perfect vehicle.

"That's it. That's the one. How much?"

"That depends. Can you tow it or am I hauling it out for you?" The rotund bearded man asked.

"I drove my shop's tow truck here. If you can just help me get on my flat bed, I'm good to go."

The man thought for a few moments. "Fifty bucks."

"Done." Linda handed him a fifty dollar bill. "Best fifty dollars I ever spent in my life."

"Go bring your truck in. I'll wait here."

Linda began to walk away. As she made her long trek back to the truck, she called Jerry.

"Hey Quasimodo. What's up?"

"Hey. I just got a really big project. Frame-off resto. Are you in?"

"Sure, I guess. Who is it for?"

"I'll explain later. I gotta go get it onto my flatbed." Linda hung up. The biggest smile she had ever smiled was on her face, and it was not going away.

"Watch your end of the table!" Donna barked at Linda as they tried to enter the incredibly narrow doorway.

"It's a good thing you don't have too much, Katie." Stephania huffed as she carried a box behind Linda and Donna.

"Thank you all so much for helping me move!" Katie's reply echoed down the hallway.

Jen carried a small, light box full of Katie's toiletries. After she placed the box in the bathroom, she started to walk past Liz who was carrying a very large and awkward box.

"Sit." Liz ordered.

"But, I could..." Jen protested.

"No, honey. Please, just sit. There are only 3 boxes left and we're done. Just relax." Liz said gently.

Jen begrudgingly complied and sat on the couch; she watched the others heave the remainders of Katie's belongings.

One by one, everyone placed the boxes in their appropriate places and then sat down.

There was a knock at the door.

Katie jumped up and answered it. She quickly flung the door open. "Hi Keith! Good to see you again."

"You too." The awkward young man replied.

He handed her two large pizza boxes. Two bags full of soda sat at his feet.

Katie eagerly took the pizzas and turned back inside. Linda jumped up and grabbed the bags.

"Thanks!" Katie said enthusiastically as she handed him money.

Keith turned and began to walk away as she shut the door.

Katie turned back and faced the group. "This is my way of saying thanks, ladies!" She briefly paused. "This is all for you! Dig in!"

The group took Katie's order quite seriously; they quickly indulged themselves in the food.

Only a few minutes into their meal, the phone rang. Linda jumped right up to answer.

"Hello?" She paused for a moment as the person on the other end spoke.

The voice on the other end seemed startled. "Yes, hello. Is Katherine available, please?"

"Oh! Uhhh...sure. Hang on for a second." Linda put the phone down and walked over to Katie. "It's for you, babe." She whispered and she brushed a kiss on Katie's cheek.

Katie rose, and picked up the phone. "Hello?" There was a brief pause. "Oh, hi Mom." She waited. "Yes, that was Linda, my new roommate."

"Roommate?" Stephania quietly asked Linda; her face conveying an expression of disapproval.

"Yeah. Katie's parents are tough. Her dad is a pastor, so she has to watch what she says. It sucks." Linda whispered in reply.

"No mom, she doesn't smoke." Katie said in the background. "No, she doesn't have throat cancer. That is her normal voice." Katie paused for a minute. "Yes mom, I know she has a deep voice. But that's…"

"They're more than tough," Jen leaned in and whispered. "That's absurd!"

Liz nodded in quiet agreement.

The group waited silently until Katie's strenuous conversation was finally over.

"Okay, mom. Thanks. I love you too." Katie eventually hung up and proceeded back to the table.

"Everything okay, honey?" Linda asked.

Katie sighed. "Yeah. Just the usual."

"Your father is a pastor?" Jen asked cautiously.

"Yeah," Katie sighed again.

"How do you plan on explaining this to your parents?" Steph asked.

"Well, my parents are in Iowa. If I can find work here in Philly after I graduate, then I won't have to answer to them anymore."

"There is a ton of work to be had around here." Maria said. "With Liz and Jen alone, I'm sure you'll be fine!"

The table broke out into a light chuckle.

"That may be true," Jen said. "But, are you going to cut off all connections with them? Do you ever plan on seeing them or speaking to them?"

"On a limited basis." Katie answered.

"I think as long as you keep a safe distance you'll be okay." Steph said. "You shouldn't have any problem finding a job and really making a good life for yourselves. You'll do well."

"Of course she will!" Linda said, pulling Katie close to her. "She's bright and talented. If she can do everything she's doing now, she'll be fine. She's awesome."

"There's no doubt that she is. We all love you. You know that, Katie." Jen tenderly chimed in again. "I'm just uneasy about this whole thing, though."

"Another One Bites the Dust" played in the background. Linda hummed along as she drank her coffee and read the paper. Katie came down the stairs in her robe; her blonde hair was flat and wet.

"Hey baby." Linda said.

Katie stood smiling at her.

"What?" Linda asked with a chuckle.

Katie giggled. "You're so cute."

Linda's face twisted into an expression of confusion. "Cute is not a word normally used to describe me."

"But you are!" Katie smiled.

"Okay, I give up. Why am I cute?"

Katie giggled again.

"What?!"

"I heard you in the shower."

Linda was puzzled for a moment. Then it dawned on her. "Oh! Jesus, I'm sorry. That must have been horrible!"

Katie laughed. "Well, it's not the best rendition of 'Eye of the Tiger,' but it was entertaining!"

Both Linda and Katie laughed heartily.

"I am so sorry. I forgot to tell you I'm weird. Are you gonna be okay with that? That you're living with a weird eighties freak?"

Katie laughed and she wrapped her arms around Linda. "That sounds absolutely wonderful!" She tenderly kissed Linda on the cheek.

"Jen fell a couple of weeks ago." Liz said as Linda turned her ratchet.

Linda looked up, and nearly hit her head on Liz's truck's hood. "What?!"

"Yeah. She called Donna. I wouldn't have known about it had Donna not called me while the Paramedics were there.

"I mean, I would have weaseled it out of her when I saw all the bruises and stuff, but she'd rather not tell me this stuff, Lin."

"You realize she's trying to protect you, Liz." Linda said. "She doesn't want you to see how sick she really is."

"That's the worst part!" Liz exclaimed. "I *do* know! I see it.

"I know it's killing her that she can't work anymore. I know she'd like to have some pride and dignity. I understand how hard she has it staying at home and struggling to do simple daily chores. She just wants things to be the way they used to be."

"Can you blame her?" Linda asked, her face practically buried in the truck's big block.

Liz paused and sighed. "No. I would love nothing more than for her to be healthy again. But dang it, Linda! Why the hell does she have to push herself so hard and end up hurting herself?! There's no reason for it."

"It's like you said, she wants to have pride and dignity. Look at you and me. Imagine how you'd feel if you couldn't dance any more. Imagine how I'd be if I couldn't be a mechanic any more."

"Hell, look at all of us. We all define ourselves by our jobs. Donna is undoubtedly a cop. Even off duty, she is still a cop.

"Maria eats, sleeps, drinks, and lives writing.

"Stephania models all over the world.

"Our jobs are more than just jobs to us. We are a circle of career-oriented lesbians. Jen just wants to be her old self...and like the rest of us." Linda explained.

"But..." Liz began to argue. She sighed heavily. "I know you're right. I wish it didn't have to be this way. I wish she could see that she's more than a shelter director."

"She does, Liz. She just misses life. She misses getting out of the house. She misses doing the things that you and I consider mundane." After a few more tweaks of the ratchet, Linda slowly stood up, put the ratchet away, and dove back in to the engine to pull the air filter.

"I'm just gonna hose this real quick," she explained as she walked over the hose. Within a few seconds, all the dirt was being washed down the bay and the truck's air filter looked brand new again. Both women were silent as Linda made her way back towards Liz.

Linda quietly placed the air filter back end and carefully closed the hood of Liz's truck. She then wiped her hands on a small hand towel, but they still were black as night. As she looked up, she noticed tears welling up in Liz's eyes. Cautious of her mechanic's hands, Linda gently hugged Liz. "It's gonna be ok, sweetie."

"One last thing," Katie said as she packed the last of her clothes. "I'm not allowed to have my cell or the internet at home. Dad says it's sinful. So we'll have to write by snail mail."

"Damn," Linda whispered, fighting back the tears. She paused a moment and took a deep breath. "Ok, whatever I have to do. I've always told you I'd do anything and everything for you." The tears won and began to run down her face.

Katie walked over to her and embraced her. She ran her fingers through Linda's hair. "It's ok, sweetheart." She whispered.

Linda swallowed. "We'd better go. I don't want you to be late for your flight."

Katie still held Linda tightly. "I wish I didn't have to go."

"Me too," Linda cried. "I promise I will write to you every day."

"I'll write you back." Katie struggled to smile. "I love you."

"I love you too, babe." Linda closed her wet, teary eyes and gently kissed Katie. She tenderly held Katie's small hand and they walked out to the El Camino in silence.

Sitting in the back corner of the shop sat the small car with a tarp over it.

"What is this?" Jerry asked as he and Linda walked towards it.

"Remember that off-frame resto I told you about a few months ago?"

"Yeah?"

"This is it." With tremendous pride, Linda pulled off the tarp. Underneath sat a rusted, dilapidated 1964 Volkswagen Beetle.

"What the hell is this?!"

"You know my girlfriend, Katie?"

"You mean your *supposed* girlfriend. The one who doesn't really exist until I meet her in person." Jerry winked at his sister.

"Shut up!" Linda teased.

"Okay, seriously. Yeah."

"Well, she's back with her folks in Iowa for the summer. I bought this for her. I wanna fix it up while she's gone and give it to her when she gets back.

"If you can help me get it off the frame, the body shouldn't need too much. I've got everything else. Frame, suspension, engine, interior...you name it. All I ask is that you please do your absolute best on the body."

"This chick better be worth it, sis."

Linda's eyes lit up. "She is, Jerr. She's amazing."

As each day slowly came and went through the summer, Linda wrote letters to Katie every morning and she worked diligently on the Beetle every night.

Though the summer seemed lonely, endless and barren, the progress on the Beetle gave Linda hope each and every day. Until the final day when it all came together...perfectly.

Linda was smiling from ear to ear having Katie ride with her again. She was so excited. Katie sat next to her with an equally grand smile.

"It's so good to be back home." Katie said.

"It is so good to finally have you back home, babe." Linda paused. "Hey, honey, did you ever get my card your last day at your parents'?"

"No. I never got anything."

"Huh, that's odd. Are you sure? It was a card, with something special inside."

"Nope. No, babe. Never got it."

"Maybe it got lost in the mail." Linda speculated just as the El Camino pulled into the driveway. The Beetle waited for them just in front of the garage door.

"Who is that? Who's here?" Katie asked.

"No one," Linda smirked.

Katie was clearly puzzled.

Linda chuckled lightly under her breath.

"What's going on?!" Katie asked.

"That's for you, babe. I've worked on it all summer while you were gone."

Katie looked at Linda with wide eyes. "You got a car and fixed it for me?!"

"Yeah." Linda said casually.

Katie was dumbstruck. "I can't believe you did that for me," she finally spoke.

"Why wouldn't I? You need a car, and I wouldn't let you have just any car." Linda winked at her. "I do love you, you know."

"I know. And I love you too! Thank you so much, babe!"

"Of course! Go check it out."

Katie ran over to a beautiful, two-tone grey 1964 VW Beetle. The lines and curves of the small car were flawless.

A dark thunderstorm cloud grey covered most of the car. The hood, roof trunk and wheel wells all boasted this rich, dark, intriguing color. A lighter, more misty grey ran the length of the body, covering the lower half of the door. The car's natural curves and chrome accents divided the two shades and enhanced the car's design. White wall tires only continued to enhance the car's appearance. A dusty rose interior completed the perfect, elegant, romantic look.

This car was definitely unique, but it was through a subtle grace that it was one of a kind.

Linda was coming downstairs, humming along to Every Rose Has its Thorn, looking forward to her morning coffee when there was a knock at the door.

She apprehensively walked to the door. She saw an average, middle aged couple through the peep hole in the door. Thinking nothing of it, she opened the door. "Can I help you?" She asked.

"Are you Linda Scott?" The wife asked.

"Yes...?" Linda quickly became leery.

The husband barreled his way into the apartment. "We're Katherine's parents."

Linda stood silently for a few moments before she realized who they were. "Oh! Uhhh...hi." She said weakly.

"We have no time for formalities," Mrs. Wolfe said angrily. "We know who you are and what you've done."

Linda stepped backwards. "What I've done?"

Mr. Wolfe glared at her.

"I'm not sure I know what you're talking about. I haven't done anything...not to Katie – Katherine."

The couple looked at each other.

"She's so deep in sin, she can't even see it." Mrs. Wolfe said to her husband.

"In the name of Jesus," Mr. Wolfe began praying. "We command these demons out!" Mr. Wolfe pushed Linda backwards. She fell onto the floor.

Linda tried to stand up again, but she was pushed back down; Mrs. Wolfe then held her down by her shoulders.

"Lord, we ask that you please save this girl. Please show her the light. Take these demons away from her. Show her your love and your grace. Show her the error of her ways..."

Linda tried to push her way up. "There is no error of my ways!"

Mr. Wolfe slapped Linda across her face. "Silence, demon!"

Enraged, Linda pushed her way up and out from Mrs. Wolfe's grip. She stepped right in front of Mr. Wolfe. "You need to leave!" She shouted in his face.

"Demon be gone!" He shouted as he once again shoved Linda down.

Linda jumped right back up. She got right into his face.

Mrs. Wolfe came up from behind and pushed Linda.

Linda turned around and pushed her in retaliation.

170

Mr. Wolfe then grabbed Linda by her arm and threw her down. He then walked away.

Linda scrambled to get back up. As she did, Mrs. Wolfe kicked her in her ribs. Linda collapsed into a ball.

Writhing in pain, Linda struggled to breathe and find the strength to get back up. Slowly, she worked her way up to her hands and knees. Painfully, she fought to maintain her balance. Just as she finally stabilized herself, from behind, Mr. Wolfe struck her in the knees with a baseball bat.

Linda fell forward with a thud. She experienced a level of pain she had never felt before in her left knee. She gasped for air.

"Get Katherine here." Mrs. Wolfe demanded as she shoved a phone in Linda's face.

Linda could hardly turn to look at her.

"Call her!" She screamed.

Linda carefully dialed Katie's cell.

Katie answered, but Linda couldn't speak into the phone.

"Babe, what's wrong?" Katie asked.

"Katie, please," Linda struggled to speak through the tears and sniffling. "Please, just come home. It's an emergency. I need you here as soon as possible."

"Ok, I'll get there as soon as I can, honey. I love you."

"Me too." Linda swallowed hard.

Mrs. Wolfe pulled Linda up. She grabbed her by the shirt collar, and threw down on the floor again. "You'd better hope she gets here soon." She sneered.

The Wolfes hovered over Linda like vultures waiting for their meal to die. Linda's sense of time was long gone. Moments seemed like hours and yet, hours seemed to be as short as nanoseconds. She sat on the floor, on her hands and knees, just trying to breathe. She prayed for Katie to come home; she also prayed for her safety.

Linda was both scared and relieved when she saw Katie finally walk through the door. As she did, Linda's elbows gave out and she lay down.

Katie gasped when she saw Linda. "What the hell have you done to her?!"

"*We* have done nothing to her. The real question is: what has she done to you?!" Katie's father barked.

Linda just lay prone, crying hysterically and unable to move.

"She didn't do anything to me, dad!" Katie shouted back.

"That's a lie!" Her mother screamed. "We know about your – about how she, she...perverted you!" Mrs. Wolfe broke down into hysterics. Through her sobs she said, "we know. We saw one of her letters. It came after you left. We saw the 'romantic getaway' cruise thing that witch sent you! You would never have done that before! She twisted you! She turned you to her perverted ways!"

"Perverted me?" Katie asked.

"They-" Linda was trying so desperately to speak, but it was difficult. "They think I hurt you - I changed you. I ruined you." She sniffled.

"No!" Katie shouted as she stepped towards her parents. "She didn't ruin me. She makes me happy! She supports me! She takes care of me! She..."

"You see that?! She even has you brainwashed!" Katie's father shouted with conviction.

"Dad, I'm not brainwashed." Katie said in a calmer, more rational tone. She walked up to her father. "She – this – Linda isn't my first girlfriend, dad. You only think I haven't dated, because that's what you wanted to believe. You remember my friend Samantha, from high school? She was my first girlfriend, dad. I've always been this way."

"No, no you haven't!" Her mother screamed with tears racing down her face.

"You are only saying that to cover up for this...pervert! Mr. Williams is a good deacon of the church. He would never raise his daughter to be gay." Mr. Wolfe shouted.

"Dad, it's not in how we're raised or that it's any kind of a choice. We were born this way. *I* was born this way."

"You were not! That is just another one of the lies this deviant told you!" He pointed down towards Linda.

"Dad, stop it!" Katie shouted. "Stop saying that about her. It's not true. I love her!"

"That's it," Katie's mother said sternly. She walked over and grabbed Katie's arm, and started dragging Katie out of the house. Katie struggled to get free. She dug her heels into the ground, only to be dragged harder. She twisted and turned and tried to loosen her mother's grip, but it was all to no avail.

"No!" Linda shouted. "Katie! Please don't..." she pleaded from the bottom of her heart. "I love you!" Linda shouted, she tried to get up, but the pain was too much.

She watched as Mrs. Wolfe and Katie disappeared just past the door.

"Lord, we pray that you save this girl from her demons!" Mr. Wolfe said before hitting Linda in the back with the bat.

Linda grunted as she lost what little air remained in her lungs.

"Show her the way and the truth and the light." He paused. "In the name of Jesus, I exorcise thee, Satan!" He struck Linda with the bat like a golfer hitting the ball for a long, hard drive.

Linda fell flat on the floor.

Mr. Wolfe continued to pray as he took swing after swing at Linda. Linda could only hear noise now. The world around her was fuzzy.

Blackness began to wash over her, but then it waned away. Linda could hear more prayers and feel more hits. Attempting to breathe became her sole focus.

Like the tide slowly coming in, Linda had waves of unconsciousness that eventually rolled back into consciousness and then back again.

Her entire body hurt and tingled. She couldn't even begin to fully comprehend the full extent of her wounds. Horrid pain leaped from her back to her knee to her head to her ribs and then back again. With blurred vision, she watched Mr. Wolfe walk away and grab the bat bag that sat just outside the doorway.

She lay on the futon, wrapped up in her blue chenille blanket. Her '80's ballads CD played "Every rose has its thorn." She couldn't even count how many times she's heard it today. She didn't care. It was a dreary, cold, rainy night. She wanted to move, but she couldn't. She couldn't do anything. Her bruises, wounds and injuries were tremendous. No words could describe her pain and misery; no actions could take that pain and misery away.

Linda just lay there, wishing there was something she could have done earlier. She went over all these wonderful, powerful statements in her head. Things that she wished she would have said to Katie's parents. It was too late now. She had no idea where Katie was, or if she was safe. She hated herself for not stopping Katie's parents. They hurt her, and there was nothing Linda could do. Not now, anyway.

She simply lay in her own pain and misery, ignoring the outside world. She didn't even know what time it was. She guessed simply because the day had turned from grey and miserable to black and miserable.

Unexpectedly, there was a knock at the door. Linda wondered who it could be. She figured it was late, and the weather was disgusting, so who would be outside now? She didn't move. Maybe it was just some mistaken person. The knocking continued.

Linda thought she heard Donna's voice. "Linda, you in there? It's raining and I want Katie inside, warm and safe, as soon as possible."

The knocking crescendoed.

"Okay, okay. I'm coming..." Linda mumbled angrily.

Slowly, painfully, Linda pushed the blanket off, and put her box of tissues down.

It was extremely difficult and painful as she rose from the futon and tried to walk. With a stumbling limp, Linda slowly made her way to the door. Slowly, and with depressed curiosity, Linda opened the door.

Donna had her arms wrapped around a blanket that encased Katie who was standing, shivering, and soaked.

"Holy shit!" Donna whispered. "Katie told me they got you too, but I didn't expect this!"

Gently, she nudged Katie forward. Katie and Linda awkwardly feel into each other, and held onto each other for dear life.

"Listen guys, I hate to interrupt you."

Linda and Katie pulled away from each other ever so slightly and they turned their attention to Donna.

"You both need medical attention. Are you both okay to get in my car and go to the hospital?"

Linda hesitated before she quietly said, "Yes."

"Okay. You guys both lean on me and we'll get you there."

Donna wedged herself in between Linda and Katie so they could both lean on her. Slowly but carefully they hobbled through the rain to the car.

Donna gently guided Linda into the back seat, and then carefully placed Katie in the front passenger seat.

She drove quickly to the hospital, not wanting them to lose any more time for medical treatment.

Once inside the hospital, Donna walked right up to the triage nurse. "Hi. My name is Detective White, with Philly PD. These two ladies here are the victims of a brutal hate crime. They need immediate medical care, but you also need to be sure to document every injury."

"Yes, ma'am." The triage nurse then called for medical staff to come get them.

"And please treat them well. They're family."

"We will," she replied.

Just then two nurses came right up with wheel chairs. They placed Linda in one and Katie in the other.

"You guys gonna be okay?" Donna asked.

"As okay as we can be." Linda weakly replied.

"Listen, I gotta go. But I'll come back for you guys later, ok? I love you both." Donna squeezed both of their hands before leaving.

They were then both whisked away for further examination and treatment.

"How does it look?" Linda nervously asked.

"Honestly? Not good." Doctor Adams said. "Your fibula is shattered just below the lateral collateral ligament. Your medial and lateral collateral ligaments, and your anterior cruciate ligament are all torn. Your meniscus has been compromised.

"You're looking at major surgery. Probably multiple surgeries. It's not going to be an easy recovery. And you will most likely have a limp for the rest of your life."

Linda looked up at him and the ugly MRI image of her knee up on the viewer. "Will I be able to work?"

"You will need to make some adjustments. It's not going to be as easy as it has been. You will need to change some of the ways you do things...compromise, adapt. You may need some extra help with things.

"As long as you follow all the post-op instructions and do your physical therapy diligently, you should be okay for the most part."

Linda inhaled deeply. "Okay. So, when can we do the surgery?"

"Well, don't rush it quite yet. We're still waiting for your blood work to come back. You just got here. You and your girlfriend are going to need some time to heal. Let's get you stabilized and strong enough for surgery first. If all goes as I hope, you will have the surgery within the week. Deal?"

"Okay." Linda agreed, fearful of her new future.

Linda's gurney was way too far away from Katie as they both lay in their room, waiting for more of their various test results.

Katie reached her arm out as far as she could. Linda could see her stretching her short arm out over the side of the gurney. Linda then extended out her arm. Their fingertips could just barely brush each other. Even with that slight touch, they could still feel the love and electricity from each other.

"Are you okay?" Linda asked for the fiftieth time.

"Yeah." Katie weakly replied.

"I'm sorry I didn't save you."

"You have nothing to apologize for, babe. My parents brutally beat you and you're going to apologize to me."

"I'm supposed to protect you and take care of you." Linda argued.

"You're just supposed to be with me," Katie answered. "Promise you will. Please stay with me."

"Of course I will! I'm not going anywhere."

"I love you, Linda. I can't imagine my life without you. Now even more so, I just want to be with you. I don't want to lose you. Please stay with me forever."

"I will." Linda smiled as best she could. "I love you, Katie. I wouldn't want to be with anyone else."

"You promise? You're not going to leave me after all this?"

Linda smirked. "Babe, you know how my parents left me when I couldn't be what they wanted me to be. You know about Brittany: how she used me for anything and everything she could get.

"I'm used to people being fake or putting limitations and restrictions on me. *I'll love you if... I love you but...* You don't do that. You've never done that. You're honest and genuine. You accepted me for the eighties freak that I am. You don't care how I dress or what I look like. You make me happy. Really, truly happy. You're the best thing that ever happened to me, Katie. So am I going to leave you after we were *both* attacked? Of course not! Hell no. This has *nothing* to do with you. You didn't do this. It's not like you used me, cheated on me or lied to me or whatever. We were both hurt today. We were in this together today and we're in this together from here on out."

"Forever?" Katie asked.

"Forever," Linda assured her.

The phone rang in Linda's ear. No answer. "Damn," she whispered to herself. "Guess I'll just have to leave a message." She mumbled. She waited for the beep. "Hi Mom, it's me. Linda." Linda took in a deep breath. "Something happened recently and I'd like to talk to you sometime. Soon, if we could. If you wouldn't mind. So... well... please call me, I guess. Bye."

She shook her head as she hung up. "That was the stupidest message I have ever left," she said to herself.

Linda nervously pulled her chair out to sit. "Thanks for meeting me," she grunted as she ungracefully sat herself down with her cane and her left leg in the brace that wouldn't allow her to bend her knee.

"What happened?" Melanie asked.

"Well Mom, that's why I called. You see, there's this girl. She's awesome. She lives with me. We've been together for a while. She is just amazing. She's a vet student at UPenn. She's smart, she's funny.

She's awesome. You would like her. Her name is Katie. She's from Iowa originally. Her parents are religious – *really* religious." Linda's voice trembled. "They...they kidnapped her and beat both of us up really bad." Tears raced down Linda's face. "And now Katie has no family. And I hate it. And I hate that *we're* not close and I don't want us to not have any family at all!"

Melanie reached across the table and held her daughter's arm. "Oh honey. I am so sorry.

"Your father and I talked after we got your message. We knew something must have happened.

"Your father told me how he really felt. How he hated seeing you so rarely. How he hated the awkwardness of family get-togethers." Melanie succumbed to tears as well. "He reminded me that you *are* beautiful, just like your name says. It's just a different kind of beautiful.

"I am so sorry, honey. For everything. We love you. *I* love you. And we *are* a family. And if this Katie girl is as good as you say, we will love her too and gladly welcome her to our family. Please be patient with me though, Linda. This is a big change for me. But I will do my best, okay?"

Linda wiped away her tears, and then reached across the table to wipe away her mother's tears. "Thanks, Mom!"

"Okay, here we go." Linda looked over at Katie and smiled. "I love you."

Katie looked back and smiled. "I love you too, babe." She paused. "You're nervous. What are you more nervous about, spending time with your parents again or having me meet your family?"

Linda thought for a few taciturn moments. "I don't know!" She laughed.

"It's gonna be fine, babe." Katie winked.

"Okay, let's go in." They got out of the car. Linda took Katie by the hand and led her into her parents' house.

Tentatively, Linda opened the door. They both slowly stepped into the house. Before them, Melanie, Chuck and Jerry all stood in a row.

"Mom, Dad, Jerr. This is Katie. Katie, these are my parents and my brother, Jerry." Linda said.

"Hi Katie. It's a pleasure to meet you." Melanie said.

Chuck firmly grasped Katie's hand. "Nice to meet you, young lady."

Jerry reached out and grabbed Katie, squeezing her with a giant hug. "Welcome to the fam," he said.

Once released from Jerry's arms, Katie went back to Linda. The family all walked into the living room.

"So Linda tells us you're a vet student." Chuck started the conversation.

"Actually, I just graduated. I am staying at Penn and will be doing a double residency."

"What do you mean?" Melanie asked.

"The two things I love the most are birds and surgery. So, I am doing a residency in avians and exotics and another residency in surgery."

"So you will be board certified in two areas?" Chuck asked.

"They let you do that?" Melanie jumped in.

"It's not the norm. Not by any means. I did really well as a student, and a few of my professors wrote wonderful letters of recommendation. So, yes, in the end I will be board certified in two areas."

"What are your plans, then?" Chuck followed up.

"I will gladly take one of my two goals. Either, open up my own practice where I can tend to all kinds of animals and do surgeries there. Or, work at Penn or one of the bigger specialty practices and work in both the exotics department and the surgery department." Katie explained.

"You have some big dreams there, young lady."

"I do. But it's worth it. To do what you love is...priceless. To be able to do what I want is well worth all the hard work."

Chuck smiled at Katie.

"How did you and Linda meet?" Melanie asked.

"I worked over at Mario's Pizza while I was in school."

"Oh, Lin's favorite!" Jerry exclaimed.

"Yeah." Katie chuckled.

"I see. Well, no explanation needed there!" Melanie quipped.

"How many times did you see her there before you finally agreed to a date just to get her out of there?" Jerry teased.

"I believe dinner is just about ready. Let me go check." Melanie excused herself.

"Be right back, babe." Linda whispered to Katie. She stood up and followed her mother into the kitchen.

"She is wonderful!" Melanie softly said. "This is so much better than I ever could have imagined. I am so happy for you, honey." She embraced her daughter in a tight hug.

"Thanks, Mom." Linda smiled.

The Model

by

Lauren Shiro

Dedication

To my grandmother for always believing in me and being a bright ray of sunshine for all of us in the family. You inspire and encourage us all. You bring love and positivity to everyone you meet. You are a gift, you are an angel. I love you very much!

The Model

It was just another day at The Taco Shop in the mall. At sixteen, Stephania hated working, but she hated school more. Thankfully, school was a moot point. Her family was too poor for her not to work.

Her father, Harold, had passed away from an unexpected heart attack a year earlier. With four children to raise, no education and weak linguistic skills, Gabriela was overwhelmed. She had a job, but it only paid minimum wage. Gabriela, Steph's mother, could hardly pay to keep a roof over the family's heads. Stephania had no choice. An education was selfish; her family needed food.

"Welcome to the Taco Shop. May I help you?" Stephania greeted the next customer. Simply another nameless face; another mall rat who foolishly thought this was authentic Mexican food. As much as Steph didn't like her job, she certainly didn't envy the woman on the other side of the counter.

"Wow. You are beautiful." The middle-aged woman said. She was a rather plain, unremarkable white woman with curly salt-and-pepper hair. Steph would think nothing of her if not for the kindness that emanated from her dark brown eyes.

"Thank you. What can I get you?"

"How old are you?"

Stephania sighed. What was this woman's problem? "Sixteen. Do you want a double stacker taco galore? It's only $5.99 with a large drink."

"Hmmm. Why aren't you in school?" The woman was beginning to annoy Stephania now.

"Because I'm here," she quipped quickly.

The woman stood silently for a moment. After a brief pause, she spoke. "Okay. Well, here's my card. Feel free to call me whenever you're not here." She handed Steph a small, dark business card. Stephania simply tucked it away in her pocket without so much as a glance. "And I'll have a number three combo meal, please."

Stephania turned from the woman to begin *finally* making her meal.

Steph stared at the business card under the dim light of the lamp in her room. *Joanne Wilcox – Wilcox Talent Agency, representing models, actors and singers in the greater Philadelphia area since 1975.* Why would she have given her this card? Steph wasn't a model, an actress, or a singer. This woman must be delusional. Still, there was that look in her eye. What would it hurt to actually call her? Steph wouldn't actually lose anything, right? Maybe she would just give this woman a call. Maybe.

Steph hung up the phone and ran into the kitchen, calling for her mother. "Mamá, esta mujer es un agente de talento. Desea que sea un modelo. ¡Puede conseguir los trabajos profesión de modelo para mí y yo haré mucho dinero! Esto ayudará la familia".

Gabriela looked at her daughter, confused. "¿Qué?"

Steph handed her mother the business card. "¡Mira! Esta mujer." She realized she never told her mother about her encounter with Joanne. "Me dio su tarjeta un par de hace semanas. Acabo de la llamar. ¡Dijo que soy hermosa y puedo ser una modela y la marca mucho dinero! El dinero que puede ayudar la familia. Pero le necesito firma papeles. ¡Deme por favor permiso a hacer esto! ¡Por favor!" She pleaded. All she needed was for her mother to sign those papers and she would officially be a model. Just one signature could change the family forever. Her one signature could mean fame and fortune for them all.

"Yo no me fío de esto." Gabriela protested.

Why didn't she trust this? It was the miracle they had always prayed for! "¡Mamá, por favor!" Steph begged.

"No."

Stephania needed to think of something – some kind of compromise. She wanted this so desperately. "Pues, continuaré trabajar en la tienda y obtener el dinero y la marca allí mientras hago esto, ¿bueno? Esta manera la familia todavía tiene mi profesión de modelo de incase de ingresos no paga. ¿Esta bien?"

"Quiero penseralo."

It was the most Steph could ask for. Her mother would at least consider the notion of her working at The Taco Shop and modeling as well. She sighed heavily, hoping her teenage dreams would come true. "Gracias, Mamá."

"Okay, this is just a test shoot. Relax and have fun. You don't have to do anything too crazy." Joanne gently coached Steph.

"Okay," Stephania nervously replied. She was in a large, warehouse type of building. There were lights sitting several feet in the air on giant stands. Some looked like normal lights; others were in giant frames, in some kind of cloth or material boxes, and more in round reflective metal bowls that looked like satellite dishes on the apartment building where she and her family lived. Behind them were racks of clothes that seemed bigger than her family's whole apartment. It was all so overwhelming and surreal for Stephania. She never imagined that she, the little poor Hispanic girl from the barrio, could ever be a model.

"Ready?" The awkward man with thick glasses asked from behind his mammoth camera.

"Uh, okay." Steph's voice trembled.

The lights all around her flashed at once as she simultaneously heard the camera's shutter. Shocked by the brightness of the lights, Steph closed her eyes and winced.

"It's okay." Joanne whispered. "Just relax. Have fun."

Steph opened her eyes. She took in a deep breath and smiled right as the lights and shutter went off once again.

"Hi, I'm Chrissy." The exquisite blonde weakly shook Steph's hand.

"Stephania. Nice to meet you."

The two models walked over to their chairs and sat down. Within seconds, two quiet unknown people began fussing with the girls' hair.

"How long have you been modeling?" Chrissy asked with an air of arrogance in her tone.

"Two years. I started when I was sixteen. You?"

"I also started when I was sixteen. That was *four* years ago." Chrissy bragged.

"Wow. That's great," Steph replied both awe-struck and sarcastically.

185

"Are you coming?" Chrissy impatiently asked.

"Yes, hang on!" Stephania called back as she struggled with her belongings. She clumsily ran to catch up with Chrissy.

"Come on, let's go!" Chrissy sauntered away as Steph continued to struggle and trip her way out to the car.

The car ride was a long, awkward one. Steph sat nervously on the other side of the bench seat. She had never been to a party like this. There were going to be some of the best models and photographers from around the world at this party. Aside from Chrissy, whom she had only just met this morning, Steph did not know a soul that would be there. She nervously wondered what they were like. She questioned how they would perceive her, if they would like her. She had no idea as to what to expect.

Stephania nervously played with her hands as these questioning thoughts raced through her head on an endless loop. The infinite ride suddenly ended in front of a night club.

Chrissy wasted no time in grabbing Stephania's arm and dragging her out of the car.

Inside was a dimly lighted can of sardines. Dance music played at a deafening level. People squished and squeezed their way around each other. Tall, lanky, beautiful people hugged and air kissed each other in some unusual ritual. Steph immediately felt out of place. She was introduced to countless people whose names she could never decipher over the loud thumping beat of the music. Somewhere in the crowd, she lost Chrissy. She awkwardly managed her way around through the throng of people alone.

She had been uncomfortably standing silently alone for a while when she felt an arm on her shoulder.

"There you are!" It was Chrissy.

Stephania initially breathed a sigh of relief in seeing a familiar face, but then she noticed something was different about Chrissy. Her words were a little garbled. Her eye lids were half shut and her eyes looked glazed. Her face almost seemed to droop. Something must have happened; she didn't look anything like this earlier.

"Come with me!" Chrissy said in a caricaturesque manner.

Stephania allowed herself to be dragged through the mob. She had no idea where she was or where she was going until Chrissy flung her into the bathroom and slammed the door closed behind them.

"Look!" Chrissy squealed. She pulled out a small baggie with a white powdery substance in it.

"What…? What is that?" Steph knew the answer, but she secretly prayed she was wrong.

"You're so funny!" Chrissy laughed as her body moved and twisted in unusual ways. "Come on, try some!"

Steph backed away. "I don't know…"

"You know what's great?" Chrissy slurred her speech. "With this, you don't need to work out. You can eat whatever you want and you'll stay skinny with this. Woooooo!" She sang.

"Really?" Steph leaned in closer. "I don't have to watch what I eat? I really don't need to work out?"

"Naw! It's all good. All the best models do it. The photographers too! You'll get in with the best of the best!"

"I will?" Stephania's eyes lit up with excitement.

"Yeah! You'll be hanging with all the top people! So, you wanna try some?"

"Uh, okay." Stephania nervously replied.

"Here!" Chrissy stuck a rolled up dollar bill in Stephania's face.

"Oh!" Steph jumped back a little to gain some space.

Chrissy poured out the white powder and neatly arranged it in a long thin line. "There you go!" Chrissy said, moving her arm in a Vanna White-like motion.

Stephania nervously put the dollar bill to her nostril and lined herself up with the long line of cocaine. She took in a deep breath, trying to work up the courage. With her second breath, she began inhaling the powder. It raced up her nose causing an unusual tickling sensation as she inhaled. She hadn't even finished the line when the room started spinning. Stephania felt a giant surge of energy race into her brain. "Whoa!" She stumbled into Chrissy's arms. She paused, looking up at her. "You're beautiful!" She pulled herself up and just leaned into Chrissy, kissing her.

Both inebriated, the two continued in a sloppy but erotic kiss. Their arms clumsily felt their way around each other's body. Somehow, Steph managed to undress her. They awkwardly touched and pleased each other in the bathroom for the rest of the evening.

Stephania stared at the piece of paper. *This could not be right. There was no way it was right. How could this be? This isn't real.*

She dialed the office.

"Wilcox Talent Agency. This is Vanessa."

"Vanessa, is Peter available?"

"Peter Gordon? May I ask who is calling?"

"Stephania. Stephania Henderson."

"Okay. Please hold one moment."

Stephania kept her gaze on the check that was being gripped tightly by her small hand.

"Peter Gordon."

"Peter, it's Stephania."

"Hi Stephania. What can I do for you?"

"It...it's this...check. This can't be right. Did I really just make...?"

"It's correct."

"Huh?"

"It's right, Stephania. That check was written correctly. That is the amount."

"But, I..."

"Welcome to the business. If you do well, you get paid well. Take it and use it as you please. Just take this as a lesson. Stay professional. Keep doing well. Take care of yourself. Work hard. There is plenty more of where that came from, so long as you genuinely earn it. Deal?"

"You bet!" Stephania squealed. "Thank you!"

She ended the call and then began to jump up and down around the room. After she winded herself a bit, she sat back down and picked up the phone again.

"McCarthy Realty. This is Lanna. How may I help you?"

"Hi Lanna. My name is Stephania Henderson. I would like to buy a house."

"Okay, well I think I can help you with that. What are you looking for in a house? What do you like? What don't you like?"

"Oh, it's not for me. It's for my mother. I want it as far away from Kensington as possible."

"Well, there are plenty of houses in the greater Philadelphia area. I'm sure we can find something good for her. Would you be able to come down to the office some time so we can start looking at properties?"

"Sure! Can I come right now?"

"Oh! Okay. Sure."

"I'll be right there!" Stephania hung up. Still clenching the check, she grabbed her purse and keys and ran out to her car.

Stephania brushed through her wet hair, carefully working every knot out, until it was straight, sleek and perfect.

188

As she walked into the living room, the computer signaled an e-mail had just come in. She walked over to the computer and leaned over the chair. She wiggled the mouse until the screen came up.

Hey Chrissy!

Attached are some of the raw, unedited images from our shoot yesterday. And, of course, I have the others that are just for our eyes only!

Hit me up any time you want to shoot again, or...ya know.

Talk to you soon,

Tommy

Tears instantly filled Stephania's eyes and blurred the computer screen. Chills ran up her body. Her chest felt heavy, and her heart was pounding so much that it was literally painful. She couldn't breathe.

This was the worst feeling in the world. She trusted Chrissy. She loved her and she had for two years. She thought they had a great relationship...perhaps even perfect. She knew how lonely it could get shooting in various locations and being apart, but she had always been faithful.

How could his have happened? Why couldn't Chrissy have been faithful? What was wrong – what was missing that it drove her to cheat?

Was she wrong? Had she jumped to a conclusion? Did she misread the e-mail? Tommy was a big name in the industry. He wouldn't want to potentially ruin his reputation. Nor would Chrissy. Maybe she just misconstrued the whole thing.

Stephania tried to breathe deeply and get herself to relax. This had to be wrong. There was no way it was true. Chrissy would never cheat on her! She just needed to take a deep breath and get her imagination under control.

Chrissy methodically prepared the lines. Stephania hovered over her, watching her meticulous movements.

Alexander walked in and saw the two of them. "Almost ready?" He asked as he prepared the camera.

Stephania nodded, her eyes still fixated on Chrissy and the magical white powder.

A few more seconds passed by and Chrissy then announced that she was ready.

"Well please, ladies first." Alexander insisted.

Steph and Chrissy looked at each other. Steph motioned for Chrissy to go first. She knew that if Chrissy didn't, she'd lose all courage.

Chrissy grabbed the short straw and quickly inhaled the first line. Without missing a beat, she handed it off to Stephania.

Steph grabbed the straw stub and placed it at the base of her nostrils. Her heart instantly began to race. She took a few quick, shallow breaths and then she inhaled. The fine particles twirled and tickled their way up her sinuses and into her brain. She immediately felt...fast, excited, superhuman. She felt a burst of energy and she liked it.

With giddy exhilaration, she handed the straw to Alexander. He, too, quickly inhaled the Cocaine and joined in the exuberance.

The trio all began to jump and dance around the studio.

"Okay, okay. Let's do this." Alexander said. "Chrissy, you go stand over there; and Stephania, you kneel. Let's see what that looks like." His speech was incredibly rapid – almost too fast to understand.

Chrissy and Steph bounded to their positions and struck poses.

"That's it!" He exclaimed.

They began rapidly shooting picture after picture. The bright lights only fed everyone's energy. Shot after shot, pose after pose. Each picture just built up the excitement exponentially.

They had been shooting for a while. Stephania found herself in an unusually difficult and nearly contorted position. She was breathing heavily, but couldn't stop smiling. She looked up at Chrissy. "I can hardly breathe."

"I know, right? This is awesome!"

"No. I mean it. I can't breathe." She felt a cold sweat coming on. The pressure on her chest grew and grew.

Chrissy's face dropped. "What's wrong? You look pale."

"Stand up." Alexander commanded as he walked towards them.

Just as she did, Stephania felt very dizzy and light-headed. She stumbled over and fell into Chrissy before she just crumbled to the floor. The world around her turned black. She couldn't see, but she could still hear Chrissy and Alexander.

"Help! Get some help, Alexander! Call an ambulance! Stephania!"

Then the sounds around her became fuzzy too.

"Stephania?" A quiet woman's voice asked.

Stephania struggled to open her eyes. It was hard to breathe. She could hear and feel the world around her. But her eyes would only open for a moment before rolling back in her head. She felt anxious and unsettled. She wanted to open her eyes. She wanted to feel normal. Her body fought her. A heavy weight rested on her chest. Her arms felt tangled in different plastic wires.

She fought with every ounce of strength to pry open her eye lids. For one brief euphoric moment, she had a blurry vision of the world around her. Everything seemed to have a light blue tint. There must have been windows off to her right because a very bright light came from that way. A woman who looked to be a small brunette stood near her, but Steph could not make out her face. She was lying down, but what little she could see didn't seem familiar.

Just as she was beginning to feel some level of comfort from seeing everything, blackness once again enveloped her.

The oxygen mask was cutting into her nose. Stephania pulled it forward to give her face just a minute's reprieve.

"No, no, no." A woman in scrubs leapt forward to place the mask back over her face.

Stephania sighed heavily. "I was just…" What was the point? This woman didn't care. She didn't want to hear her excuses.

"Do you know *why* you're here?" She asked.

Stephania studied the nurse. Her skin was a dark, rich mocha. Her black hair was short but cute. She was a petite woman; her scrubs complimented her small figure.

"No." Stephania said. It winded her to speak.

"You had a heart attack."

Stephania sat forward. "What?" Her voice creaked out.

"You had a heart attack that was induced by cocaine use. You're what? In your early twenties? You're a young girl and you just had a heart attack. You need to sit your pretty little ass in that bed ad keep that mask on. You're lucky you're alive. You need to get off that stuff." The nurse glared at her.

Stephania leaned back onto the bed and cast her gaze onto the floor. It was easier to stare at nothing than to look at that nurse and know she was right.

Stephania felt like she was flying through the corridors of the hospital. The person pushing her wheelchair seemed to be racing. She didn't care, though. She was happy to be getting out.

The wheelchair zipped around the last corner. There, on the other side of the clear sliding doors was Chrissy waiting in the car. That was a sight for sore eyes. Stephania's freedom was there, just on the other side of the door.

Suddenly, the speed dropped to a crawl these last few feet. Inch by inch her freedom got closer, but it wasn't enough.

Finally, the chair stopped and the orderly put on the brakes. He came around and offered his hand for Stephania to stand up. She rose and took small, quick steps towards the car. He opened the car door for her and guided her in.

"Thanks." Steph mumbled. She pulled the door shut.

"You ready?" Chrissy asked.

"Hell yes. Just get me home."

Stephania plopped on the couch. She turned on the television. She didn't even care what was on. Today's shoot was one of the longest and definitely most physically challenging shoots she had ever been on. She was exhausted and sore. All she wanted to do was absolutely nothing.

Her mind began to fade into nothing when the phone rang.

"God damn it," she whispered. "Hello?"

"Hey baby!" Some strange woman said.

"Uhhh...who is this?"

"It's Ellie!"

"Ellie? Ellie who?"

"Chrissy?"

"No, this is..."

The woman hung up.

"Stephania." She hung up her phone. She sighed heavily. She wished that it wasn't true, but it was. She had feared this for a long time.

Maybe they meant a different Chrissy.

No. She knew better than that.

Maybe, Chrissy purposefully gave her bad information because she didn't want to see this chick again. Maybe this was the last time. Stephania hoped with all her might that it was.

"Have a seat," Peter guided her into his office. He gently closed the door. "How are you doing, Stephania?"

"Good, good. Thanks. So, what's going on?"

Peter sighed as he sat down. "It's come to my attention that you...may not have been at your best on that last shoot."

Stephania's confused expression spoke for her.

"Warren told me you were..."

Stephania stared at him.

"You were...high." Peter paused for a moment. "He told me you were high on something. What? I don't know."

Stephania opened her mouth to begin to speak.

"I don't want to know. Don't tell me." Peter rubbed his face with both of his hands. "Remember I told you to stay professional. I told you to take care of yourself and to always work hard. You're slipping. As long as you continue with this, you will lose job after job. You'll gain a reputation in this business, and not a good one. The money that helped you to buy your house, your mom's house, the cars...all of it will be gone. And then what?

"It's not like you have a college degree to fall back on. Do you even have your GED yet? What are you going to do? How are you going to take care of yourself? How are you going to take care of your family? What kind of life are you going to have? Nothing. Is that what you want, Stephania? A life of nothingness?"

Stephania tried to speak. She took in air and then coughed. "Chrissy," she choked.

"You need to get away from her. That girl is bad news. She is not going to help you. Not in any way. She will ruin your career and she will gladly ruin your life with her lies and drugs if you stay around long enough."

Stephania sat, petrified.

Peter leaned in and grabbed her hands. "Listen. I am saying all of this from a point of love. I'm worried about you, Stephania. You're a beautiful young girl. You're a good person and you have a lot of talent. I don't want to see you throw all of this away because of stupid, selfish people. Just be careful."

Stephania breathed deeply. She nodded her head. It was all she could do.

The coffee pot sat silently this morning, as it had for so many days – weeks, really. Stephania moped around the house in her robe.

193

Chrissy was back in Europe and the time apart was killing Stephania. She craved Chrissy's presence so desperately. Stephania flopped down in front of the computer. She clicked on the internet. Surely she could find something to distract her.

Her stomach rumbled. She was hungry...very hungry. *Ugh,* she thought. She desperately needed to distract herself from her loneliness and her hunger. She began to meander through the internet.

The phone rang unexpectedly and jerked Stephania out of her slump. She jumped and the chair rocked backwards for a moment. She gathered herself together and answered the phone. "Hello?"

There was silence on the other end of the phone.

"Hello?"

Now it sounded like someone was breathing deeply...or even crying. Still, no one spoke.

"Hello? Is anyone there?"

Finally, through the sniffles, she spoke up. "St...Stephania?"

"Mom? Is that you? Mom, what's wrong?"

Her mother wept.

"¡Mamá, por favor! ¿Qué lo ocurrió?"

"Álvaro murió." She cried out.

"What?! No! No, no, no! That can't be true! Digame, Mamá, que no es la verdad."

"Es la verdad." Her mother was crying so hysterically, Steph could hear her struggling to breathe.

"Stay there! I am coming home! I will be there as quickly as I can!" Stephania hung up the phone.

She leapt out of the chair, grabbed her coat and literally ran out the door to her car.

Gabriela stood with her head down, her three daughters embracing her.

"I cannot believe this happened." Stephania's sister, Erendiria, said.

Yoana turned to Stephania. "You are next if you keep this up. You need to stop."

Stephania lifted her head and looked at her.

"I mean it." Yoana said. "Was it not bad enough we lost Dad at an early age and now Alvaro? Don't put Mamá through anything more. Please, I beg of you."

Stephania looked around. Erendiria nodded her head.

Her gaze turned to her mother.

In slow motion, Gabriela raised her head. Her dark brown eyes were bloodshot from crying. Dark, heavy circles weighed her eyes down. Her rich olive skin looked tired, worn, old. Her once jet black hair was now streaked with silver. Her face, no longer a joyous one, told a story of sorrow. Without saying a word, her eyes told Stephania everything she thought.

"Lo siento, Mamá. Nunca más. Lo prometo. Nunca me hará daño como este. De hoy en adelante, jamás me consume cocaína."

Gabriela looked hard at Stephania for several long moments. She finally said, "Gracias."

"Where are you?" Chrissy whined into the phone.

"At Mom's, I told you. Are you coming?"

There was silence on the other end of the phone.

"Chrissy, my brother just died. We are having the funeral tomorrow. I would like to have you here with me. Please come."

"Steph," she sighed. "I can't. It's just…I…that…uhhh…"

"What are you trying to say?"

Chrissy paused for several moments. "No. Just…no."

"Thanks for being here when I needed you the most!" Stephania ended the call and cried.

She heard the back door open. She slid herself around the tree more; her back was now facing whoever just came out. Stephania tried to control her tears. She didn't want anyone to know she was crying.

"Stephania?" Yoana gently tapped her sister's shoulder.

"What?" She angrily sniffled.

"Are you okay?"

"Fine." She stared ahead, refusing to look at her youngest sister.

"It's that Chrissy girl, isn't it?"

"So what if it is?"

Yoana came around her side and looked at Stephania. "You know we don't care, right?"

Stephania stood speechless.

"We don't mind. Not Erendiria, not Mom, not me. We don't mind. It's just…"

"Her." Stephania answered.

"She has been nothing but bad news for you. And look. Your brother dies and she doesn't even care."

The tears won, Stephania could no longer hold back.

"She doesn't care about you. She never has and she never will. You can be gay, just find someone better. Please."

Stephania couldn't bear to look her sister.

"We do love you...and accept you. We all just want the best for you." Yoana put her hand on Steph's shoulder before finally walking away.

A cold misty rain fell from the grey December sky. Stephania was hunched and huddled as she stomped her way towards the large stone building. A woman sat under the overhang smoking a cigarette.

"Are you here for the meeting?"

Stephania's eyes peeked out from above her scarf. She nodded her head.

"It's a good place. They really help."

Steph just studied the woman.

She was a woman, probably in her mid-forties. Her hair was poorly dyed black. Light brown eye brows sat over her dark green eyes. Her face was worn, but warm. She exuded a sense of peace...something that Steph greatly longed for.

"It's scary. I know it is. I've been there. I walked through those doors for the first time eighteen years ago. I just keep coming back. It's what's kept me clean for all these years. Believe me, if it can help me, it can absolutely help you."

Stephania shivered.

"Okay. Let's get you inside. My name is Judy." The woman stuck out her hand.

"Stephania." Her answer was muffled by her scarf.

They shook hands.

"Come on," Judy guided her into the Church's heavy wooden doors.

"So you're not gonna do it?!" Chrissy shouted as she walked a few feet behind Stephania.

Steph whipped around. "No. No, no, no. I told you once. I will tell you a million times. You can drag this out as long as you like. I don't care. The answer is still no."

196

"God you're weird! You are so fucking weird! I don't get you! I never did! You never make any sense! What the hell is wrong with you?!"

"I don't know. A lot, I guess."

"You are just not normal!" Chrissy screamed and stomped off.

Fighting back tears, Stephania tried to breathe deeply. Trying to remain calm, she grabbed the phone. She dialed quickly.

"Hello?"

"Judy?"

"Yes."

Stephania sighed a sigh of relief. "It's Stephania."

"Hi Stephania. What can I do for you?"

"Well, I'm not sure. I...I don't know. I guess I'm just weird. It seems I'm too eccentric. People don't seem to get me. Sometimes I feel like no matter what I say, I'm just misunderstood. Maybe I shouldn't say anything at all."

"Let's take this in steps, shall we?" Judy started. "You say you're weird and eccentric. First off, who decides what is or is not normal? Who dictates what constitutes weird?

"Eccentric? Okay. Let's just say that you *are* eccentric. What's wrong with that? It means you're unique. You have character, you have depth. What's so bad about that? I'd much rather be unique than be like everybody else. I would rather someone called me eccentric than run of the mill. I don't think that's a bad thing. Do you?"

Stephania sniffled. "No, I guess not."

"You need to be you. You were created to be Stephania. Be who you are. Do what you like. Live *your* life, not somebody else's. Remember, 'to thine own self be true.'"

"Okay."

"Along with that goes saying what you think. You have every right to express your thoughts, feelings and opinions. You said you think you shouldn't say anything at all. Don't ever not speak. Not talking will only build things up inside you. One day, you will simply explode because no one can keep everything in. Nor should they. It's toxic! Say what you're thinking. Express yourself. Talk about your feelings. It's so very important for all of us – including you – to be able to say what's on their mind. Don't be quiet to benefit others. Speak for yourself."

"So whatever I think, whatever I feel, I should say it?"

"Yes."

"What if other people don't like my opinion?"

"Tough. They'll figure it out. They will either accept and respect your opinion for what it is, or they'll just go away. Either way, it's on them. Not you. You have a right to express your thoughts, feelings, questions, concerns...whatever! Say what's on your mind. People will understand and respect you for it."

"They will?"

"Like I said, they either will, or they'll eventually leave. And if they are the type to leave, they're not the kind of people you want to have in your life anyway!"

"Yeah. I guess that's true." A smile slowly crept across Stephania's face.

"Steph, you are a beautiful young woman inside and out. People like you for you. And people *do* want to hear what you have to say. Don't ever hold back on account of other's people's opinions. Be who you are and say what you need to say. Remember, we love you for you."

"Thanks, Judy. I needed that."

"My pleasure. You go have a good day now, okay?"

Stephania's smile grew. "I will. Thank you."

"I gotta get out of here," Steph whispered in Chrissy's ear. She wedged, wiggled and wormed her way through the masses of women, children, balloons and toys. The cold air hitting her as she opened the door gave her a great sense of refreshment.

"What's going on?" Chrissy asked.

"I can't do this. Surrounded by these women and all those kids..."

"You don't like kids now?"

"I was never a big kid person."

"You raised your sisters and brother!"

"Yeah I did. Out of obligation."

"Raising kids is raising kids, isn't it?"

"Are you insane? Absolutely not! I helped my mother out because Dad died. Yes, I took care of them. I made sure they were clean and fed. I made sure they had everything they needed. I also worked so that we could pay the bills. It was tough, but we managed. I gave them what they needed. But these gringa mothers are very different. They're all fawning over these kids giving them every little thing they *want.* They give two year olds freakin' cell phones! It's ridiculous."

"Gringa mothers?" Chrissy glared at her.

"Honkeys? Is that better?"

"So, they're gringas and honkeys, too?"

"Yeah. They're both."

"They can't be both! Are you Hispanic or Black? Make up your mind."

Steph's eyes narrowed. "Both," she grumbled. "And those rich white girls are being just plain stupid with all their 'ooh, this' and 'ahhh, that' shit."

"Those *stupid, rich, white girls* are my friends." Chrissy hissed back.

"You are the company you keep," Stephania sneered.

"Well, I'd rather keep their company than yours!"

"No skin off my back, cusca." Steph turned and began walking down the sidewalk back to her apartment.

The Philadelphia Pride Festival was huge. The city streets were lined with people, booths, and confetti. There were drag kings and queens all over. Rainbow balloons were tied to pretty much everything.

People. Lots of people. People of every color, every orientation, and every type filled the streets.

Steph had really just come to watch people. She didn't like the noise and hubbub. She just wanted to see what it was like. If she was going to define herself as a lesbian, she thought this would be the best way to educate herself on the gay community.

As she walked, she noticed the HRC booth. The signs with the equal logo were familiar to her. Steph noticed a few random people and representatives from the organization were all talking. Curious, she made her way over to the booth.

"Well hi there!" A male rep said to her. "My name is David. How can I help you?"

"I'm not quite sure." Steph started. "I'm just coming out. I've seen your equal sign all over the place, but I don't quite know what it means or what you do."

"Well, we are a group that fights for all rights for the LGBT community. From discrimination laws to marriage equality, raising awareness...you name it."

"So, you're a charity?"

"Not exactly. We are a not-for-profit group, but donations are not a tax write-off, I'm sorry to say. But that doesn't mean that our work is any less important."

"Okay, so I am just coming out as I said. I don't know what I can do to help you or help the community."

"It really doesn't take much. What kind of work do you do?"

Steph shifted her weight. She was a little apprehensive about answering this one. "I'm a model," she said hesitantly.

"In that kind of position, being seen all the time, the best thing you can do is to be a positive example of our community. Just presenting yourself in a positive, professional manner all the time will boost the image for the entire community. Like I said, it really doesn't take much."

"Well, that's easy enough. But, what else can I do? If there are discrimination laws and such, I want to fight that. I'm mixed and I know what prejudice is like..."

"Using your talents in any capacity would help, I'm sure."

"You mean like doing shoots for you or something?"

"If you can, that would be great!"

"I don't know if it would be a problem with my contract or not. I would just like to help out."

"We appreciate your offer. I would advise you to speak to your agent and see what they say. And we can certainly look into opportunities for you as well."

"Here's my card," she said as she presented him with a business card. "Please feel free to contact me any time."

"Thank you so much for your offer." He replied. "We will certainly see what we can do."

Just then a woman - a very masculine woman - entered the tent.

Another HRC rep walked over to her. "Hi there. How can I help you?"

"Uhhh...I'm not sure. I just figured I would stop by and see what you guys had going on."

"Well, specifically for Philadelphia and Pennsylvania in general, we are fighting to pass laws that would protect members of the LGBT community from getting fired based on their gender and sexuality expressions."

The tomboy's face contorted in confusion.

"Take yourself for example. Is that how you normally dress? Is that what you would wear to work?"

She looked down at herself. She was wearing a large blue, baggy tee-shirt and jeans. "Well, sorta. I wouldn't wear this to work, per se."

"Did you know that you could be fired from your job for dressing in such a gender neutral or even more masculine manner?"

"That would be pretty near impossible." The woman replied. Her voice was deep and scratchy.

Stephania had to stop, turn and listen to the conversation.

The rep seemed rather perturbed by the woman's answer.

"And why do you say that?" She asked with a bit of a snarl.

"'Cause I own my own shop. I don't think I would fire myself over my clothes." She laughed.

"Well, not everyone has that luxury and they could potentially be fired for dressing in a way that is comfortable to them but does not necessarily fall into typical gender-specific attire." The HRC woman lashed back.

"What kind of shop do you own?" David now asked.

"Car shop. I'm a mechanic."

"Is your shop LGBT exclusive?" He asked.

"No." She answered apprehensively.

"But you are LGBT friendly." The female rep said.

"Well, yeah. I have your sticker on my door and stuff."

"Oh you do?" David asked. "That is probably one of the best ways to help us in our political fights. If you show that you support us, and your clients can see that, you are helping to spread awareness and political change."

"What else can I do? I mean giving you guys money is fine, but are there other ways or other things I can be doing to help?" The woman asked.

"Well, this nice young lady just gave us her card. She's a model and said she would love to do some shoots to support the HRC." David said.

The woman turned to Steph. "You are?"

"Yes." Steph nervously replied.

"Ya know, a lot of my clients drive classics and hot rods. We should have you shoot with some of our cars."

Stephania paused for a moment. "How many is a lot? How many classic cars are we talking about? A dozen? More? Less?"

"I think I have at least twenty five right now. Why?"

"Well because, if you have that many cars, we could actually shoot a calendar. Me with your clients' cars. And we could sell those calendars and then donate the proceeds to HRC."

"What a great idea! That's awesome!" The gamine briefly paused. "I'm Linda." She extended out her hand.

"Stephania."

"See. This is great! You are both using your talents to help support us so that we can ensure you have equal and protected rights." David said.

"This was rather serendipitous." Stephania stated.

"Uhhh...yeah!" Linda agreed.

"Here's my card." Stephania said, handing Linda a business card. "Give me a call some time and we'll see what we can do."

Linda smiled. "Sounds great!" Linda tucked Stephania's business card into her wallet. She smiled and then walked away.

"Well, I'd say that was fairly productive." Steph said to David.

"I'd say so!" He replied.

"This was great. I hope we can make this happen. I guess I will be in touch. Thanks!"

"Thank you! Have a great day and congratulations on coming out!" David called out as Stephania walked away.

"Peter Gordon."

Oh thank goodness he answered. "Hi Peter! It's Stephania."

"Hiya Steph! What can I do for you?"

"Well, I have an odd question."

"I wouldn't expect anything less from you," he jokingly retorted. "What's up?"

"Would you mind if I did a charity shoot? I met a girl at Philly Pride. She's a car mechanic. She works on classic cars. She was gonna donate her time and her shop. Her clients were gonna donate their cars, I was gonna donate my time. And we were gonna make up calendars and then use the proceeds to support something like HRC. Is that cool?"

"I think that's a wonderful idea! It gives you good press, it supports the community. I love it. I have your back on this! Good job!"

"You're sure? There are no problems with me doing this?"

"No! None at all. Well done, Stephania."

A giant smile overtook her face. "Thanks, Peter."

"It's not that you wouldn't do an excellent job, Miss Henderson. You are clearly more than qualified. It's just that...well, you're too...ethnic for the campaign. What we're looking for is..."

"What you're looking for is some skinny ass white girl. A little blonde haired, blue eyed twig. I get it."

The man on the other end of the phone was silent.

"You know, it's not like I'm that dark. But just because I have black hair and full lips. Just because my boobs actually fill a bra cup and I actually have an ass, I'm too thick and too 'ethnic' for you. Okay.

Whatever. If and when you are looking for a real woman and someone who is professional and truly representative of women everywhere, call me." Steph hung up.

She probably shouldn't have said what she did. But she was so sick of this! How many times had she heard this before? Being mixed was so...odd. The photographers and companies that used her loved her. Those that didn't used her ethnicity against her. Stupid prejudices. She hated it all. She didn't need this stupid campaign anyway.

Just as she took in a deep breath to calm herself, her phone rang.

"Hello?"

"Hi, Stephania?" The voice was deep and vaguely familiar.

"Yes. Who is this?"

"This is Linda Scott. I own a garage. We met at the HRC booth at pride."

"Oh that's right! Hi! How are you? I am so glad you called. I am having a terrible day!"

"You are? I'm sorry. What happened?"

"I just got turned down for a job with a major fashion company. They said I wasn't pretty enough. Can you believe that?! How could they say that to me? Do you think I'm not pretty enough?"

"What?! Oh no! Not at all! I think you're beautiful."

"You do?"

"Yeah!"

"Do you think I'm pretty enough to date?"

"Uhhh...yeah."

"You hesitated. Why did you hesitate?"

"Well, you're just not my type, that's all."

"Not your type?! What do you mean I'm not your type? What? Why? Is it because I'm mixed? It's because I'm mixed, isn't it. That is what always does me in."

"What?! No! Not at all!"

"Well why, then?"

"Honestly? You're too...tall." Linda chuckled. "I like short girls."

"You do?" Stephania asked cynically.

"Yeah. I've always been tall and I just think it's...weird to be with someone my height or taller."

"So you would like me better if I was short?"

"I like you for you. I just date short girls. Is that okay?"

Stephania laughed. "I think so. So, now, why did you call me?"

"Oh! Uhhh...I don't..." Linda struggled to remember. "Oh yeah! The shoot!"

Both women laughed.

"So, I have fourteen cars definitely lined up. I just wanted to know what your schedule looked like and where I can find a good photographer."

"Wow! I'm impressed. You've done a good job. Thank you."

"You're welcome. But what about a photographer?"

"Oh, I know a great guy! He would do an excellent job. I will call him. And scheduling...Let me look. I think I have some openings in August. Will that work for you?"

"I think that my clients and I are way more open and flexible than you are. You tell me what works for you and we should be fine." Linda replied.

"Let me look and ask my photographer. Can I call you back?"

"Of course! Call me back once you know and we'll get it all set up."

"Deal!" Steph exclaimed.

"Okay. Talk to you soon." Linda replied.

"Bye!" Steph said. A smile had finally come back on her face.

Linda came back into the room with beers in both hands. She handed them out to Liz, Jen and Maria and lastly Stephania. "Here," she said to each of them as she handed them out.

"So, how do y'all know each other?" Liz asked as she pointed at Linda and Stephania.

"Steph's a model." Linda said. "She shoots with some of the classic cars I work on for HRC."

"HRC?" A confused look washed across Liz's face.

Stephania could not believe that Liz had never heard of HRC. "Human Rights Campaign." She said brusquely. She was shocked to see the puzzled look on Liz's face. "The sale of the calendars is donated to them for LGBT rights."

"Oh," Liz replied.

Ignoring the tall redhead, Stephania turned her attention back to Maria who sat next to her on the couch. "Tell me more about you," she leaned in closely to Maria.

Maria simply looked at her. "Why? I am nothing interesting. We are just here for the game. What would you want to know?"

"Anything and everything! You're a writer. That is fascinating to me."

Maria shook her head. "Why are you here?"

"To watch the game." Steph replied somewhat perplexed. "You?"

Maria studied Steph. "To spend time with my friends. Jen has been a good friend of mine for years, and her partner Liz is a good friend now too. I just want to enjoy my time with people that are close to my heart."

"Linda is my friend," Steph replied. "I like her very much and I consider it an honor that she invited me here. I don't get much time to develop real friendships; so I, too, value times like this. But you intrigue me. I feel a connection to you. I simply want to get to know you better."

Maria's expression loosened up.

"Look, give me a chance. I am not what you think I am. Go out with me. Once. Just one date. You won't be sorry."

Maria glared at her.

"I won't beg, but I can promise you, you will not be disappointed."

Maria sighed heavily. "Alright fine. One date. Now, can we just watch the game, please?" Maria acquiesced.

Linda quickly glanced at the large television just past her right shoulder. "Oh hey! The game's started, you guys."

The group of women all turned their attention to the Super Bowl game that was now underway.

The phone rang three times.

"Classic Car Care." Linda eventually answered.

"Hey Linda?"

"Yeah?"

"It's Steph."

"Oh hey, Stephania! How are you?"

"Good. How are you?"

"Fine, thanks. What's up?"

Stephania closed her eyes and hoped this would go well. "Listen, my mechanic just got laid off. The garage she's been working for is closing and she needs a job. She's been great with my car. I know how busy you've been. Any chance you'd want to take on another mechanic?"

Linda remained quiet. It seemed an infinite pause before she finally answered. "Uhhhh...sure. Yeah. Have her come by so I can meet her and show her around."

Stephania smiled. She was so excited to help both of her friends. "You are the best! Thank you! You won't regret it!"

"Okay."

The last detail to truly seal the deal struck Steph. "Oh, and one more thing!"

"Yeah?"

"She's hot!" Stephania giggled and hung up. She could hardly wait. She knew this would be beneficial for both Brittany and Linda. To see them both succeed brought her tremendous joy. She loved helping people she cared about. "This is gonna be awesome!" She shrieked.

She danced her way out the door. Today was going to be a great day.

Maria sat across from Steph, dressed in a beautiful black sweater and grey dress pants. She wore black thin framed glasses which caused Stephania to look in her eyes even more.

"Thank you for giving me a chance," Steph said as the waitress placed glasses of water in front of them.

Maria sat motionless.

"Look, I promise you, I am not what you think. Yes, I work in an industry that is all about appearances. Yes, I need to be vain to make a buck, but that does not make me a bad person. I have been working since I was sixteen. My father died when I was fifteen. I watched my mama struggle to feed us and keep a roof over our heads. I worked to help my mother. I appreciate my family. I have given back to my mother for all that she did for me. And you know what? I will keep giving to her for as long as I can. I know the value of friends and family. And even more so because I travel so much. I love my friends and family. I am a very dedicated person. I value my relationships. I value my time with people. People are important to me. I have been cheated on. I know what that feels like. To feel like you're not enough. Not good enough, not pretty enough. To feel unwanted – totally rejected. I get it. I would never want to cause anyone that kind of pain. I know that people look at me and think I am some superficial bitch. But I am not. I am more than that. I *do* have a brain and I need one. I could be beautiful today, but ugly tomorrow. So I need that brain to be able to support myself for when my looks fade. You're a writer. You use your brain. Your paycheck isn't dependent on your looks. You are valued for who you are, not what you look like. People look past your appearance to find out who that woman behind those glasses really is. Nobody gives me that chance. People only take me for face value. They think I am too stupid. But I *can* speak and I *can* write *and* I have thoughts and feelings. I am a person, not just an image. So if you think I am some kind of vain, selfish, self-absorbed, superficial idiot, you are wrong."

Maria sat back and smiled. "It's very nice to meet you, Stephania."

Liz, Jen, Linda, Maria, Stephania and Donna sat around the table.

"This is nice. I like this." Liz said, smiling.

"It is always good to be in the company of family," Maria agreed.

Stephania moved her chair in even closer to Maria and she rested her head on Maria's shoulder.

"Thanks for inviting me." Donna said to Linda.

"Yeah, any time."

"Hi ladies. What can I get you for drinks?" A young waiter asked the group.

Stephania sat right up and shouted, "An apple-tini!"

"A Corona, please." Maria looked up at the young man.

"I'll just have a Bud," Linda said.

"Make that two, please." Donna requested.

"I'll just have water." Liz said.

"Can I also have a water, but could you put lemon in mine?" Jen asked.

"Certainly!" The young man flashed a smile and quickly disappeared into the restaurant.

"This is going to be a good night." Maria said, nodding and smiling at them all.

"Okay, so there's my mother, Gabriela..."

"And your sisters, Yoanna and Erendiria. I think I got it." Maria chuckled.

Stephania's brow furrowed. "What?"

"You are so cute. Why are you so worried? Everything will be fine."

"How can you be so sure?"

"I would imagine that if you are introducing me to your family, you must think we have a pretty good relationship." Maria chuckled.

"Besides, I know you're worried about the past. But that's done and over with! And am I really like her in any way?"

"No." Steph huffed.

"See!" Maria paused. The car rolled into the driveway. "This is a beautiful house! I think you've done well by your mother, sweetheart. And I'm pretty sure she'll agree. Especially after today." Maria winked at Stephania.

They ambled up to the front door. Steph's chest tightened. She suddenly felt light-headed and in need of air. Her heart was racing. She felt sick. Her nerves were getting the best of her. Could she really do this? It was all too much. Maybe they should just go home.

Just as Stephania's fear climaxed, the door opened.

Gabriela peered around from the behind the door. She smiled when she saw Maria. "Hola."

"Hola señora Henderson..."

"Gabriela." She corrected Maria.

Maria smiled. "Hola, Gabriela. Es un honor y un placer de conocerle. Me llamo María."

"Bienvenido a mi casa, María." Gabriela turned her attention to Steph. "Bien hecho, mija. Me siento muy orgulloso de ustedes. Yo al igual que ella. ¿Qué hacer?"

"Escritora," Stephania squeaked in between shallow breaths.

"Muy bien." Gabriela smiled for several moments.

Slowly, heart race came back down to normal. Stephania was finally able to take in a deep breath of relief, and then she, too, smiled.

Steph looked at Liz. She was pale and looked sick.

This was horrible. How could this have happened? She inhaled deeply before knocking on the door.

After a nerve-wracking infinity, Linda opened the door.

She looked shocked to see them.

"Can we talk?" Stephania asked.

"Uhhh...yeah. Come on in." Linda stepped back so they could come in. "What's going on, guys?"

Liz and Steph looked at each other one last time before they sat down on the couch.

"Well, umm..." Liz started.

Stephania could hardly breathe, but she didn't want Liz to have to be the one to tell Linda. "No, let me tell her. It's my fault."

Linda turned and looked at Steph intensely.

"Linda, it's about Britt." She said.

"Britt?! What's wrong?"

"She's fine. She…" Stephania was clearly at a loss for words. "She's not who you think, Linda. If I had known what I know now, I never would have introduced you."

Liz looked down at the floor. "She made a pass at me, Lin." She said quietly.

Stephania whipped around and stared at Liz. "Made a pass at you? She fucking fondled you!"

"What?!" Linda asked in utter shock.

"She did," Liz said dolefully. "She's been trying to get me down there when you're not around. I called this morning to have you check my brake line. She told me you'd be in. So, I went down there thinking you'd be there. And you weren't. She said you had gone home sick. I told her to just leave a message for you to call me when you felt better. She told me that she didn't want me to have a wasted trip. I told her it was no big deal. She insisted that she could do it. I told her I didn't mind. I tried to be polite and explain to her that I really only wanted you to work on the truck. And I don't know…during the whole thing she kept moving around. She somehow cornered me."

Linda's face dropped.

"And then she kissed me and she started to grab me and…" Liz's words hung heavily in the room.

"Liz got out," Stephania said quietly. "She got out okay and then she called me." She took a deep breath. "She told me what happened. I called Britt just to see if she would say anything. She acted all nonchalant on the phone with me. She said there was nobody there and that it was pretty much dead." She closed her eyes and then rubbed her forehead with her hand. "She did tell me, though, that she has a thing for Liz and that she really wanted to…well, you know." Stephania shifted in her seat and finally just sat up. "When I asked her about you, she said what you didn't know wouldn't hurt you." Steph slowly rolled her head to the side to look at Linda.

Linda bit her lip, trying not to cry.

"I'm so sorry, Lin." Liz said.

"No, I'm sorry." Stephania said. "I am so sorry I ever introduced her to you, your shop, everything. This is all my fault. I am so, so sorry. I would never have done this if I had known she was like this. Please forgive me, Linda."

Linda stood like a statue in her own living room. Tears flowed freely from her eyes.

"Lin?" Liz asked as she stood up.

The silence was stifling.

Liz and Stephania quickly glanced at each other. They both stood up and walked over to Linda. Stephania wrapped her arms around Linda and Liz embraced them both. They held her tightly, trying desperately to take away her pain.

Stephania was leaning into Maria as they sat and watched a movie together. Stephania breathed in deeply.

"Are you ok?" Maria asked.

"Couldn't be better," Stephania replied. "I just love being with you. You're so grounded. I always feel peaceful when I'm with you. I love it."

"I'm glad you do."

"You are exactly what I need in my life."

"I'm glad," Maria repeated herself.

"I want to have this every day."

Maria quietly observed Steph.

"I want to have moments like this all the time. I want the stability and contentment I have with you."

Maria looked down at Stephania, comfortably resting with her head on Maria's chest and her long, lean body stretched out sideways on the couch. In near perfect timing, Steph looked back up at her.

"I want us to move in together." Stephania spoke quietly.

Maria looked at her silently while Steph gazed deeply into her dark brown eyes.

"You've become a part of my life, my family. You're like no one I've ever met before. You accept all my eccentricities. You love me for more than just what I do and how I look. You understand the importance of family and fidelity. You make me happy and I want to make you happy."

For several moments, the room was silent.

Maria inhaled deeply. "You are like no one I have ever met before. You are unique. You are brave and stubborn. You have way more energy than anyone I have ever met. You are beautiful inside and out. There is an age difference, but I don't notice it. Everything just feels right with you. You are my family, too. I would be honored to share my life with you, Stephania."

Stephania's face lit up. She had a smile that was never going to leave. "Thank you. Te quiero."

Maria smiled back. "Te quiero."

Stephania looked at all the women around her. Katie was cute and quite complementary to Linda. Katie was short, with an adorable round face, and beautiful long, blonde hair. Liz sat next to Katie, dwarfing her in a nearly comical way. Donna had just come off a shift and looked worn out.

Stephania couldn't help but notice that Katie was looking at her rather intensely. Stephania decided to just stare back.

"I am so sorry," Katie said. "You just look so familiar. I'm just sitting here trying to place your face."

"Well now I'm gonna seem like a pompous ass!" Stephania replied. "You *have* seen me, I'm sure. I'm a model. You can place my face all over Philadelphia...all over the world, really."

"A model? That is so neat! I've never met any kind of celebrity before," Katie said excitedly. "I'm from Iowa. There are no celebrities there," she chuckled. "You have a very unique and exotic look. I could see how you would do so well as a model."

"Thanks. I am unique. My father was half-black and half-white, and my mother was pure Salvadoran. That's where I get my rather unique features."

"And personality traits," Maria chimed in.

"Oh hush you!" Stephania retaliated. "So, you're a vet student at Penn, huh?"

"Yep," Katie was glowing with pride.

"It's great that you're a vet student." Liz said.

"Thanks," Katie said.

"Of course you do! Now you know someone who can care for your herd." Steph joked. The table broke out into laughter.

"Herd?" Katie asked.

"We have seven cats," Liz explained.

"Seven?!" Katie was in shock.

"Seven?!" Stephania repeated Katie's question. "Last I knew you had six - the three boys and the three girls."

"Well, the boys have won," Liz explained. "We now have four. A neighbor found a little black and white Maine Coon kitten running around the neighborhood. She was able to nab him, and guess who the first people she thought of were?" Liz smirked.

"What's his name?" Maria asked.

"Teddy Roosevelt. 'Cause he is fearless, and he ain't afraid to speak his mind!" Liz answered.

"You see," Jen spoke quietly. "I used to be the director of an all feline shelter in Florida. Cats have always been my passion, and so I took in countless kitties over the years."

"Yep," Donna interrupted. "I have them to thank for Taffy."

"And we have Tito Puente." Maria added.

"Well, sort of." Stephania explained. "We'd love to take him in, but Maria is highly allergic. So, she named him, but he stays with Liz and Jen."

"Ay, sí. Mi Tito Puente..." Maria's voice trailed off as if she was daydreaming.

"Sí, sí. Tu Tito Puente. El único hombre que quieres." Stephania mumbled to Maria jokingly.

"What are you saying?! Keep it in English, girls!" Liz scolded. "Anyhoo, because of Jen's amazing work and passion for people of the feline persuasion, we now have *seven* furry children running around the house."

"Wow. That is amazing." Katie said with great enthusiasm. "I'll be more than happy to help out with the troops. And maybe if you know any good rescue organizations here in the city, we can work something out there too!"

Liz nodded in approval. Without any hesitation, she raised her glass and said, "To Katie!"

Jen interrupted. "Wait! That's not all! *We* have an announcement to make. My amazing woman just became the new Prima Ballerina for the Pennsylvania Ballet!"

"Liz! Why didn't you tell us?!" Linda asked.

Liz simply blushed. "I auditioned today and wasn't supposed to hear back for like two weeks, but the guy called me while I was riding home on the train."

"Wow! That's awesome!" Stephania exclaimed.

"Here's to Katie *and* to Liz!" Linda toasted.

"Now you know another celebrity." Donna joked to Katie.

"Indeed! Congratulations, sweetie." Stephania said.

It was around ten in the morning, but both Maria and Stephania were still walking around the house in their pajamas.

Maria had decided to work from home since the girls had been out so late.

Stephania was taking it easy since she had the shoot with Linda tomorrow. She had just leaned back in her chair, propped her feet up on her desk and took a sip of her coffee when the business phone line rang.

"Hello?" Stephania answered after hurriedly swallowing the very hot coffee. She tried not to cough into the phone.

"Hi, is this Steph-ah-NEE-ya?" The woman's voice on the other phone clearly struggled with the pronunciation of Steph's name.

"Steph-AHN-ya." She corrected the other woman. "Yes, this is she."

"Hi, this is Susan from Peter's office."

"Hi Susan, how are you?"

"I am doing well, thanks for asking. I'm calling for Peter. He's home sick with the flu." Susan explained.

"Oh poor Peter! If you talk to him later, please tell him I hope he feels better."

"I will," Susan replied. "Anyway, we just got a call for a shoot for you that Peter thinks you'd be very interested in."

"Okay, go on."

"Well, you were requested for a cover shoot of...Curve Magazine."

"Are you kidding? You're kidding, right? This is some kind of a prank, isn't it? A belated April Fool's? Peter would do something like that..."

"No."

"This is for real?!"

"This is for real." Susan answered.

Stephania could not believe this. There was no way this was happening. "You're sure they wanted *me*?"

"Yes, they wanted you. They've seen your portfolio and your wonderful work for the gay community. They would like to do a cover shoot and an article."

Steph gently put the phone down on the desk and then proceeded to scream and jump around the room.

Maria scurried in to come see what was wrong.

Steph waited a moment, took a deep breath, and picked up the phone again.

Maria just stood there, puzzled.

"I'm sorry, Susan. I just needed a moment," Steph cleared her throat. "Peter was correct. I would love to do this shoot." She could hear laughter on the other end of the phone.

"Great! I'll have one of the Curve reps call you and we can get you all set."

"Thank you." Stephania said, trying desperately to maintain her composure.

"Sure. We'll talk again soon." Susan hung up.

"Would you care to explain why you gave me a heart attack?" Maria demanded.

Stephania put the phone down. "Well…" She said slowly, playing this out. "I got an offer for a shoot and…"

"And?" Maria cut her off.

"It's for the cover of Curve! They want to do a shoot and an article!"

Now it was Maria's turn to scream. She hugged Steph and the two began to dance around the office.

Finally out of breath, Maria said, "This has been your dream for years! That's great! I'm so happy for you. Congratulations, baby. So when is the shoot?"

"One of the reps from Curve will call us. Knowing everyone at Peter's office, they'll call later today."

Maria squealed with excitement.

Stephania paused, and then her eyes lit up. "I'd better hit the gym! I have to look good. I'm about to be on the cover of Curve!"

She slammed her coffee mug down, gave Maria a peck on the cheek and ran out the door.

Stephania sat motionless in the chair, as she had done so many times before. Some woman was pulling and moving globs of hair. She couldn't see because the make-up artist stood right in front of her, painting away.

"Liz, Linda, get your butts over here!" Stephania called out, hoping that they could hear her over the rest of the crowd.

"What is it?" Linda's low, raspy voice asked.

"Well, there's something I need to tell you both."

"And that is…?" Liz inquired.

"I'm about to be on the cover of Curve!"

Liz and Linda shrieked in delight.

Despite her urge to jump, Steph didn't move, lest she entangle everyone, including herself and the hair and makeup assistants.

"That is so cool!" Linda exclaimed.

"When? Where? What?" Liz asked, the words tripping out of her mouth because she spoke so quickly.

"Well, I got the call yesterday morning. The folks at Curve are flying me out to LA for the shoot in three weeks."

"Wow! That's great!" Liz said. "Is Maria going too?"

"Yep! I insisted that they at least fly her out, and they agreed!"

Linda winced. "Is she gonna try to see her sister?"

"Not that I can imagine. Maria let that one go a long time ago." Stephania answered serenely.

With that, the makeup artist had finished. "Done!" He exclaimed as he jumped back to revel in his artwork.

"I got about two minutes here and I'll be done with your hair, sweetie." The stylist said.

"Good! Let's get this shoot rollin'!" She called out.

Steph walked east down Spruce Street. She passed by the Veterinary Hospital of the University of Pennsylvania. She smiled, thinking of Katie working inside the massive building.

She crossed 38th street, and walked towards her utopia, better known as "Wawa." With child-like excitement, she opened the door.

As Steph slowly meandered down the few aisles in this relatively small store, she spotted Katie about to check out. "Hey, Katie!"

Katie looked up, surprised.

"Oh, hey!" she said. "What are you doing over here?"

"Sadly, this is the nearest Wawa that I know of," Stephania explained. "And...I'm addicted to Wawa."

They both laughed.

"Do you have a few minutes, or do you need to go back to VHUP?" Steph asked.

"No, I've got some time. I'm actually not on for another...forty-five minutes? So, yeah, I've got time." Katie checked out. She then walked over to the coffee station to wait.

Stephania's arms were overflowing with goodies from Wawa.

After she checked out, Katie looked at her skinny, model friend in great surprise.

"I know," Stephania said before Katie could even speak. "I'm telling you, I can't help myself."

"And the eggnog? Did you really need two whole gallons of that stuff?! " Katie asked. Her tone was light and jovial, but she still expected an answer.

"I know, but it's so damn good! I just work out extra hard when I have this." Steph answered with a giant grin on her face.

215

"Good enough." Katie laughed.

As they walked back towards VHUP, Steph asked, "Know any spots where we can sit?"

"Well, there's a small café and sitting area on the second floor."

"I'm not sure I wanna bring all this crap up stairs with me."

"I'm not opposed to just sitting on the curb in the VHUP parking lot," Katie offered.

"That's more my speed." Steph agreed.

The pair slowly sat, placing their bags on the ground. There wasn't much room.

Without even taking a breath, Steph dove into one of her bags and pulled out a cup of soup she had purchased. Instantly, she opened it and began to eat.

"So, what's up?" Katie asked.

"Well," Steph said between large spoonfuls. "Everybody likes you. We all think you're great, and a perfect match for Linda."

"Thank you!" Katie exclaimed.

"You're welcome." Stephania quickly ate another overflowing spoon of her soup. "I'm just a nerd, and I'm overly protective of Linda."

"You are? No offense, I know Donna is, but you too?"

Steph nodded her head.

"Okay." Katie said nervously.

"Look, Linda met her last girlfriend on account of me, and things got bad. It's all my fault, and I feel terrible about it. Linda says she doesn't blame me, but I blame me. So, I feel I owe it to her to watch out for her best interests."

She could see the confusion in Katie's eyes. "Okay, look. I had met this gal Brittany years and years ago. Long before I met Maria or really hung out with the gang. She had been my mechanic. We tried dating briefly, but were way too different, but we remained good friends. Anyway, she lost her job at her garage. By this time, I had shot a calendar or two and the first person I thought of was Linda. I just thought it would have been nice for Linda to have another mechanic to take some of the load off. Brittany had always done great work on my car, so I thought nothing of it. Out of her friendship to me, Linda let Brittany work for her. Well, one night, they were working late, and Brittany started hitting on Linda. Linda didn't like to mix business with her personal life, but Brittany was a very persistent person. Very persistent. So, Linda finally gave in."

"That night?" The surprise was audible in Katie's voice.

"Yeah. Brittany was *that* determined."

"Holy crap!"

"Yeah, you're not kidding. So, they started dating. Things were going ok. Linda didn't seem overly happy, but Brittany was so ridiculously happy that Linda played along.

"The problem was, it was an all act."

"Oh no." Katie muttered under her breath.

"First, Brittany was using her job at the shop to get to Liz. She would try to schedule Liz to have work done on her truck when she knew Linda wouldn't be around. Liz doesn't let *anyone* but Linda touch that truck. That's how they met, and Linda was always going to be Liz's one and only mechanic. One day, Brittany was actually successful in getting Liz down there when Linda wasn't around. Coming from Lansdale, that was a big trek for Liz."

"Yeah! No kidding."

"So, Liz sees that Linda's not there and she just makes small talk with Brittany. Time passes and Linda still isn't at the shop. So, Liz asks when she'll be back. Brittany told her Linda took the day off, but that she was in charge and could work on the truck for her. Liz politely said, 'no thanks,' and started to walk away. That really pissed off Brittany. So she grabbed Liz's arm, just started kissing her and trying to cop a feel."

Katie's jaw dropped.

"Liz got away, and flew outta there! She told me, and we were unsure if we should tell Linda. By the time we decided we should, it was too late."

"Why?" Katie asked inquisitively.

"Well, by that point, Brittany had really wormed her way into every aspect of Linda's life. She used that to her full advantage. She had been stealing money from the shop; she had turned a lot of customers away, so Linda was losing business. You name it. So when Linda called her out on this, she took all of their tools, all of the money, every little thing that she could. She totally destroyed Linda's shop. Donna and the Philly PD got called in…it was all fucked up. She ruined Linda's life and then she ran off."

"Oh, shit," Katie whispered.

"Yeah. Linda was devastated. It had been the first, and last, time she allowed another mechanic to work in her shop, and the first time she mixed business and personal life. It bit her hard. For Linda's safety, Donna took her in for a while and then Linda moved. That's why she lives so close to you. She moved her into UCD, into that apartment on Pine and 46th. She had to start the business all over and start her life over. Obviously, things have gotten better for Linda over the years, but I still worry about her a lot."

"Years?" Katie asked.

"Yeah, I think it's been about two, maybe two and a half years since all this happened. Linda has not dated since. Well, you're the first since Brittany."

"Wow!" Katie said in utter amazement.

"Look, I don't think you're gonna do that. You don't seem like the hurtful, manipulative type. You're working really hard towards your own goals and all that. I just want you to know that we are *all* watching out for Linda, ok?"

"Okay, no problem." Katie answered with conviction. "You know, Stephania, I am falling madly in love with Linda. And all I want to do is build a good life with her. I promise you, I have no plans of hurting her in any way. I totally understand and respect your concern for her. And actually, I appreciate it. It's good to know that she is loved and cared for. Shows me what kind of friends you guys really are. And I like that." She smiled. "So, thank you, really." She quickly looked at her watch. "I hate to be rude, Steph, but I gotta go inside. I only have five minutes before my rotation starts."

"Oh, sure. I should probably get this eggnog into the fridge pretty soon, anyway. Either that, or into my belly!" Stephania laughed.

They both slowly stood up and hugged. Stephania watched Katie walk back into the hospital before heading back home.

"Honey, are you ready? We can't miss this flight!" Steph called out, as she struggled with her heavy suitcase.

"Coming!" Maria called back.

The two women each ungracefully fought with their suitcases... eventually they met up in front of the door. They paused, looked at each other, and lightly laughed.

"Here we go!" Steph said exhaustedly.

She opened the door and once again, they scuffled with their luggage.

Stephania's big day was finally here. She nervously fiddled with her belongings in the suitcase, trying to do something with all of her anxious energy.

Finally, there was a knock on the door. The driver had come to get them.

"Maria, the driver's here! We gotta go!"

Maria came from out of the bathroom, with her cell phone glued to her ear. "No, you go, honey. I'm going to stay here." Maria looked like she had been crying.

"Honey, are you okay?"

"Yes, I am fine."

"Are you crying?"

"Oh no! No, I'm fine. Just tired. You go on."

"But honey, they said you could come on set. They said they might even use you in the article!" Steph argued.

"No, no. I'll just be in the way. You go."

"Okay." Steph replied as she closed her bag. "You're sure?"

"Yes."

Stephania took her bag and began to walk out the door. "I love you!" She whispered to Maria, and then she disappeared.

Stephania looked at herself in the brightly lit mirror. The makeup artists had slathered thick layers of color all over her face for this shoot. Her face was unrecognizable. Steph turned her head ever so slightly. Even her profile didn't resemble itself. It was a far cry from where she had begun.

Stephania stood and positioned herself in various poses. She stretched her long, lean body into various beautiful positions. From the simple to the dramatic to the ridiculous, she struck pose after pose and made them all look good. Her face and eyes exuded her energy and intense emotion.

Even the slightest angle change of the tilt of her head created an entirely new image. Being conscious of every inch of her body, she posed for shot after shot after shot. For hours she shot. It was exhausting and exuberating.

After her shoot, Steph guzzled a bottle of water and sat down with one of the journalists.

"What is it like being on the cover of a magazine, but perhaps a magazine that's not necessarily a big name in the mainstream?" He asked.

"Absolutely wonderful! This has been my dream. It didn't matter if I was on every other magazine cover or none at all. For me, this means I have arrived."

"How or why is that?"

"For as much as I am in an industry that focuses on appearances, to be a part of a cause that I believe in is the greatest honor. To be a face of the LGBT community and to represent us in a positive light means that I am doing good work as a model. I'm not just taking pictures, I'm making a difference."

"Tell us who you are."

"I'm really not anyone special. I'm just a poor girl from Kensington. My father died when I was fifteen. My mother worked her ass off to feed and care for us. Being the oldest, I started working at sixteen to help my mother out. I never graduated from high school, but I did eventually get my GED. I was discovered at age sixteen and have been modeling ever since. I got lucky. I got out. I used my money to help my mother and siblings, to get them out as well. Everyone but my youngest brother survived. He died from a drug overdose."

"Now, didn't you struggle with addiction as well?"

"I did. Alvaro's death was a wakeup call. I had been lucky in that nothing serious ever happened."

He interrupted her. "I heard you had a heart attack at twenty-two from your cocaine use. Is that wrong?"

"No, it's true. But I was lucky enough to not have any long-lasting effects from it. I walked away unscathed. So, I feel like I didn't have any real serious close calls or serious problems from it. Anyway, losing my father was bad enough. But losing my baby brother broke my spirit. A big piece of my soul died that day. His name means guardian, and as his older sister, I failed to guard and protect him. I vowed that day that his death would not be in vain. I have been sober ever since. I attend twelve step meetings and keep a good support system. I focus on my family and not myself now."

"It seems family is all encompassing for you. Not just blood, but friends...people, really. You now focus on helping a lot of people. For example, your charity calendars for HRC began as an idea – just something you and a mechanic thought up. It quickly became a local legend and eventually has become an annual national event. Tell us more about that."

"It's so funny. I met one of my dearest friends at Philly Pride one time years ago at the HRC booth. We started talking and came up with the idea. We used her shop and her clients' cars. The photographer donated his time and equipment; we were able to produce those first calendars at a pretty reasonable rate. And it just grew year after year. It's a really fun project. A lot has changed, but we still use my friend's shop and one of my other friends' trucks is used every year as well. It's nice to know that a project we enjoy is helping to make a difference for our community."

"It does. It definitely does. So, as we just said, family is very important to you. And you talk about blood family and family of choice. Tell us about your family now."

"Well, my mother and I talk every Sunday. That is our ritual. My sisters and I remain fairly close. I talk to both of them fairly frequently as well. I have a wonderful partner. We've been together for a few years and we have a great life together. And we have some friends that I consider to be my extended family. I am definitely blessed."

"Most people look at you and hire you based on how you look. But, who is the person behind those pictures? What are your hopes and dreams?"

"To make a difference. To not just be another pretty face. But to represent something; to help bring about positive change. To stay close and loyal with my friends and family. To live a good life."

"I am calling this article, The Modeling World's Greatest LGBT Secret Weapon. Because you really are fighting and creating some wonderful changes for our community. Thank you."

Stephania came back to the hotel late, and exhausted. Her excitement still over-rode her fatigue. It had been a tough shoot, and she was surprised by some of the questions the interviewer asked, but still, it had been a wonderful day.

"Honey, you still up?" Steph called as she entered the room. She stopped just inside the door. She could hear Maria quietly sobbing. She left her suitcase by the door and gently walked into the room.

Maria sat on the edge of the bed, crying into her hands. Slowly, she looked up.

"Honey, what's wrong?" Stephania asked with great concern.

Maria spoke slowly through her sobs. "My mother passed away. I was listening to a message from Marisol when you left this morning."

"Oh, honey!" Steph sat next to her, and gently rubbed her back.

"Did you call her back?"

"Yes," Maria sniffled.

"How was she?" Steph inquired lovingly.

"Cold and rude." Maria answered, her pain obvious.

"Are they going to hold a wake or a funeral?"

Maria wept harder. "The funeral is Sunday."

"Okay." Steph soothingly replied. "Are you going?"

"Yes, of course I am going! This is my mother!" Maria answered angrily through the tears.

"Okay, sweetie. In the morning, I'll put the extra nights on the card, ok? We'll just stay here, and we'll leave Monday."

"No, Sunday night." Maria insisted.

"Okay, Sunday night." Steph responded gently.

They sat in silence, save for Maria's sobs. Steph kept her arm around her all night.

Maria and Stephania left the store with new funeral dresses in hand and started walking back to the hotel.

As they walked in the late afternoon California sun, Steph began to wonder if she should even go tomorrow. "Maria, do you think it's a good idea that I go?"

"Of course! You are family."

"I know, but with your sister… And I'm part of the problem…"

"Do you want to go?" Maria asked harshly.

"Well, yeah."

"Do you love my mother?"

"Of course!"

"Then you're coming." Maria stated firmly.

Steph sighed and said, "Okay."

Steph stayed back just a few steps. She watched Maria reunite with her family. Maria had dark olive skin, but even she seemed pale comparative to her LA relatives who had clearly been living outside under the California sun.

Cousins, aunts, uncles, and friends who hadn't seen Maria in ages all embraced her greatly. They cried together; told each other how much they missed each other.

Stephania was surprised at how well she had been accepted with open arms by everyone in the family. The feeling in the house was warm and accepting. They were all having a beautiful moment. Everyone except for Marisol who conspicuously went outside and walked around the backyard of Aunt Pura's house aimlessly.

Maria decided to be brave, and she walked out to the backyard. Stephania watched from a window. She saw Marisol getting more and more animated; she appeared extremely agitated. Steph decided it was her turn to go outside.

"Maria, you are not..." Marisol started. She stopped and looked as Stephania made her way towards them. "No, not you. Get out of here."

Stephania kept walking towards her.

"Get out of here!" Marisol shouted.

"No," Steph said. "I am going nowhere. I am staying right here. This is my wife's family, and I love them like my own. We are all mourning a great loss."

"Wife?! She is not your wife. You just call her that so feel better about yourself, puta." Marisol snapped.

"Puta? Puta?!" Steph roared. "Yo no soy una puta. Tú no puedes aceptar la vida de tu hermana o su amor para otra persona." She spoke callously and over-articulated as she got right in Marisol's face.

"You are an ungodly whore!" Marisol muttered as she began to walk away.

Stephania's long arm reached out and grabbed Marisol by the hair. She pulled Marisol right in. Their faces were inches away from each other. Stephania breathed heavily as she looked down at Maria's sister. "You want talk about God, bitch? Let me tell you a little something about God. God is love. Plain and simple. So, let me ask you something: who is more like God? Someone who loves another person and lives the kind of life that God wants us to, or someone who spreads lies and tries to divide a family? That's not very God-like, now is it?"

Marisol tried to wiggle away, but Steph's grip was far too strong.

"You lied to your own mother just because you can't accept your sister's life. Was it because you were jealous of their close relationship? Was it because you were jealous of your sister's success? Or was it because you tried to cover your own insecurities?"

Marisol didn't move.

"Ya know what, Marisol? I don't even really care. The whole family knows about your lies now. We don't need to know why. But everyone in that house now sees you for the selfish, hurtful bitch you really are."

Stephania released Marisol's hair. Marisol had been pulling forward, so she fell forward when Steph released her. Marisol quickly got up and brushed herself off. She turned and gave the two women a cold, hateful stare, and then walked away.

Maria walked up and grabbed Steph's hand. "Thank you."

"You are my family, and I would do anything for you. I told you I wouldn't let anyone hurt you. Even if it is your own sister. Family is the most important thing."

Maria looked up at Stephania. "Yes it is." Her voice cracked and one lone tear rolled down her face.

"I love you." Stephania said as she squeezed Maria's hand.

"I love you too," Maria whispered. "Let's go back inside with the rest of the family."

Stephania sat down and curiously picked up the phone. She dialed the number. He answered after three rings.

"Thank you for calling the Human Rights Campaign. This is David speaking. How may I help you?"

"Hi David! This is Stephania Henderson."

"Oh my gosh! Hey! How are you? I love hearing from you, but it's not often enough!"

Steph chuckled. "Thanks, David."

"So what can I do for you?"

"Well, I have an odd question. I was wondering if there was some way we could do something... different... with the calendar money this year."

"Depends on what it is, I guess. What are you thinking?"

"Well, two of my friends were savagely beaten in a gay bashing. Linda, the gal who owns the shop where we shoot the calendar is one of them. The other is her partner. They have major medical bills from the hospitalization, surgeries, lost time from work...you name it. I was wondering if we could use the money to help them."

"Hmmm."

Stephania started to worry.

"I would have to talk to my supervisor to figure out how we could do that. It's not something I'm used to by any means. But that doesn't mean we can't. I'd want to help anyway, but especially considering that it's Linda. I'm sure we can find a way to make that work."

"That would be great, David. It really would. I greatly appreciate that."

"Yeah, no problem. Let me see what I can do and I'll get back to you, okay?"

"Sounds wonderful! Thank you!"

"You're very welcome. Take it easy. I'll talk to you soon."

"Okay. Thanks again. Bye."

She hung up and in perfect timing, Maria walked in. Steph looked up at her from her chair.

"You made the call?"

Steph nodded.

"Good. And it will all work out."

"One way or another."

"Good!"

"Yeah. I'm happy about it."

"Me too." Maria smiled.

"You know, I like this."

"What?"

"Our family. We have my mom and sisters. We have your family now. And we have the gang. Our family of choice. I just...I like this. I feel like our lives are really full and complete."

"That's because they are." Maria winked at her.

"I love you, Maria Lopez. And I love the life we have together."

Maria smiled down at her. "Me too."

More Great Books by Lauren Shiro

Unbreakable Hostage
Lareina Oliveira; she wants to share her passion for math. So it is back to school for Lareina... a tough Ph.D. program. A classmate is captivated by Lareina's beauty and intelligence, and despite her repeated refusals to his attentions, he kidnaps her! Only her determination and wits can save her...

Imperfect
Carol Mathers, in her mid-thirties, a highly sought-after IT guru in St. Louis. She has built a great life for herself with her partner, Alexandria, even though the two face prejudice as lesbians, and as an interracial couple -fighting tragedy and sometimes, triumphing amidst the chaos...

Impeccable
Carol – abandoned - waiting... for what, she couldn't know. She couldn't see that there was more life waiting for her. Carol is forced to face the demons of her past as well as begin to face life without Alex. Struggling to make sense of it all, Carol experiences her new life and all of the highs and lows that come with that life.

Short Stories

Amnesie, a short story

What happens to love when life changes? Two women in love, one debilitating change...

Trajectory, a short story

Joe Davis has spent the last four years of his life behind a scope as a sniper for the Detroit PD's SWAT Team. A fateful call sends Joe and his team deep into the Detroit Ghetto; and reminds him that there is more to life than what's on the other end of his gun.

Lauren Shiro

Love without Boundaries

In celebration of her one year wedding anniversary and recent political changes that legalize her marriage, author Lauren E. Harvey (L. E. Harvey) and Vanilla Heart Publishing are excited to announce the re-releases of her books and a brand new series of Loving Her singles under her (legal) married name, Lauren Shiro.

Lauren Shiro was published nationally for the first time at age fourteen. Since then, her work has been published in newspapers, magazines, literary journals, and even textbooks.

In 2006, she began writing fiction and she hasn't stopped yet. From her set of intertwined short stories in *Loving Her*, to the powerhouse duo of *Imperfect* and *Impeccable*, Lauren has written stories that are sure to touch your heart. Lauren continues to write stories of love without boundaries.

When she's not writing, Lauren works as a licensed veterinary technician. In her spare time, she enjoys everything from wood working to roller derby. She resides in Rochester, New York with her wife and their menagerie of furry and feathered friends.

Visit with Lauren
Email AuthorLaurenShiro@gmail.com
Facebook Facebook.com/LaurenShiro77
Twitter twitter.com/AuthorLShiro @authorlshiro
Blog LaurenShiro.blogspot.com
Website LaurenShiro.com